THE
MILK
CHICKEN
BOMB

ANDREW WEDDERBURN

COACH HOUSE BOOKS, TORONTO

Published with the assistance of the Canada Council for the Arts
and the Ontario Arts Council. Coach House also acknowledges the
assistance of the Government of Ontario through the Ontario Book
Publishing Tax Credit Program and the Government of Canada
through the Book Publishing Industry Development Program.

LIBRARY AND ARCHIVES CANADA CATALOGUING IN PUBLICATION

Wedderburn, Andrew, 1977-
    The milk chicken bomb / Andrew Wedderburn. -- 1st ed.

ISBN 978-1-55245-180-9

    I. Title.

PS8645.E27M54 2007   C813'.6   C2007-901577-8

for Scott Black and Mike Schulz

Are you lost?

The headlights sting my eyes. I keep my hand in front of my face, squinting. My backpack digs into my shoulder, too much stuff packed in there I guess: sandwiches, my Thermos, some comic books. I wasn't really sure how long I'd be gone.

I squint into the headlights and try to yell over the big, loud truck engine. I'm just out for a walk, I say.

A what?

A walk, I shout.

It's true, I've been out here for a while, walking up the gravelly side of the highway. I'm not sure how long. Long enough to get right out of town, past the Welcome to Marvin sign, past long dark stretches of ditch, barbed wire fences, and now and then a driveway, with a floodlight at the end, up above a farmhouse door. The wind whips grit up off the road; it gets into my teeth, makes it hard to breathe.

The passenger door opens and a woman gets out. She walks over and squats down in front of me. Lines around her eyes, puffy cheeks. A blue bandana wrapped around her head, a starched blue dress.

You can't just walk up the highway in the middle of the night, she says, you'll be run over by some maniac. No one knows how to drive around here.

The truck is huge, not a pickup but a big blue farm truck, a red hood, a wooden box with sides tall enough to hold cows. A man with a thick brown beard and denim overalls sits at the wheel. In the back of the cab are five kids, all of them in crisp overalls and checkered shirts. Behind them I can see dark shapes. Wooden crates, hay, egg cartons, chicken wire.

Get in, she says, get in. Shoos me up into the cab, between the quiet kids. No one says anything while I squeeze up onto the seat. I look for seatbelts but there aren't any. The woman climbs into the passenger side and slams the door. Some maniac would have just run you over and not even noticed, she says. Just driven right by, like they'd hit a badger or a porcupine.

Just out for a walk, I say.

The man shrugs and puts the truck in gear. We drive off, everybody quiet, no radio. The kids sit still and don't say anything. Their chins dip and then they jerk awake, wide-eyed for a while, until they start to doze off again.

It sure is dark all over, driving up the highway. Sometimes headlights whoosh past and you have to squint. You can see them coming, the sky over a hill getting brighter, then two white circles that sting your eyes and cut the whole road away, leaving little blue spots. We drive past the old chicken farm. Long rows of black windows with a white glare. I wonder what happens inside the chicken farm at night – are all those chickens sleeping? Or are they up, working on their big escape? If you stand outside the long chicken-farm walls, you can probably hear them inside, clucking, scratching at the concrete floor with their dirty chicken feet, trying to find a way out. Standing on each other's backs, trying to reach the windows. Trying to lift the latches, before tomorrow when the lights come on.

We pull off the highway into the Aldersyde truck stop. Even this late, trucks are parked at the diesel pumps. Teenagers with red shirts under heavy red and black jackets climb up on the big rig tires to clean windshields. The father rolls down his window, waves a hairy hand toward the diesel pump.

We're on our way back to the colony at Cayley, he says. We can drop you off wherever you live, though.

Well, the thing is, I was on my way here.

He narrows his eyes at me.

I was just out at a friend's place in the country, and I was on my way here to get picked up. I just live over in Marvin.

You were in the middle of nowhere.

Yeah, I went up the wrong road. But this is where I'm supposed to get picked up. Right here at the truck stop. Turned out perfect I guess.

His wife shrugs. I don't know, she says, how often do you find children out by the highway in the middle of the night?

You're from Marvin, he says, so we'll take you there.

But they'll be looking for me here, I say. They'll get pretty worried if they show up and I'm not around.

The Hutterite shrugs. He pulls crisp five-dollar bills out of his wallet and holds them out the window for the gas jockey. I climb overtop of the quiet kids and out the door.

Inside the truck-stop restaurant old men hunch over their coffee cups, faces pressed close to sports pages, want ads, laminated menus. I wander over to the counter and pull myself up on one of the round stools. Put my chin down on the counter, careful about the old coffee rings and sticky spots. The waitress cocks an eyebrow at me. I listen to the truck drivers mutter to each other. Over by the door a heavy trucker plugs quarters into the pay phone. Drums his thick fingers on the plastic. The waitress picks up a pot of coffee, sniffs at the steam. Makes a face and pours it in the sink. I watch her for a while then slide back off the stool.

The toilet in the washroom has a sign taped to the tank: Out of Order. I have to stand on my tiptoes to reach the urinal. On the brown tile wall there's a checklist: paper towel, soap, washed. Some checkmarks and initials. A vending machine: instant tattoos, and Mixed Adult Novelties, and something called a RoughRider. A picture of a blond woman with bare shoulders, her head thrown back and her mouth open.

I come back and there's a piece of pie on the counter, where I was sitting. The waitress sits on the other side, her chin propped up on an elbow, sips ginger ale from a straw.

I don't have any money.

I wouldn't worry about that, she says. Where do you live?

In Marvin.

How'd you get here?

I was out for a walk.

That's a long way to be out for a walk.

I guess.

Eat your pie, kid.

I unzip my backpack and get out a comic book. Flip the pages and eat pie. In the city under the ocean, the Under Queen gets ready to unleash her tidal wave on the Surface. But millions of people live on the coast! She catches the hero and ties him, upside down, above a vent in the molten crust. The Under Queen laughs and laughs. I guess if I ruled the city under the ocean, I wouldn't much care about the Surface Dwellers either.

I watch the gas jockeys outside, pumping gas. One of the gas jockeys props open the hood of a car, peaks around the side to see if the driver is paying attention. The driver just sits there in his car, drumming his fingers on the wheel. The gas jockey goes back behind the hood, where the driver can't see him, and yawns. Stretches. Scratches the back of his neck. After a while he closes the hood, gives the driver the thumbs-up.

The gas jockey looks up and makes a face. Drops his squeegee. Points. Truckers put down their forks, look up. Their eyes get big, their mouths drop open. The tidal wave rushes in above the fields, over across the highway. Fence posts and cows and pickup trucks all pushed along in front of the massive, boiling wave. Everybody screams and drops everything, truckers turn and run, and inside we get under the tables and hold our hands over our heads as that wave comes crashing down.

Where were you walking to? asks the waitress.

I shrug, eat some pie. It's pretty good pie, not too sweet. I guess a lot of people like really sweet pie, but I can only eat so much of it.

Well, I thought I'd go to Calgary. I'm looking for a job.

She chokes. Lays her hand flat on her chest. Takes a deep breath.

How old are you?

I'm ten.

Right. Ten.

The bell above the door rings and in comes Mullen's dad. I turn around so that he won't see me, but you just can't pull one over on Mullen's dad. The older gas jockeys all stand up to say hello, slap him on the shoulder. He starts to take off his jacket. Sees me and stops laughing.

I play with my pie. Mullen's dad sits down on the stool beside me, has to pull his long, skinny legs up into the tight space. The waitress sits up. Straightens her apron. Mullen's dad pulls off his black toque, sets it on the counter beside him.

Having some pie? he asks after a while.

Yeah.

Apple pie?

Yeah.

He looks up at the waitress. Hello, Hoyle. Nods his head toward the coffee pot. She pours him a mug. He pushes away the little bowl of creamers. Has a little sip.

Long way to walk.

I got a ride.

He was asking for a job, says Hoyle the waitress. Starts to say something else and he looks at her and she stops. I play with my pie, tap the crust with the bottom of my fork. He sips his coffee. Then he pushes the cup away.

Finish that last bite, he says. I stab it with my fork. Put it in my mouth. Mullen's dad pulls out his wallet, unfolds the leather. Hoyle shakes her head. He shrugs and puts five dollars down on the counter. She shakes her head again, and he pushes the bill toward her. Pulls his toque over his hair.

Come on, he says. I zip up my backpack and follow him out the door.

We drive out the back highway, past the old magnesium plant, its dark windows all empty, its chain-link fence locked up. The new Meatco plant is all lit up in the distance, big white lights in the parking lot, the parked trucks, everything new, big. We drive and all the farm lights are out now and it's just our headlights on the narrow highway, fences, ditch garbage. Mullen's dad drives with one hand, elbow up against the window, his other hand resting on the gear shift. He whistles to himself. Rolls his shoulders, like his back hurts.

In High River some cowboys sit outside the bowling alley and drink beer out of stubby bottles, their shirts unbuttoned in the cold. We stop at the traffic lights, the only set in town, red.

Hey, open the glovebox, says Mullen's dad. Get me that pen. I open the glovebox: a map of Calgary, a socket wrench, some crumpled candy wrappers. I hand him a blue-capped ballpoint pen. He puts it in his mouth and grinds the plastic between his teeth. Mullen's dad is always chewing on something: straws, keys. Sometimes he chews on pencils and gets little flecks of yellow paint on his teeth.

We drive past Lester's Meats, the parking lot all empty for the night, a few dirty cattle tucks under the single light post. Proud To Be Union Free Since 1977. I wrinkle my nose at the smell.

So I pulled the toboggan out of the garage the other day, he says. It's not doing so well. Bottom's all scratched up. Were you guys riding it on ice last winter?

There wasn't snow for so long, I say.

I was thinking of getting Mullen a new sled for Christmas, he says. You think he'd like that? The sort with runners, that you can steer. You guys could ride one of those anywhere.

Christmas is pretty far away, I say.

Yeah. Christmas is pretty far away.

We drive through the dark, past wooden gates, long driveways. People put wagon wheels on their gates, their names on wooden arches over the road. We drive through the dark and the circles of light, under posts, around driveways. We drive through the snow and onto the highway in the dark. We get back to Marvin and Mullen's dad drops me off at my house.

You want me to come in and say something?

No, I say, it'll be okay.

It's pretty late.

It doesn't matter.

I close the door of his truck and wave goodbye.

We ought to make the lemonade sweeter, Mullen says.

Most of the leaves are already brown and falling off the trees, all the way up the street. In school we colour pictures of autumn leaves: brown and yellow and red and orange. None of the leaves on Mullen's street turn red, though, or orange. Just brown and yellow and then they fall off the trees and get wet and soggy and stick in the grates. They stick to the roofs of people's cars.

We ought to make the lemonade sweeter, says Mullen. Now that it's fall. I bet people would buy more lemonade if it was sweeter.

That sweet stuff is for kids, I tell him. We're after the adult audience. Real classy. Mullen pours himself a glass and puckers.

You're sure out early this morning, says Deke Howitz. Leans on his fence. Deke Howitz hasn't shaved this morning, and his hair is greasy and not combed. Eyes red like he's been up all night. Hey, Deke, Mullen says, do you think we ought to put more sugar in the lemonade? Deke shrugs. I don't know anything about lemonade. Shouldn't you be in school? School doesn't start for another forty minutes, Deke. I know I wouldn't be up this early if I didn't have to, says Deke.

He waves us over to his fence. Leans over and reaches back into his scruffy blue jeans for his wallet.

Did they come, Deke?

He coughs and grins. Opens up the worn leather wallet, flips through the little plastic flaps with his driver's licence, his credit cards. He pulls out a little paper card.

Davis Howe Oceanography, Mullen reads, Davis Howe, CEO. What's a CEO, Deke?

That's me, kid. Sole owner and proprietor.

I don't get it, says Mullen. Why do you have a different name on your Oceanography business card?

Because they really stack the deck against you when you've got a name like Deke Howitz. Everybody just thinks you're some hillbilly. Some real asshole.

So the bank will loan you the money now? The money to buy your submarine?

All I'm saying is that Davis Howe is a lot more likely to get $400,000 from the bank than Deke Howitz is. He puts the card back into his wallet. Now I just have to get my suit cleaned.

Is that the suit you wear to pay your parking tickets?

Yeah, that one.

I thought you had a washing machine in there, says Mullen. I thought you even had a dryer.

Sure, says Deke, but you can't wash a suit in a washing machine, it gets all rumpled. I'm rumpled enough already. Hey, Mullen, is your dad home? I need to borrow his jerry can. He's already gone to work, says Mullen. Deke leans on his fence. I need to borrow his jerry can before McClaghan comes around for the rent, says Deke. Just the four-litre would do. He's already gone to work, says Mullen. Deke goes back into his house. After a while the windows start to steam up.

Hey, buy some lemonade, best on the block. People mostly ignore us. They pull by slowly in cars, their dogs' faces pressed up against the glass, panting. They walk by reading newspapers or just looking at the sidewalk.

Across the street Mrs. Lampman tugs on the rusty hinge of her mailbox. Hey, Mrs. Lampman, you want some lemonade? She shuffles through her mail, skirt creased, hair frizzy. It's too cold for lemonade, she says, you should get a coffee pot. Well, Mrs. Lampman, we're not allowed to drink coffee, and besides, we've got the best lemonade, and people love it even if it's cold. Mrs. Lampman roots in the pocket of her jacket, finds some credit card receipts, a sticky mint, a kleenex, a dollar. Here, give me some lemonade. Hey, Mullen, get Mrs. Lampman some lemonade. Mullen blows a bubble.

Selling lemonade is a lot easier in the summer. In the summer we hardly have to ask people; they cross the street for lemonade, their quarters right out of their pockets. We had a big grasshopper problem this summer, I guess worse than a lot of other years. Grasshoppers all over the lawns and in the gravel, grasshoppers in garden hoses, in dog dishes and mailboxes, trapped underneath newspapers. Anywhere you went you could hear them, scritching and hopping, rattling around like pennies in a jar. All the cars on the street had grasshoppers ground up in their tires. We had to put tinfoil over the lemonade jug and wrap the lemons in cellophane. Grasshoppers jumped on and off the tinfoil, like popcorn.

Mullen's dad pokes in the black mailbox. Lifts the metal flap. He pulls out a few letters, looks at the addresses. Puts one of them in his mouth and the rest in his back pocket. He takes the letter out of his mouth and tears it in half. Tears it in half again. Stuffs the torn paper in the front of his blue jeans.

Mullen's dad is probably the tallest guy in town. He comes out of the house, stretching his skinny arms way up above the top of the door frame. He scratches his chin. He puts his hands on his narrow hips and leans backward, rolls his shoulders around.

How's the old man's credit?

It's fifty cents a glass, Dad.

Come on. You know I'm good for it.

Dad, you've got a job.

Mullen's dad sits down on the curb. He takes a toothpick out of his shirt pocket and sticks it in his mouth. Mullen pulls a plastic cup off the stack and digs his tongs into the ice bucket. Takes his dad a cup of lemonade. Then he gets a duotang out from under the bag of sugar and makes a tick on his dad's tab. Mullen won't ever let me look at his dad's tab; I can only guess how big it is. Someday he's going to pay it, though: a jam jar full of quarters, five-dollar bills tied into lumps with elastic bands. Enough nickels to fill a Thermos. We'll both buy new bikes, with handbrakes, not the back-pedalling kind, when Mullen's dad pays his tab. Buy every new comic book the week it comes out, with plastic bags so they don't get sticky and torn up. We'll skip school and buy slurpees and boxes of Lego, and if they throw us out of school we'll laugh, on account of our financial security. I think they ought to try and throw us out of school. We'll just make the lemonade better.

At 8:20 we take down the signs: Lemonade! and No Dogs Please. We take the cooler and the lawn chairs into Mullen's garage. Mullen's dad lets us leave the cinder blocks and the plank on the lawn. We go to school.

At school all the Dead Kids from up the hill take off their outside shoes and put on their inside shoes. White with stripes and velcro instead of laces, or high-tops with thick laces that are always clean. Inside the school it's dark and hard to see, especially after having been outside for so long. Kids move around in the dark like they're underwater, bubbles rising from their yappy mouths.

Today I figure the whole school is underwater and all the Dead Kids are jellyfish, and you can't touch a jellyfish 'cause you'll get stung, see. Good thing I've got my snorkel and my flashlight. I figure some conquistadors must have sunk around here somewhere. Jellyfish come close and I duck and pivot like they taught us in basketball. Jellyfish stare at me with their buggy jellyfish eyes, floating on stalks in the murky water. A bell rings, it must be a fishing lure; all the jellyfish start floating off in the same direction. I bet it's a trap, I bet there's nets and harpoons waiting down the hall. They clog up the hall, all their oozy tentacles get caught up into one big jelly lump. I bob along behind them, breathing through my snorkel, in, out. Far enough behind that when the fishing starts, I won't get trampled if they panic. I wonder if jellyfish panic when harpoons start sticking into their crowd, when brother and sister jellyfish get hauled up all of a sudden, out and away. Or maybe they just bob along stupid-like, waiting, bubbling, not knowing any better, until the harpoon gets them right square.

Pete Leakie sits on the sidewalk, legs spread out, drawing with chalk. Hey Pete, what are you doing? Drawing, he says. He rubs a stub of chalk into the grainy concrete. A house, with orange flames, and people sitting on the roof. Are they yelling, Pete? They're laughing, he says. See? See all the smiles? Why's the house on fire, Pete? Pete shrugs.

Pete reaches into his knapsack, blue and full of holes, reaches in and gets some green chalk. Starts drawing green circles above the house. Where's Mullen? asks Pete. Mullen's at home, I say, doing the dishes. Mullen's dad makes him do the dishes? Sure, I say, every night after supper. Pete starts drawing green X's inside the green circles. What are you drawing now, Pete? Well, the house is on fire, says Pete.

Pete wears sweaters and glasses and has two chins. There's yellow chalk smudged in his black hair, and chalk handprints all up and down his overalls. Chalk on the arms of his black-rimmed glasses. Last year, when Mullen and I got sent up for putting wallpaper paste on all the shower floors at school, Pete brought us potato chips in the detention room. Pete Leakie isn't a Dead Kid. He's all right.

Pete shuffles backward on the concrete; he sticks a piece of blue chalk into his mouth and creases his forehead up all critical-like, examining his work.

Do you know how to draw horses? Pete asks me. I don't like drawing horses, I tell him. Yeah? What do you like drawing? You know, I say, the same old stuff. Today at school I drew some rhinoceroses. No kidding, says Pete. Yeah, no kidding.

I look at my watch. If Pete Leakie were a Dead Kid, it would be a whole different ball of wax. If Pete Leakie were a

Dead Kid we'd just talk about Mr. Weissman's math class and how many problems there are to do. A Dead Kid would be shifty and stuttery, 'cause Dead Kids don't much like me and aren't supposed to talk to me. But a Dead Kid would never draw on the sidewalk with chalk, so Pete Leakie's not so bad.

Mullen comes around the corner. Hey, Mullen, Pete Leakie says, your dad makes you do the dishes every night?

Oh yeah, Mullen says. We make quite a mess, the old man and me. Spaghetti sauce and baked-on cheese. Stacks of dishes up past your head.

Don't you have a dishwasher? Pete asks.

We got a sink. Mullen looks down the street, looks at his watch. A sink and one of those wire brushes, with the soap inside.

My parents bought a new dishwasher last year, with the tax-return money, Pete says. You don't even have to rinse the dishes off first, just put them right in. That's great, Pete, Mullen says. Yeah, I say. Great, Pete.

Mullen's got that look, that look he gets, like the time he found the boat at the bottom of the river, or when he wanted to start collecting flyers from all the offices on Main Street. It doesn't do any good to ask him, Hey, Mullen, why do you want to fill garbage bags with driver's-education pamphlets and pizza-delivery menus and bible-retreat brochures and mortgage application forms? He'll just get that look. I bet they'd have a lot of flyers at the IGA, he'll say, I bet they've got all kinds of flyers there.

Mullen grabs my elbow and whispers, Hey, do you know where we can get a telescope?

A telescope?

Yeah, he says, we oughta go and do some what, some surveilling.

I've got some plastic binoculars, I tell him, but they're at my house.

We have to go now. She might leave any time.

Who might leave?

Mullen stretches his arms up above his head and his black T-shirt tugs up above his belly button. Gosh, Pete, Mullen yawns, it sure has been something, watching you draw, but we have to go. See you around.

Yeah, Pete Leakie says, see you guys around. Pete Leakie finds his orange chalk. Starts drawing an orange octopus on the sidewalk.

Where are we going, Mullen?

We have to go surveil, he says. Down the street, across from the post office.

There isn't anything across from the post office.

There is now.

You can smell the Russians' barbecue all the way up the street. We walk up the sidewalk and there they are, out in their yard, sitting in their lawn chairs, reaching over now and then to prod at the steaks sizzling away on the grill. Most people have already put their barbecues back into their garages on account of it being fall, but the Russians do everything later than everybody else. They probably won't put up their Christmas lights until two days after Christmas again this year, and then leave them out until June. They wave with their brown beer bottles.

Hey, Mullen, Vaslav hollers, where's your dad?

Still at work I guess, he says.

Solzhenitsyn sticks his hands into the pockets of his skinny jeans. I left work an hour ago, says Solzhenitsyn, and he had already gone.

Well, Mullen says, I don't know then.

Tell him to come over when he gets home, Solzhenitsyn says. Solzhenitsyn works with Mullen's dad at the meat-packing plant, smashing ice. Every day they get into the truck together, wearing their overalls and rubber boots, and drive out of town, almost to High River. They smash ice with sledgehammers, in a small steel room, and come home red and sweating, with sore backs and wet socks, ice in the toes of their boots and seams of their blue jeans.

We walk down the alley instead of down Main Street, 'cause we like to throw rocks at garbage cans. Mullen gets a few pretty good dents into a stainless-steel can outside an empty garage. I like the sound the plastic cans make when you hit them with a rock, especially if they're empty. Even though it's only six, the sun is starting to go down out on the other side of town, where the foothills start. Sometimes Mullen's dad takes us for drives out into the hills, up past the provincial-park line, and shows us the forest-fire watch towers and abandoned farmhouses and other good stuff.

As long as I can remember, the windows in the building across from the post office have been covered with paper like you wrap boxes in at Christmas to mail to Ontario. We sit on the sidewalk in front of the post office and Mullen takes some comic books out of his backpack. Here, make like some dumb kid, he says. We make like to flip through comic books but peek over the tops at the woman in the window.

She doesn't look like other women, the woman in the window. The women down at the hair salon or the drugstore wear sweaters and short jackets, with blue jeans. The women at the United Church wear gold earrings and black blouses. Mrs. Lampman across the street always wears a blazer when she teaches social studies at the school. The woman in the window across from the post office wears a sweater, but it fits different than any I've ever seen. Looks thin, and when she moves, it holds on to her. She wears a grey skirt that goes down to her ankles but stays close to her thighs and the backs of her knees. Her hair is pulled back into some sort of clip, but it sticks out in all sorts of directions, trying to escape.

What do you think she's doing in there? I don't know, Mullen says, peeking over the top of his comic book. The room is empty, bare drywall with putty patches showing, and the electrical sockets unfinished, hairy clumps of wire. She wanders around with a tape measure. Measures a wall and writes on a pad of yellow paper tucked into the belt of her skirt. She sticks the pen behind her ear and frowns.

I bet she's from the city, Mullen says. That's how all the women look in the city. I sat on a bus in Calgary with two women like that. All pretty and high classified.

She drops her tape measure and lights a cigarette, a long, thin one. Smoke mixes in with the sawdust in the air. Mullen flips a few pages of his comic.

We watch her for a while. She writes stuff down and holds her hands in front of her face like a square, at arm's length, looks at the walls through the square. She doesn't ever look out the window. People drive by, and if they know us they wave. Nobody cares if Mullen and I sit on the post office steps and read comic books, 'cause nobody cares what we do, so long as it isn't causing public mischief. That's what the caretaker at the First Evangelical Church said when they made us appologize about the flyers. That we were causing public mischief. Public mischief, it turns out, is when you climb up on the roof of the school with three garbage bags full of flyers, fold them into paper airplanes, and throw them at Dead Kids. Even if you only get through half of one bag in two hours. They sent us up for that: for skipping class and making a mess of the playground. They said taking that many flyers was like stealing, even though flyers are free and in piles that say Take One. And after we'd cleaned up the whole playground we had to go down Main Street and apol-ogize at the insurance office, and the bank, and the First Evangelical Church. When they told Mullen's dad he laughed, but the way people sometimes laugh on television, when you can tell they're only actors.

I have to go home soon, Mullen.

No, come on, she's still doing stuff, he says. I bet she'll smoke another cigarette soon. Look, she has sawhorses in there. You think she might saw something up? Maybe she's got one of those circular saws.

I have to go home, Mullen. Seriously.

Since when does it matter when you go home?

I stand up and hand him his comic. I'll see you tomorrow.

Yeah, tomorrow.

I walk down to the end of the block and turn around. Mullen's still sitting there, pretending to read his comic, watching the woman in the window.

An old man with patches on his elbow leans on McClaghan's counter, looking at the lighters in the rotating shelf. One of those flat hats on his wrinkly old head, all covered in buttons. Annual Rotarian Convention, and Legion Number 19, and Vets Get Set. He takes a scratchy old Zippo lighter out of his jacket. A flint, he says to McClaghan, I need a new flint for this.

Where'd you get this? McClaghan takes the lighter, turns it over. Mail order?

Antwerp, says the old man, I got it in Antwerp. Pressed into my hands out of gratitude.

McClaghan spits in his jar.

McClaghan's jar is the worst thing in town. You always have to go to McClaghan's hardware store after school, though, for model-airplane paint or thirty-five-cent gum or hockey tape, so you always have to see the jar. He leaves it on the counter right beside the hockey cards, this beet-pickle jar two-thirds full of old-man phlegm, brown tobacco juice, stubby toothpicks. He takes it everywhere. Any time you walk by, there's McClaghan out on the step, under the 40% OFF sign, listening to his radio, spitting. But spitting on the sidewalk is bad for business I guess, so he spits in the jar. You can hear it all up the street, the hack and plop of old-man spit landing in that beet-pickle jar.

McClaghan rummages in his drawer. Pulls out envelopes, paper boxes. Opens them, frowns, puts them back. The old man puts all his nickels on the counter, one at a time, lining them all up and trying to get them all straight, but his hands shake and push the nickels all over the place.

In McClaghan's hardware store they've got everything you could ever want. Table saws and new bicycle chains, and four-man tents and car batteries, rubber boots, fishing rods, pickaxes and wheelbarrows – everything. Stacks of plywood and two-by-fours, router bits, camping stoves and jerry cans. They've got a paint-shaker, just about the loudest thing I ever heard, shakes so fast you can't read the label on the can. And all that stuff is great, but the best part about McClaghan's is fireworks.

So, McClaghan, Mullen says, pulling his elbows, his chin, up on the counter. McClaghan's counter is way taller than it needs to be. How about some of those roman candles you've got back there? I bet those pack a whole bunch, yeah?

McClaghan wraps his fingers around the jar. Out. Both of you, beat it.

How much does one of those big boxes cost, anyway?

Split, kid! McClaghan barks. We scoot outside. Sit down on the sidewalk. People sure get worked up about stuff, says Mullen. Hey, you want to come for dinner with the Russians? Me and my dad are going over, well, pretty quick I guess.

Yeah, that sounds pretty good, I say. We walk past the Lions Club playground. Two kids crouch on the teeter-totter. Neither one wants to go up because they know the other will hop off and crash the hard seat down on the hard ground. They just bob up and down, glaring at each other, never quite leaving the ground.

Hey, Mullen, what's Solzhenitsyn's real name? I don't know, he says, I thought Solzhenitsyn was his real name. I saw some other guy on TV with that name, I say, some famous Russian from history. Mullen throws a rock out across the street. They can't both have the same name? Course they can't have the same name. You never met anyone named Benjamin Franklin, did you? Or Genghis Khan? I met a Benjamin once, Mullen says. Back in Winnipeg in the second grade. When his front teeth fell out no new ones grew back, so he had fake teeth. He could take them out. You can't name your kid after somebody famous, I say. It's not allowed. That's why you have to get a birth certificate when you're born, to make sure that you've got an allowed name. I don't know what Solzhenitsyn's real name is; that's what my dad always calls him, Mullen says. All the other Russians call him Solly. Is that an allowed name?

Mullen's dad comes out of his house carrying a bunch of TV trays tight against his chest. Closes the door with his hip. Walks out onto the sidewalk, past Deke's. Pushes open the little wooden gate with his hip. The Russians' lawn is about as dead as everybody else's on the block, except for Mrs. Lampman's maybe. In the summer she always digs little patches along the path, plants sweet peas. Everybody else on the street is doing pretty good if they keep their lawn cut. Pavel and Solzhenitsyn sit in their lawn chairs around the barbecue, their heavy jean jackets buttoned all the way up in the cold, brown beer bottles tight in black gloves. Vaslav sits on the step, his belt undone and his big stomach pushing the bottom of his sweater up over his belly button. He's working on his novel. Drinks beer and scribbles on a huge pile of paper in his lap. He scratches his forehead with his pen, leaves a blue line.

Hey, you ever torn the corset from the heaving chest of a kidnapped virginal millionairess?

The kids, says Mullen's dad. Starts to unfold TV trays.

The kids have never torn the corsets off anything. I'm trying to get the facts straight. So as to be historically accurate.

They've got a lot of buttons on them. Those corsets. It would take some tearing.

Right, says Vaslav, it sure would.

Does the virginal millionairess have a name? asks Mullen.

Well, I've got it narrowed down to a short list of about eighteen. Has to have the right tone, see. I've left it blank so far in the manuscript. He holds up the top few pages and, sure enough, the pencil script is full of blank spaces. It's got to go well with all the other words, see, he says, especially the ones I use a lot. And it's got to evoke the proper balance of Victorian restraint and bottled passion. Voluptuous without being lusty, see. Owing to the virginalness of the character.

Pavel takes the lid off the barbecue and starts to turn chicken legs with his black-ended tongs. He squints with his one eye, making sure he gets the legs okay with the tongs. His glass eye looks off somewhere else, never quite in line with the real one. Solzhenitsyn goes back and forth to the refrigerator inside, bringing out all kinds of food: jars and jars of all kinds of pickles, and plates with different coloured strips of fish, covered tight in plastic wrap. A bowl of hard-boiled eggs. Him and Mullen's dad talk all serious-like, in between bites of pickled beets and anchovies, lots of big serious words, like newscasters on television.

Vaslav reaches across them for a pickle. Hey, he asks Mullen's dad, is there hot water in your house?

Hot water? Sure there is.

Vaslav sticks the pickle in the side of his mouth. Wedges a beer bottle against the arm of his lawn chair, hits it with the flat of his palm, pops the cap off. I called McClaghan three times last week about the hot water, he says through a mouthful of pickle. Each time he tells me to leave it alone. If it ain't broke, don't fix it, he says. I told him an ounce of prevention is the whole cure and he hung up on me.

Our hot water is fine, says Mullen's dad.

Our hot water is fine too, says Pavel. Vaslav makes a face. Pass me the herring, he says.

You left work early, says Solzhenitsyn.

Mullen's dad opens another bottle of beer. Shrugs. Sometimes you've got to leave work early. Solly drums his pencil on his knee.

I can't tell who's skinnier, Solzhenitsyn or Mullen's dad. It's hard to imagine the two of them with sledgehammers, in a steel room, smashing blocks of ice. It must get slippery in the ice room. The floor must get slushy and deep, like outside the curling rink in March, when the weather starts to break.

Earl Barrie got hit by a side of beef just before three o'clock, Soltzhenitsyn says.

What?

A frozen side of beef. Took a wrong swing and hit him in the head. Luckily, his hard hat –

And he's ...

Jarvis and I drove him to the High River hospital. Had to clear all the empty egg cartons out of the cab and lay him across our laps. His head in Jarvis's lap and his feet sticking out the window. To keep his head steady. He got conscious every now and then, went on and on about spanking his wife. Lord, just let me spank my wife again, he'd say. Jarvis had to put the talk-radio station on.

Earl hates talk radio.

Right. Kept him awake. So he went off about how much he hates talk radio, and how he wants to spank his wife, all the way to High River.

Why does Earl Barrie want to spank his wife? asks Mullen.

His dad glares at Solly. I don't know, Mullen. He must have taken quite a bump. Pretty delirious.

Days I can't find Mullen I like to walk over to the gully and throw rocks. There's this grocery cart in the gully I like to throw rocks at. Rattles real good when you hit it. Or I like to walk over to the football field and watch them building houses in the new subdivision. Some of them wearing hard hats, with stickers: Safety First, and 1,000 Consecutive Hours. They've got heavy belts and hammers. If Mullen and I had hammers and tools like that, we could build all sorts of stuff. We could get shovels and dig out the back wall Underground. Dig tunnels and other rooms: a library for our comics and a workshop for all the building we'd do. We could build shelves, put down a plywood floor. We could put down roofing felt so we could take off our shoes and not get slivers. We could build a wall, like the fur-trading forts in social studies class, with sharpened logs, and a drawbridge. Then we could just stay down there and do whatever we wanted. Grown-ups from the school could come by and hammer on the log walls and we'd just ignore them from inside our underground fort. They'd fall into the sharpened logs underneath our drawbridge and we'd laugh and laugh.

After recess, all the Dead Kids stop what they're doing: hanging up coats or unlacing boots or popping open the rings of their new binders. They start to point and then realize what they're doing, and stand there, looking awkward. A few binders pop, like grasshoppers jumping.

Jenny Tierney walks to her coat hook. Hangs up her black leather purse. Takes off her black jean jacket. She looks around the hallway and all the kids have to pretend like they weren't staring at her, get back to taking off their boots or getting their textbooks off the shelf.

Jenny Tierney is the only kid who gets sent up more than me and Mullen. But me and Mullen get sent up for dumb stuff, like wallpaper paste and soap flakes and racing toilet-paper rolls down the staircase. Jenny Tierney told a kid to stick scissors into an electric socket, and he did. Jenny Tierney is twelve years old and still in the fifth grade, like us. She's two inches taller than me and four inches taller than Mullen. Jenny Tierney hit a kid in the face with her math textbook so hard he has to wear glasses now. They didn't even send her up for that, at least not like we get sent up, cleaning chalkboards or washing the windows on the school buses. She had to sit in the office for hours, and her parents had to come and sign forms. I remember her math book sitting on Mr. Weissman's desk, the brown paper cover with a dark red splotch. Some people say that every time Jenny Tierney hits a kid with her math book, she peels off the brown paper and puts it in a scrapbook. She's got pages and pages of other kids' bloody noses, beat into brown paper.

We all rush off to class with Jenny Tierney watching us. She waits until we're all on the way off to class before she follows, her hard-heeled boots ringing on the tiled floor.

In the morning we sell lemonade. I stir in sugar, the wooden spoon tight in my mitt. You can't just pour in the sugar and stir, or it all settles at the bottom. You have to do it slow-like: a little water, a little sugar, a little more. Mullen doesn't like to stir 'cause he says it takes too long, but I don't mind. Who's in a rush? Some water drips off the spoon into the sugar, makes little grey clumps. I try to pick them out and sugar gets all stuck in my mitt, bits of mitten fuzz stick in the sugar. I take off my mitt and drop a fuzzy sugar clump onto my tongue.

The trick is making sure you don't get any seeds in the pitcher. I pull off my mitts and squeeze the wedges into my palm. The slimy little seeds squirt into my hand. They try to slip through my fingers. They want to get into the lemonade. Lemon seeds are tricky like that, they know that everybody hates them, so they try to sneak up on people. Because if no one wants you, you might as well ruin it for everybody. If they get in there they'll hide behind the ice cubes and wait, then sneak into your mouth and spread slime all over your tongue, make you gag and choke, and they'll laugh and laugh, jump down your throat, right into your stomach, and who knows what they'll get up to down there. I squeeze the juice into the pitcher and throw the slimy seeds out on the road. That'll teach them.

Deke pulls up in his rumbly car. Deke drives a silver El Camino, the only one in town. Everybody always stops and points when Deke drives by, slow-like, window rolled down and elbow sticking out. He leans out the window with an unlit cigarette stuck to his bottom lip.

What are you kids doing?

Well, Deke, we're making lemonade. Figure we'll sell some and then go to school.

You should come for breakfast with me, says Deke. Thought I'd get some breakfast. He bats at the cardboard air freshener, knocks it up against the windshield. You sell any lemonade today?

Nah, I say.

That's 'cause it's too cold, Mullen says.

It's because people are chumps, I say. They don't appreciate the value of our product.

We sold a glass to Constable Stullus yesterday, I say. He was measuring between people's cars and the curb with a tape measure.

That son of a bitch gave me a ticket, says Deke. Next time put vinegar in his lemonade. Or bleach. That'll teach him.

What do you want, Howitz?

Deke bats the air freshener. Just seeing how the boys are doing.

Mullen's dad lifts the top of the mailbox with his index finger, peeks inside. They have to be at school, Howitz. Don't have time to go running around. Yeah, sure thing, says Deke. Mullen's dad goes back inside.

Let's get some breakfast, says Deke. The cigarette still hanging off his lip. Hey, Mullen, you want some breakfast?

Mullen whistles. Well, the thing is, Deke, my dad doesn't like you very much.

No, Deke says, I guess he doesn't.

So I ought to just stay home and go to school.

Think you'll sell any more lemonade? I ask Mullen.

He snorts. Nobody's going to buy any damn lemonade.

Well, I guess not. See you at school.

Yeah, says Mullen, school.

So I was at the post office, getting my mail, Deke says, driving down Main Street. He takes a black plastic comb out of his jacket, starts combing his hair, one hand on the wheel.

From the P.O. box? I ask. Yeah, from the P.O. box, says Deke. The Davis Howe Oceanography office. And you know the building across the street from the post office? That empty building with the papered-over windows? They aren't papered over anymore, I say. Deke puts his comb back into his pocket. Chews on his cigarette filter. That's right, he says.

There was some woman in there a few weeks ago, I say. She had a measuring tape. Measured everything. Is that right? Deke says. Yeah, measured the walls and the doorways and the spaces between the electrical outlets. You ever seen her before? No, Deke, I never saw her before. No, Deke says, neither had I.

The car stalls at a stop sign. Aw fer Christ, Deke says. He grinds the engine a few times. When the car finally starts, it coughs like an old woman at the drugstore, like a good throatful of snot. Maybe we should let her warm up a bit first, Deke says.

I yawn. Yawn so wide it makes my head ring. I hold a hand up in front of my mouth.

Holy, kid, says Deke. Need a little shut-eye there?

I guess so, Deke, I say. Yawn a little more.

What are you doing getting up so early anyway? Looks like you need some more sleep. What good's it do, getting up hours before you need to go to school?

Sometimes you're just up, Deke. It's not like I don't want to be sleeping.

I know I'd be in bed if I could be. Hey, you want to see my vacation pictures? They're in the glovebox.

Deke's glovebox is full of maps: Lake Athabasca Region, the Columbia Ice Fields. There's a packet of photos from a drugstore in Calgary.

Pine trees and mountains. Deke holding the camera out in front of him, in front of a waterfall. Where's this, Deke? That's just outside of Dawson City, he says. In the Yukon. I flip through the pictures. A moose on the highway. Other cars all stopped around it, people standing around taking pictures. Doesn't get much more beautiful than the Yukon, says Deke.

I like driving in Deke's car 'cause the seats are wide and scoopy, with leather padding. Deke's car smells like Deke: cigarettes and chocolate bars and cardboard air fresheners shaped like pine trees. His Banff park passes take up a quarter of his windshield: 1973 through 1986.

We stop at the truck stop in Aldersyde. Just leave your lunch box in the car, he tells me. All the guys at the truck stop know Deke. They punch him in the shoulder and tell him jokes – they must be pretty funny I guess, 'cause everybody laughs. We sit down in the coffee shop. I try to get a look back behind the counter but I don't see Hoyle the waitress anywhere. Everything else is pretty much the same, though. Deke scratches his cheek and they bring him a cup of coffee. Scratches the bridge of his nose. They bring me hot chocolate, with little marshmallows.

That guy's got a real chip on his shoulder, Deke says, blowing the steam off the top of his coffee. You know that, kid? A real chip. You have to watch people with attitudes like that.

Mullen's dad used to be a geologist, I tell Deke, in Winnipeg. He used to know where oil was. You ought to see all his books – shelves and shelves of them, the hardcovered kind, without jackets. With the names stamped onto the sides.

Deke sniffs and sips his coffee. Guys like that, he says, where do they get off? It's not like I don't work damn hard. What was he doing living in Winnipeg if he was a geologist?

I dunno, Deke. My hot chocolate is still too hot. I pick a marshmallow out with my spoon and slurp it up.

Mullen get teased a lot at school?

Kids tease Mullen but Mullen doesn't care, I say. They tease him a lot 'cause he's short and lives down the hill.

So they don't tease you, then?

Well, I say, I guess so. I'm his best friend. But things have been different lately. We got Roland Carlyle, this sixth-grader, sent up for mail fraud. Kids aren't so likely to tease Mullen now.

Mail fraud?

Yeah, I say, Roland Carlyle said that Mullen's dad worked at a shit house. So we spent a week stealing all the mail from the houses on Pine Street. Then we stuck a week's worth of mail into his gym locker the day we knew Mr. Weissman would be in to watch us clean them out. Nobody believed Roland when he said he didn't do it, 'cause everybody knows he's always stealing cigarettes from the IGA.

Pine Street's all the way across town, says Deke. Why did you steal their mail?

Come on, Deke. You've got to cover your tracks. Get away from the scene of the crime and all that. Besides, we'd have felt bad stealing mail from people we know.

When I was a kid, Deke says, drinking his coffee and scratching his cheeks, in the second grade, there was this kid, Link Ashcroft. How old was I in the second grade? He looks at his fingers. Eight?

Seven, I tell him. You'd have been seven.

Right, seven, says Deke. Well, Link liked to kiss girls. All the rest of us played street hockey and shot marbles and Link would just run around the playground, looking for girls to kiss. But not other second-graders. Link liked to kiss girls in the sixth grade. What grade are you in?

The fifth, Deke, the fifth.

Right, says Deke. Link liked to kiss eleven- and twelve-year-old girls, and they went along with it, 'cause they thought it was funny I guess, this seven-year-old kid. Girls would sneak off at recess in twos and threes, he'd meet them behind the gym. He'd set his little lunch pail on the ground and stand on top of it to reach the mouths of the girls he was kissing. And Link didn't just peck these girls on the cheek – why else do you think they were so excited about him? They'd hold him up, on his lunch box, and he'd put his little tongue in their mouths and go to work.

Pretty soon, girls were coming over from the junior high school, hearing about this seven-year-old who liked to make out. They'd stand behind the big blue dumpster, smoking cigarettes, waiting for Link to get out of class. Link, he didn't know what the hell was going on. They'd take his hand and put it up their shirts, kiss the kid all over. He'd come into class all covered with teenage lip gloss, smelling like menthol Matinée Slims, this big dumb grin all over his face.

You ever see that woman before, in the window?

I never had, Deke.

He dips the tip of his finger in his coffee, draws a damp line down the middle of the green table. Looked like she was from the city, he says. Sophisticated-like.

Deke sips some coffee. He tears open a few more sugar packets and stirs them in. Taps the cup with his spoon.

You know what they're doing pretty soon, kid? They're knocking down the grain elevator.

Why are they doing that?

Say it's obsolete. Say they're going to build a new community centre there, for the Rotarians.

The green elevator, I ask, or the orange one?

I don't know. Maybe both. You want to go see that? I was there when they knocked down an elevator in Okotoks, two or three years ago. A couple of guys in Bobcats, they just drove into the walls. Fell down like it was made of dry toast. You'd think that a grain elevator would be sturdier. That the walls would be thicker.

You can smell the meat-packing plant here in Aldersyde. Smells like burning, and the outhouses at summer camp. Like the elephant building at the zoo. The gas jockeys sit around outside by the propane tank. Two of them play rock paper scissors. The same guy always loses, has to go lean on the windows of the cars when they pull up. Props the gas nozzle in the sides of the cars. Cleans the windshields.

Hey, Mullen, where's your dad going? I dunno, Mullen says. Hey, Dad, where're you going? Mullen's dad throws his jean jacket into his truck.

I want you to sweep the porch. Mullen sticks his fists into his pockets, hits the back of his heel on the sidewalk. Come on, Dad. Come on. Sweep the porch and the sidewalk, Mullen's dad says, get all those leaves and twigs. Come on, Dad, it's winter. It'll snow any minute. See all those clouds? Mullen's dad pats his back pockets, takes his wallet out, looks in it. And don't just sweep everything into the gutter, he says, or the neighbours' yard. Get the dustpan. Tell you what, Dad, Mullen says. When the snow melts in March, I'll sweep the porch. Sweep it real good. Like, put it all in garbage bags. I'll put the bags on the curb, in March. Real good-like. Mullen's dad pats the front of his grey jeans, feels the pockets of his jean jacket. Your keys are inside on the desk, by the mail, Mullen says. Mullen's dad takes a pencil out of his pocket, the flat kind they sell at the hardware store, sticks it between his teeth. Put the bags in the alley, he says. And don't pick up anything sharp, like broken glass. Leave that for me. He goes into the house. Comes back out spinning his keys around on his index finger. Stops to look in the mailbox.

Mullen's dad hunches down on one knee. Show me your shoulder, he says. My shoulder's fine, says Mullen. Come on, show me. Mullen pulls his sweater up around his neck. Mmblfr, he says through his sweater. The white bandage is taped in a wide square to his pink skin with white tape. Whenever I cut myself, on the side of an open can of peaches, or in the teeth of the gate in a backyard, I always get a pink bandage, just a little sticky strip, brown and fuzzy. Mullen's bandage is white and plastic and puffy, like a jacket, and has to be held on with tape. His dad has a look at it but doesn't peel back the tape to look underneath. Don't pick at it, he says, and don't poke at it. Mmblnfrmnr, says Mullen. His dad pulls the sweater back down, careful to tug it well clear of the bandage. Mullen coughs while his dad smooths out his sweater.

It's hot, says Mullen.

You got burned, says his dad. I'll bet it's hot.

You going to be home in time for dinner? asks Mullen.

We're eating at the Russians' tonight, says his dad. If I'm not back just go over there. Take that bottle of wine, I said we'd bring one. The red one, in the rack. He pats Mullen on the head, gets into his truck. Plays with the rear-view mirror a bit. See you at dinner. Yeah, Dad, at dinner.

Where's your dad going, Mullen? Mullen climbs up on the porch railing. It creaks. I dunno, he says. Hey, you know what I found down by the river? A bucket of paint. They don't put paint in buckets, I tell Mullen, they put it in pails. Mullen reaches up, tries to grab the lip of the roof. Yessir, a whole bucket of paint, just sitting there under some leaves, by a stump. You know down by the river where we dug that hole that one time? Somebody must have dropped off a bunch of trash there.

We wander around the back of the house. Mullen's dad has a tire hung off the only tree. In summertime during storms you can hear it, banging on the tree, into the side of the fence. On the back porch there's a little table, some beer bottles neatly stacked in their cardboard boxes underneath.

We climb the fence. I hang on the edge for a second, like I always do, one leg swinging on the other side. The alley behind the yard is overgrown with old poplar trees and rose bushes; there's a chain-link fence and the big hill on the other side. Mullen pushes a piece of plywood off the fence; behind it we've got a pretty good hole cut in the chain. We get on our hands and knees and crawl through the fence, into the scrub.

What colour paint is it, in this pail? I ask. Mullen's shoelaces scurry away ahead of me. Red, he says. We crawl through the bushes until the side of the hill runs up straight vertical, where the big tractor tire is, leaned up against the mouth of the culvert. Which is how you get Underground.

Everything we keep, we keep Underground. Like the traffic pylon, and the construction light – we've had it for months and it still blinks. The orange blinking gives us all the light we need; it makes you kind of dizzy at first, but we know our way around pretty well. We have an old card table, with ring marks and a wobbly leg, and we've got some milk crates we found behind the IGA. All our stuff is stacked up against the wall there: the burnt-out fluorescent tubes and the old rake with the taped-up handle, our cattle-auction posters and our air-show posters. We've got Russian pictures that Solly gave us, of red-jerseyed hockey players and frowning statues. Square letters with English underneath: Visit Leningrad, Moscow Metro 1973. We have a Sears catalogue, the thick winter one, all the pages stuck together because of the damp. Vodka bottles, one of them filled with sand, and a tea cup with a mouse we found under Solly's porch.

We brought in all this stuff ourselves, except the old refrigerator, which was already here, leaned up on the dirt wall at the back of the culvert, the door hanging open. Bent in all funny to make it fit. The culvert is just tall enough for Mullen to stand, but I have to duck my head. Our feet ring on the ribbed steel. Mullen opens the fridge door and gets out a big white plastic pail with a steel handle. It's definitely a pail. Smears of red around the edge of the lid.

What do you want to do with all that paint? I ask. Mullen grunts and sets the pail down with a clang. Well, you know the fluorescent tubes we found behind the IGA? I figure I could go down to the railroad tracks and throw those tubes around, like they were whatsit, javelins. What about the paint? Well, he says, I figure we could pour the paint into the tubes. So they blow up when they hit the ground. I think it over while Mullen looks around for the tubes. Yeah, that sounds like fun. Yeah, Mullen says, I figure it'll be.

Turns out the tops of the fluorescent tubes don't screw off, so instead we dip the ends of them in the paint and then throw them, over in the alley behind the credit union. They float real good and you can see the red up there in the grey sky, and when they hit the ground they explode, glass bursting in a big red splash.

Isn't it ever going to snow? Mullen says.

It's not even October yet, I tell him. It isn't even winter.

Back in Winnipeg it snowed so much I couldn't pass the second grade, on account of all the not-going days, Mullen says. Dad would stand out on the balcony and watch cars slide down the street, drinking coffee, all these cars sliding in the snow and him laughing and pointing. He didn't have a job and just wrote letters all winter, trying-to-get-work sort of letters and when he wasn't writing letters he'd read the newspaper. So when I didn't have to go to school I'd just sit around with him and we'd laugh at the cars.

Mullen smears a puddle of red paint with the tip of his shoe. He knows how to make an igloo, my dad, that's how much snow we had in Winnipeg. And he'd let me build snowmen on the sidewalk in front of the apartment building. I'd put my snowsuit on and go make snowmen and he'd sit on the balcony, shout things at me. Hey, Mullen, he'd shout, you ought to give that one by the mailbox a nose. He'd throw old ball caps and carrots down to me, and spatulas and flyswatters and crummy old ties. This one day it snowed and school closed and the snowplow didn't come, nobody could drive down the street 'cause of all the snow, and I built snowmen right out in the middle of the street. Dad tossed me down some of Mom's old clothes, this fancy hat of hers with a black rim and flowers in it – I put her right in the middle of the street.

When Dad said we had to move here so he could work, I asked if there'd be snow and he said there would be, but last winter it never snowed more than an inch. School didn't even close once last year. Hey, Dad, I said to Dad, in Alberta do they have snow? And he said, Mullen, in Alberta it snows so much that everybody has to dig tunnels to get to the grocery store. In Alberta it snows so much people can't drive their cars between November and April, they have to go everywhere on snowmobiles. You won't take your snowsuit off for six months, he told me. But school didn't even close once last year.

We throw some more tubes. Paint trails drip behind them. A car drives down the alley and we run away. We forget the pail of paint.

Paul Grand comes into the hardware store, skateboard under his arm. None of the old men look up, but Mullen and I both set down our comic books, watch him. He walks through the aisles, skateboard under his arm, chews a green apple. The other skaters from the junior high are all tall and skinny, long arms, their jeans too big, holes in their black T-shirts. They wear punk-rock T-shirts with letters, DOA and SNFU and TSOL. They wear jean jackets with patches sewn on with dental floss. Paul Grand isn't tall, though. His cheeks are big and red, and he isn't much taller than me. Black sideburns cover most of his face, and his red mesh ball cap sits high on his head like someone from the Aldersyde truck stop.

Everybody knows that Paul Grand is the best skateboarder in town. Probably any other town around here too.

He walks up the aisles to where McClaghan keeps the skateboards. They lean up against the wall, the bottoms of the decks facing out, with their bright devils in monster trucks, skeletons on motorcycles. Bright wheels and plastic rails along the sides. The other skaters all go into Calgary for skateboards; they spend two hundred dollars on narrow decks with little wheels, name-brand trucks and bearings. Paul Grand is the best skater in town and he only ever rides forty-dollar boards from McClaghan's. Paul Grand can ollie without cracking his tail, it's true. Everybody always says it's impossible to ollie without cracking your tail, until they see Paul Grand do it. It probably is impossible, for anybody else. He picks up a fat board, green rails and wheels, a minotaur in a biplane on the back, steam puffs out of his nose, hoofs on the control stick. He hefts it up and down. Takes it by the nose and swings it back and forth in the aisle. Holds it upside down and spins the wheels, listens to them. Then he walks up to the counter and sets the skateboard down, wheels up.

I'll give you thirty dollars for this, he says.

McClaghan looks down. Can't you read? It's forty-five dollars.

Come on, says Paul Grand, the bearings are for shit. What kind of wood is this? Particle board?

Watch your mouth, kid. You're the one who wants to buy it.

I'll give you thirty dollars.

Forty-five. Get out of my store.

Paul takes his wallet out of his pocket, a green vinyl wallet with a sailboat printed on the flap. Takes out six wrinkled five-dollar bills. Maybe you'll sell a lot of hammers today, he says. Maybe somebody will want to buy a rake. Any of these guys buy any rakes today? He flicks the bills like a movie gangster.

Get out of my store, says McClaghan. All of you kids, he shouts over at me and Mullen, put the comic books down and get lost. He spits in his jar. Paul leaves the minotaur on the counter, picks up his old skateboard. We follow him outside.

Hey, says Mullen, I heard one of those junior high kids bought a skateboard in Calgary for two hundred and fifty dollars. Picked out all the right parts and they put it together for him.

Paul shrugs. It's just about winter. If you ride a skateboard in the winter it gets wrecked; it rusts and warps and gets wrecked. But who wants to stop skateboarding? So why buy a good skateboard? He bites off the last of his apple and throws the core out into the street.

You ought to get McClaghan, says Mullen. Everybody in town wants something bad to happen to him, all his tenants, I bet everybody else too.

My buddy had this Ford Pinto, says Paul Grand. Little tiny car. We'd all pack right in there and drive, I don't know, anywhere but here. Like in Okotoks, all the parking lots are paved, right, so we'd go there. You should see the curb cuts on the sidewalks – it's, like, everything is round. Yeah, all the people in town are like pink-stucco-garage types that yell at you for skateboarding on anything, but it's worth driving all the way out there for those curb cuts. They've got railings on the stairs. It's perfect.

The best thing in Okotoks, though, there was this lawyer, right. Had this empty swimming pool. I don't know what kind of chump builds a swimming pool in Alberta, it's not like it's ever warm enough to go swimming, but whatever. He had a swimming pool, empty eight months out of the year. We'd drive out there and skate it as long as we could, before the lawyer called the cops. It was like California. You'd get right up out of the bowl. We took pictures. Then the cops would come and you had to pile back into that Ford Pinto and drive the hell out of Okotoks.

This one time, we get there, and it's pretty late, so we figure everyone around is in bed. And it's dark and all the lights on the street are out. We get all around and my buddy Dave Wave goes in first. Takes a run back from the patio, from this lawyer-white fence, and runs and jumps into the pool on his board and hits the concrete and we all clap, quiet-like 'cause it's so awesome, and then Dave screams and falls off his board and hits the concrete and hollers as loud as he can.

So we jump in the pool and the whole thing is full of jacks. You know, jacks, like marbles and jacks, little steel jacks. He hit those and his wheels locked and he flew off into the pool and was sitting there, he had jacks stuck in his arms and his jeans all tore up. And then the lights come on and there's the lawyer, laughing, Come back any time, you punks, he said, and turned off the light. We carried Dave back to the Pinto and drove the hell out of Okotoks.

Paul Grand takes out some cinnamon gum. Unwraps a stick of cinnamon gum, then another, puts them both in his mouth.

Well? says Mullen. Did you break his windows? Steal his car? Shit on his doorstep?

Paul puts a third piece of gum in his mouth. Chews and chews. We got him with the Milk Chicken Bomb. He laughs and chews.

Mullen frowns. What's the Milk Chicken Bomb?

Paul Grand stops laughing. Turns and looks at us, like a grown-up. Kid, he says, the Milk Chicken Bomb is the worst thing. The very worst possible thing. Nobody should ever build the Milk Chicken Bomb. I don't like even knowing about it. Like, because I know, I might tell somebody, and they'll build it, and it'll be my fault. The Milk Chicken Bomb is the worst thing.

What's the Milk Chicken Bomb?

If I tell you, you'll build it, says Paul. The Milk Chicken Bomb wrecks everything. You can't clean it up. You can't ever get the building back. That lawyer tried to sell his house, and couldn't. Nobody would buy. We'd drive by and take pictures of the For Sale sign. He couldn't give that house away. If I told you, you'd build it.

I promise I won't ever build the Milk Chicken Bomb, says Mullen, I promise. Please please tell me.

Paul Grand gets up, scratches his sideburn. Rolls the skateboard under his foot. I'll see you kids around, he says. Pushes down the street, sliding around all crazy on the ice. I don't think he'll fall off, though. Ollies off the curb into the street, skates down the street. Slow and easy, even on the ice, like he'd never fall off. Like he wouldn't even know how.

The Russians let us sit in the back of Pavel's truck on the way to the Marvin Recreation Centre. Pavel keeps hay bales in the back, for weight, he says, and you can lean up against them, looking backward while he drives. Mullen's pockets are full of elastic bands – we shoot them off our fingers at light posts, stop signs, station wagons.

At the recreation centre people stand around the parking lot, lean on the boxes of their trucks, smoke. Curlers hold their cigarettes with their thumbs and first fingers, except the women from the post office, who smoke between the first and middle finger. Curlers wear heavy jackets with fleece around the collars and no gloves, big round sunglasses like policemen in movies. They smoke their cigarettes and drink beer from coolers in the backs of their trucks. Vaslav unscrews the lid of his flask and takes a long pull, then another. Kids from the church with gym bags hurry to their swimming lessons. Old men come up to the Russians and lean on Pavel's truck, pat them on the shoulders. Good group this year, eh? No goddamn picnic. Pavel comes back outside with forms on a clipboard. Everybody takes turns signing with a green stub of pencil tied to the clipboard with a string.

Solzhenitsyn is the skip, and Vaslav is the third, and Pavel is the lead. Their new second is a bald man with a moustache, he comes over and shakes their hands and mumbles behind his moustache and they all slap him on the shoulder and shake his hand. He signs the forms with the stubby pencil. Vaslav passes him the flask.

You going to win today, Vaslav? I ask.

Vaslav makes a hacking sound. People in this town, he says, they don't know from curling. Couldn't give a damn. They don't even name their brooms.

Does your broom have a name, Vaslav?

He reaches into the back of the truck and pulls out a curling broom, long and white-handled, a black cloth sock pulled over the bristles. This here, he says, is Anna Petrovna, the best curling broom in southern Alberta.

Hey, Pavel, Mullen says, does your broom have a name? Yeah, Pavel says, Broom. He takes a drink out of the flask and laughs.

Inside it's hard to hear, with all the overhead fans and people talking, and everything smells like cigarette smoke and chlorine from the swimming pool. Some Dead Kids from the sixth grade stand around the pay phone by the concession stand, take turns listening and snickering. They flip through the phone book and make phone calls with nickels, say things I can't hear and then laugh and hang up.

In the rink curlers wander around, stretch with their brooms, rub their sliders with the sleeves of their jackets. The United Church curlers stretch on the floor, with purple stickers on the chests of their sweaters: My Name Is and the Alberta Natural Gas genie, like they make us wear at school when we go on field trips. They laugh and eat cookies. And the Golden Oldies hockey team that Mrs. Lampman's husband plays with, in their high-topped sneakers, laughing and holding their beer guts. Steadman's Drugstore always has a team and Ackmann's Arena and Mill Store always has a team. They slide up and down the ice, some of them with flat black-bristled brooms and some of them with yellow long-bristled brooms.

When do you play, Solly? asks Mullen. Solly sits on a bench, stretches out and touches his toes. Touches his forehead against his knees. You know, he says, eventually. Go get some snacks. Go play marbles or something. He sits up, reaches in his pocket. Pulls out fifty cents and catches it back in his fist.

Out-turn, says Solly.

Come on, Solzhenitsyn, just give us the money.

I hold up my arm, like he does when he wants Pavel or Vaslav to throw an out-turn.

Good, he says. Okay, take-out.

Mullen shoos me aside. He sticks out his tongue and pretends like he's got a curling broom. Taps it on the ground in front of him, then heaves it up like a baseball bat and swings.

Right, perfect, says Solly. He opens his hand and Mullen grabs the quarters. Vaslav and Pavel pass the flask around. Who are you playing? I ask. Solly points over to the RCMP team, all of them drinking coffee out of paper cups. The tips of their moustaches get damp. You going to beat the cops? asks Mullen. Yeah, Solly says, we're going to beat the cops. Their second's got no shot and their skip ought to stick to desk work.

What about the United Church? I ask. Will you have to play them? Just one match today. We'll play them in a few weeks. Today the posties are going to make a mess out of the United Church, says Solly. All that ideological moderation is bad for your concentration. It's the Pentecostal church you've got to watch. Mullen rubs his hands together. Right, the Pentecostals. Right.

Some second-grade kids play marbles over by the water fountain. Flick their glass cat's eyes and speckled eggs at each other. You hit a marble and it's yours, and if the other marble is bigger you've got to hit it more than once. All the kids keep their marbles in purple bags with drawstrings – they get them from their dads once the rye whisky is all gone.

Mullen watches them playing marbles for a while. He starts flipping one of his quarters. Flips it and catches it, like he's going to call heads or tails. Eventually the second-graders stop shooting marbles and look up at him.

United Church match is about to get going, says Mullen. Against the posties. Gonna be a good one.

The second-graders look at him funny. What?

They're just about to start. How many ends do you think it'll go?

The kids keep on looking at him, really confused. The kid with the most marbles snaps his fingers. Come on, let's play marbles. Hey, come on.

What are you doing? I whisper to Mullen.

Well, we've got a good hand here, he says. We can stand to lose a few until we spot out the way things are going.

What are you talking about?

You know, he says. Covering our bets. Doesn't Deke always talk about covering bets? All right, he says to me, you've got to drum up some interest. You know, get kids running their mouths about the matches. Who's throwing how many ends and all that stuff. Get their fingers itchy. Hey, grab that empty can of nuts, he says to me.

Mullen, kids don't want to bet on curling.

Sure they do. He shakes the last few crumbs out of the can. Think of all the jerky and chips they could buy if a big score comes in.

Curlers start to shove all the rocks from the house back down the ice. They get down and stretch, up off the ice, their brooms down flat on the floor. The United Church reverend has a big yellow beard, round wire glasses. Pats the other curlers on the shoulders. The post-office skip slides down to the other end of the ice, a quick step and then a long slide, leg trailing behind her.

I dig in my pocket. Pull out a dime. I drop it in the can beside Mullen. Tell you what, I say, I bet the posties really sock it to them in the first end.

Ooh, Mullen says, big bet. That's some tough talk. Some tough talk.

The kid with all the marbles starts to say something, but one of the other second-graders cuts him off. What, all those ladies? With the sweaters? You think they're going to win?

I think they'll at least finish the first end ahead.

No way, says the kid. They're all girls. The other team only has one girl. No way they'll win.

Mullen shrugs. Rattles the can. The second-graders look at each other, then they all pull dimes out of their pockets.

Kids press their faces up to the glass, their runny noses make streaks. The church throws first. The reverend stands down in the house, broom forward. The organist sets up to throw, drags herself back with a little wheeze, slides out of the hack. Purple sweaters rub their black-bristled brooms, shuffling down the ice. On this side of the glass you can hear the reverend shout, Sweep! He waves his arms for them to stop. The rock slides, too fast, just outside the last ring.

We're set, Mullen, I whisper to him. Aw hell, Mullen says. What? Over there, he says, points to the back corner, by the door of the swimming pool. Aw hell, I say.

Jenny Tierney sits on a milk crate, sucking on a red straw. Chews it. She takes a box of mint dental floss out of her pocket, reels out a skinny white stretch. She ties a dental floss bow around her right thumb, loops it around the back of her hands, ties it again around her other thumb. Makes a cat's cradle.

You kids here to sell lemonade or something? Jenny asks. Tugs her cat's cradle taut. I don't think curlers much like lemonade. Mullen takes a penny out of the jar, flips it. We came to watch our friend Solzhenitsyn. He's the best curler in town. Jenny takes one of the sides of her cat's cradle in her teeth, tugs it down over the backs of her hands. What the hell is curling? Is it a sport? I see old men who drink too much. Do they fall down? Do we laugh?

The first end finishes: three postie rocks in the first two circles. The church isn't even close. All the people inside put down their Styrofoam cups to clap and whistle. Mullen rattles around the can while the curlers push the rocks back against the boards. Well, what do you know about that? He grins at the kids. What do you think? I bet the reverend there pulls it together this time. The kids just look at him.

Uh, that was all the change I had.

Yeah. Me too.

Hey, says one of the kids to one of the others, I want to play you for that giant creamy. They walk over to the other end of the bench and get back to marbles. Mullen puts his chin on his hand and shakes his can.

Over on the next rink the Russians start up against the RCMP. There're quite a lot of people sitting on the benches for this one; everyone in town knows that the Russians are just about the best curlers around. Mullen and I sit right against the glass.

Curling takes a long time. Television hockey games and Sunday-afternoon football might feel long, but curling takes forever. If the Russians weren't the best curlers around it wouldn't really be a lot of fun. Every draw Pavel throws curves right in, pulls around other rocks like there's a magnet in it. Vaslav brushes real careful, hardly even totters. Flicks Anna Petrovna from side to side. At the far end he leans on Anna, catches his breath. The second stares down the ice and strokes his moustache. Rubs his bald head, slides careful up and down the ice, broom resting over his shoulder. In the sixth end Solly knocks four RCMP rocks out into the boards. The constables all groan and shake their heads. People on our side of the glass whistle and cheer.

Outside, Mullen hangs a chocolate cigarette off his lip. Lets it stick there by the paper. He upends the nut can: a dollar-eighty. Next time, Mullen says, I guess we'll have to plan it a bit better.

Jenny Tierney throws some rocks at the side of the building. You should have bet their marbles, she says. Jenny Tierney throws rocks like she doesn't much care where they end up, just pitches them underhand. But hard. They leave little chips in the paint of the wall. She stops and lights a cigarette.

What you got there, she asks. Chocolate? Real tough kid.

Real tough girl, says Mullen. Next time you should bet on some curling. Get a bit of the action. I mean, I don't know if it's a sport or not, but you could at least have the guts to put some money down on it.

Jenny cocks an eyebrow, bites her tongue like she's thinking about something. Then she spreads her feet and hits Mullen between the eyes. He yells and falls down. Slowly, like she isn't in a hurry, she sits down on his chest. Grabs his wrists and wedges them under her knees. Mullen hollers and she hits him a few times in the face, her fists coming right up above her shoulders. Then she stands up. Rubs her hands on her jeans and goes back inside.

Hey, Mullen, you okay?

My nose is bleeding.

Yeah, your nose is bleeding.

Is my lip bleeding?

Your lip is bleeding. Come on, we'll go inside. We've got to clean that up before it gets on your shirt.

Mullen sniffles, rubs his eyes. Blood drips on the concrete. How come it never snows in this stupid province?

We sit in the bathroom, he sits up on top of the sink. I mop his face with a wet paper towel. In the curling rink people whistle and clap.

It starts to rain. Rains and rains, for days. Nobody can say why. On Main Street people stand around under the eaves of their shops, in heavy winter jackets, holding newspapers over their heads. People watch the rain and talk about it. No sign of stopping, they say, no sign at all. It rains and the rain freezes; ice floats in puddles in the gutters. Ice on the picnic tables. The doors of people's cars won't open, on account of the ice. Mullen and I get a patio umbrella from the Russians, for the lemonade stand. A picture of a sunset on top.

And then there's the Ant People. The Ant People come and twist the tops off all the fire hydrants. The Ant People bite trees in half with their giant ant jaws; the trees fall and cut power lines, crush cars. People run around in the street, Help! Help! they all scream, while the Ant People storm through the aisles in the supermarket, smash all the ladders at the fire hall. The Ant People start fires. Their six buggy, hairy legs and their squishy, slimy abdomens. They build an anthill in the parking lot of the recreation centre out of mattresses and car seats, chesterfields, deep-freezes. The anthill towers up into the sky and everybody cries and hides. Why, oh why, they cry. Why did these awful Ant People come? When will they leave?

I hide in the gully, in the old tool shack. I cover the windows with some classified ads and make a fire, like Mullen's dad taught me. Building up a little teepee out of twigs. It gets pretty loud at night, down in the gully, with all the burning and shouting and eating alive up the hill. I cover myself in old newpaper and the red sky shines through my newspaper curtains. I wonder if Mullen and his dad got away from the Ant People. I bet them and the Russians hightailed it out, drove up on the sidewalks in Mullen's dad's pickup truck, running over Ant People, kicking them in their six ugly eyes when they tried to climb on the running boards. I bet they're all the way up to the Yukon by now, sleeping under the stars, in the box of the pickup truck.

The Ant People won't come into my gully; it's too narrow and tricky. I ought to be pretty safe here for a while. It's too bad when everybody's dead and gone, but sooner or later the anthill will collapse in on itself, trapping all the monsters inside. It'll be them hollering, shrill ant hollers. I'll roam around town, through all the broken buildings. I'll eat dry cereal in the empty IGA. I'll be pretty sad, I figure, being all by myself.

Jesus, kid, says Deke, in his undershirt, holding a can of beer. Jesus, you're soaked. What the hell are you doing out in the rain?

I was waiting for the bus, I say. You know, the Greyhound stop at the Red Rooster.

The bus? It's late, kid, it's past nine. Get inside.

I duck under Deke's arm. Stand on his welcome mat, dripping. Deke shuts the door. Christ, don't move, he says, I'll get you a towel. He runs down the hall. Deke's house is warm. Hey, Deke, I say, it sure is warm in here. What the hell were you doing, he shouts, waiting for the bus in the rain? He brings me a towel, thin, with a windsurfer on it. A windsurfer, blue waves. I take my shoes off; Deke wraps the towel around my shoulders.

Deke must have cleaned his kitchen. The dishes sit on the counter in neat piles on tea towels. All the beer cans stacked in the corner. Deke opens the fridge and gets another can of beer. He gets out a bottle of root beer, a real glass bottle with a cap. You like root beer? Yeah, Deke, I like root beer. Sit down, he says. You want a glass? No thanks, Deke, no thanks. He looks in a drawer, in another one. He wedges the bottle cap against the side of the counter and hits it, pop, with the heel of his fist. The cap hops off, rattles onto the floor.

What's all this? I ask, climbing onto a chair. His table a mess of paper, some of it scribbled and some of it typed. Yellow envelopes and a page of stamps. Deke hands me the damp bottle. My paperwork, he says. He snaps open his can of beer. Use the towel, he says. Don't drip on anything. This all for Davis Howe Oceanography? I ask. He picks up a piece of paper with holes on the side, like comes out of a computer.

This here is a statement on release against collateral. And this is an affidavit asserting my financial security. I put my lips on the bottle and slurp, the fizz tickles my nose.

You're shaking, kid. Look at you. Use the towel to dry your hair. What were you doing at the bus stop?

Waiting for the bus.

Which bus? You mean the Greyhound that leaves from in front of the Red Rooster?

I guess so, yeah.

Where were you going?

I don't know. I rub the top of my head with the towel. Down the hall, you can see the the parts of Deke's house that aren't finished. There's a lightbulb hanging on a string, and electrical sockets that stick out of the wall. The walls aren't painted, they're that drywall, with putty patches here and there. Here in the kitchen the walls have wood panelling, only I don't think it's real wood. It's the shiny kind, like it's been covered in plastic. A calendar hangs above the sink, with red circles around the days, and arrows pointing from one day to another. The refrigerator hums. I can hear the dryer, spinning and thumping.

On the fridge, held on with magnets, pictures of submarines. Cut out of newpapers, or glossy from magazines. Some look like they were cut from calendars. The tops of submarines sticking out of the water, or submarines under the ocean, surrounded by rocks and coral. There's a picture, I guess you'd call it a shipyard: a submarine inside a huge building, like a barn. All covered in scaffolding. Men with craggy faces stand around holding wrenches and electric drills.

I took the bus to Swift Current once, Deke says, for a job. Hey, Deke, they said, why don't you come out here to Swift Current for some skilled labour. You know what they had me doing? He takes a long drink of beer. They had this stack of plywood. Twenty feet high. It'd been used as forms laying down the second floor of this elementary school, and it was all full of nails. I took the bus fourteen hours into the middle of goddamn Saskatchewan for skilled labour and they had me pulling nails out of plywood for nine hours a day. You know what that is?

What's that, Deke?

That's bullshit, kid. Complete bullshit. Deke drinks some beer. How's your handwriting, kid?

My handwriting?

Here, he says. He hands me an envelope with a plastic window – you can see the red letters inside. He gives me a pen. Write your name, he says.

I write my name on the back of the envelope. Deke whistles. How come kids always got such neat handwriting? When I was a kid I sure had neat handwriting, all straight and even like yours. Look at it now, he says, waving one of the yellow pads. Even I can't read a word. You want to do me a favour?

Sure thing, Deke. I sip some root beer.

I need you to be a stockholder, he says. All you've got to do is sign some forms.

A stockholder?

Yeah, he says, in Davis Howe Oceanography Ltd. He shuffles through the stacks of paper. I figure if I can convince the bank I've got some investors, they might loosen up with the dollars. They don't give $400,000 to just anybody, kid.

I haven't got any money, Deke. I'm a kid, kids can't be stockholders.

Deke finds some paper, longer than usual, like the foolscap we get at school for writing stories. It's not like we're going to put your picture on the form, he says. You won't really be a stockholder, I just need your signature. You have a signature, kid?

I do, Deke.

Here, he says, pointing with a pen. On this line. So, what are you out so late for anyway?

I wrap the towel around my head, the way women in shampoo commercials do. I don't want to talk about it, Deke.

You boys get sent up? he asks. The dryer buzzes. Deke gets up, goes around the corner. Is that why you were at the bus stop?

I don't want to talk about it, Deke.

There's still a big empty spot in the middle of Deke's bookshelf. Deke used to keep fish. He had this big aquarium, a lot of litres in it, he had blue pebbles and real plants, and a treasure chest that opened and closed. Mullen and I came over to help him strain the pebbles in the sink. You should get a diver, we told Deke, and a castle. The pump he bought didn't work, though, and all the fish suffocated. Fish need air, I guess, even in the water, which is why you have to run a hose into the treasure chest in your aquarium. To pump in the air.

Hey, Deke, I say. Seeing as I'm a stockholder in your oceanography company now, why don't you tell me the story about the submarine again?

Kid, he says, I've told you the story about the submarine seventy times.

A stockholder, Deke. With a signature.

Hey, says Deke, you want some more root beer? He comes around the corner and bangs his knee on the lip of the table. Hops over to the fridge. He sets his beer down on the counter and opens another one with one hand. Know what? I haven't got any more root beer. How about some cocoa? You like cocoa? I've got a kettle. Whoever heard about rain in November anyway? It's bunk, kid. He crouches down and roots through a cupboard. Pulls out a cutting board, a box of cereal, an electric knife. Thought I had a kettle, he says.

Deke walks over to the filing cabinet, holding his knee. Takes a key out of his pocket and fiddles with the lock. He gets out a file, brings it over to the table.

Do you know where Uzbekistan is, kid?

I don't, Deke.

Hell, he says, *I* don't even know where Uzbekistan is. But I've been there. Skilled labour, they told me. Real top wage, real good work.

Uzbekistan isn't really a place. The Uzbek Soviet Socialist Republic – that's a place. That's where I've been. Quite a mouthful, eh? But everybody there, they call it Uzbekistan. Someday, they say – they get all serious when they talk about it – someday, they say, we'll live in Uzbekistan.

So it's in Russia.

Right, says Deke. Out there in the desert in Communist Russia. Now, kid, there are a lot of crooked people out there. You've got to be careful believing what people tell you. I met some characters in Calgary who claimed they had a licence from the Soviet government to set up an oil exploration company out there in the Uzbek desert. They were going to run a pipeline. Showed me all sorts of maps and graphs. Great opportunity, they said; all they needed was some skilled Western types to come along and help get things rolling. Guys with real oil-patch experience. Guys like me.

And you've got real oil-patch experience, right, Deke?

I've got real every kind of experience. So there we are, out there in the desert. First thing is, they're building a high-rise, thirty storeys, right there in the middle of the tundra. Housing for the pipeline workers. Well, turns out after an all-night plane flight and a few days' drive through I don't even know where, steppes they call them, and I get to the site and it seems there's been a filing error. No one there knew I was coming. They already have enough, what do you call them, Uzbeks around. So every morning I'd have to get into my boots and my thermals and gloves, and get my shovel. Go from floor to floor, shovelling snow out the window. The building kept filling up with snow, see, owing to all the uncovered windows. Deke drinks some beer. You ought to see that, kid. Snow flying out the window, thirty storeys up, the sun coming over the steppe or whatever you call it. Snow falling in sheets, all the way down.

Is the submarine in Uzbekistan, Deke?

The Uzbek Soviet Socialist Republic, Deke says. Well, one day I show up to work, only the place is crawling with soldiers. Soviets with rifles and a lot of angry guys waving paper around. I guess there wasn't any licence after all, just a lot of hot air. Don't know how you'd be dim enough to try and pull a stunt like that over there in Communist Russia, but then again, this is the same outfit that flew me halfway around the world to shovel snow out of windows. Well, I made it out without catching any notice, drove myself back to the nearest city, where we'd flown into. Had to do a lot of waiting around and arguing to convince anybody to send me home. But it's in the airport there that I meet Alev. Alev Ahmedivich Mohammed Djazic – how's that for a mouthful, eh? And Alev Ahmedivich Mohammed Djazic is trying to get out of the Uzbek SSR too. He tells me about the submarine. How he'd got it at a surplus auction on the cheap, owing to the officer serving as auctioneer being given over to nervous fits. Nervous fits and no one else came to the auction. The naval command, though, didn't much approve of the sale and were trying to track him down. He had his submarine hidden somewhere in Turkey. Wanted to unload it cheap. Believe me, kid, $400,000 may be more money than I've got, but it's goddamn cheap for a surplus Soviet diesel submarine.

Deke gets up, looks in a cupboard. Pulls out some white sugar cubes in a bowl. A jar of nuts. The Uzbeks, they drink coffee out of tiny cups, he says. And all the women keep their heads covered. It's hot, kid. Real hot. I mean, I was there in the winter and it was pretty cold, but they told me that in the summer it gets real hot. He drinks some beer. Spills a bit on his chin. He yawns.

What I need, Deke says, looking around his house, is somebody who can work detail, with wood. I'm good with the wiring and the drywall and all that, but I'd like to peel off the laminate, get some real sharp work done. No more of this low-rent shit. No wonder nobody gives me any money, kid. No wonder. How old are you?

Ten, Deke. I'm ten. And a half.

Ten and a half, Deke says. He pulls a cigarette out of his shirt pocket. His fingers shake. Ten and a half.

Deke puts the cigarette in his mouth but doesn't light it. He closes his eyes. I sit and watch him, with his eyes closed, till his chest starts moving real slow-like. He sniffles. Hey, Deke, I say. He doesn't say anything. Hey, Deke, I think I ought to go home now. Unless it's all right if I stay here? Deke's chest rises and falls. He snorts.

I turn on Deke's TV. At home I'd have to be in bed by now, but I figure since I'm staying with a grown-up, it'll be all right if I stay up awhile. Besides, if I go to bed now, I'll just be lying there, wide awake. It's no good, lying there not sleeping, feeling itchy and twitchy, twisting all around, your mind all busy and worrying. It's the worst feeling. It's better to just stay up. Sure, I'll be tired tomorrow, but I'm pretty used to being tired.

On TV there's a Western. A cowboy, beat up, hunched over the saddle of his horse. The cowboy rides into town and everybody hides. The priest locks the door to the church. Kids hide under the planks in the sidewalk. The cowboy gets down off his horse, woozy-like, you can see how he's all beat up. Draws his gun and stands there, in the middle of the town. Waiting.

At school today I'm pretty lucky that I'm invisible, 'cause the Dead Kids have got all frozen, like snowmen. They wobble back and forth, holding their lunch pails with their scraggly stick arms, the carrots on their faces drip. They can't talk, the frozen Dead Kids at school today, on account of their frozen mouths I guess. They all yowl and howl, and lurch around. Good thing I'm invisible today, so they leave me alone. At recess I sit under the stairwell and read some comic books.

Not very often, but sometimes, I spend the whole day under the stairwell. I'll bring some comic books in my bag, or draw. Giant octopuses maybe, they're always good for a laugh, or I also like to draw flying saucers wrecking cities with their death rays. I like to draw rockets, fat in the middle, with fins. Sometimes I like to sit under the stairwell and bounce my tennis ball, real quiet-like, 'cause they always come looking for me when I'm not in class. It's pretty hard to pick the right stairwell where you won't get caught right away.

Mr. Weissman draws shapes on the chalkboard. Stops now and then to push his heavy glasses back up his nose. A quadrilateral has four sides. A square is a kind of quadrilateral. A polygon has more than two sides. Is a quadrilateral a polygon? I know he told us, but I can remember only so much math.

Mr. Weissman draws and talks, shapes and numbers, his back to us. I think he forgets we're here. At first I thought geometry would be fun, with the drawing, with the rulers and compasses, but it turns out it's just another trick to make you do math.

Dwayne Klatz pulls the point out of a ballpoint pen. Taps the hollow plastic tube on his desk. He tears a page corner out of his science book. Rolls it between his fingers.

And this shape? asks Mr. Weissman. A polygon, somebody says. A trapezoid, says somebody else.

Dwayne Klatz may not be such a Dead Kid. He fidgets in class. Taps the side of his desk. Drums his fingers. Dwayne Klatz always wears overalls, he's always pulling stuff out of the big pocket in the front: red Monopoly hotels, hockey cards, elastic bands. He chews the paper in his mouth. Works his jaw, chews and chews. Looks over at Mullen sitting in front of me. Grins and shows the paper between his teeth.

Mullen looks around the classroom. Points to the front row, where all the front-row girls sit, writing in their coiled notebooks with their long, sharp pencils. Girls always have long pencils with sharp points. Never short little stubs with flat lead. They never chew the ends or bite off the erasers.

Dwayne puts the pen tube in his mouth. Turns his head from side to side, the tube sticking straight out like a cigar.

Takes a deep breath and poot, the spitball flies across the room. Sticks to the back of Jill Johnson's chair. Some kids snicker.

Mullen pulls the bin of his desk open, quiet-like. Some kids keep all their stuff in stacks in their desks: one stack for brown-papered textbooks, one for glossy workbooks, one for paper folders. Mullen doesn't have stacks. Mullen has a pile. Clumps of loose-leaf poke out the sides of his lined scribblers, duotangs stuffed into his science text. Mullen doesn't have a pencil case, just pencils, short pencil crayons, pencil shavings, sticking out all over. Pulls out a sheet of white binder paper, points to his mouth.

No, foolscap, whispers Dwayne Klatz. The few of us paying attention narrow our mouths. Mullen looks at Klatz for a while, then slides a pile of paper out from the bottom. Foolscap with blue lines.

The three kinds of triangles. Remember? What did we call them?

Mullen crumples a long sheet of foolscap into a ball, slow enough to stay quiet. I rattle my desk a bit. Mullen squishes the ball as much as he can, which isn't really so small. Opens his mouth, pops the whole ball of paper in.

Isophocles, says Pete Leakie. Mr. Weissman's shoulders slump a bit.

Mullen chews and chews. Keeps his eyes on Dwayne Klatz, who keeps nodding, a little smile on his face. Klatz has a big black mole on the side of his cheek, right in the middle. Looks like it might crawl away at any moment, down his long, narrow head. Mullen chews and chews. Opens his mouth – the paper's all soft, the blue and pink ink runny and soggy. Dwayne Klatz points to the front row, but Mullen shakes his head. Takes another sheet of foolscap. Crumples it, slow again. More kids watch now, a few slow to catch on, a few leaning right in. Mullen opens his mouth even wider, puts the second ball in with the soppy pulp already inside. Chews slow-like. Works his mouth around all the crumpled edges. Breathes heavy through his nose.

Mr. Weissman draws the angles between the sides of his triangles. Mullen chews and chews, crumples up more foolscap. Dwayne Klatz stands up and waves his arms, then sits back down quick when some of the Dead Kids near the front turn in their seats. Mr. Weissman turns around. Mullen sinks down in his seat, cheeks full, pulp around his lips.

Which is the longest side of a triangle? One of the front-row girls puts up her hand. The hypotenuse! Mr. Weissman nods and turns back around. A kid starts to laugh and Dwayne Klatz drags his index finger across his throat, like in the movies. Mullen chews and chews. Crumples up another sheet of foolscap. Has to spread his lips apart with his fingers to fit it in. He can't really chew anymore, can't close his mouth.

How many? mouths Dwayne Klatz.

Mullen looks off to the side, thinking. Then he holds up four fingers.

Mr. Weissman, says Randy Schloz, his hand up.

Now, what do you think happens when we add up all the angles inside a triangle? What do you think the sum will be?

Mr. Weissman?

Yes, Randy?

Mr. Weissman, Mullen is eating paper.

Mullen, don't eat paper, says Mr. Weissman. He doesn't turn around. Draws a triangle on the board, careful to make the lines straight. Draws little arcs inside the corners. Draws a question mark in the middle.

Mullen gets out of his desk, walks over to Randy Schloz's desk. Randy sticks his hand as far up as it will go. Mullen reaches down and pulls open the desk bin. Neat piles inside, a stack for workbooks, another for paper. Some pulpy spit drips out of his open mouth into the desk.

Mr. Weissman, says Randy.

Now, this is a right-angle triangle. So we already know how many degrees in the corner, right?

Mullen opens his mouth as wide as he can. The paper lump is too big to come out. He sticks a finger into the side of a cheek. His eyes bulge out and you can see his stomach heave. He bends forward. Dwayne Klatz gets out of his desk, comes over and wraps his arms around Mullen's stomach. Randy Schloz tries to slam his desk bin shut and Dwayne Klatz squeezes Mullen around the middle. He gags and retches out a four-foolscap mess of soggy paper goo all over the inside of the bin. Kids yell and gag and Randy Scholz starts shouting, Mr. Weissman! Mr. Weissman! Mullen threw up in my desk! Dwayne Klatz lets go of Mullen and they both stand there while Mr. Weissman sets down his chalk, walks up the aisle between the desks. Looks over top of his glasses into Randy's desk.

He threw up in my desk, see? He did it on purpose.

Good thing Dwayne was here to save me, says Mullen. I could have choked. Thanks a lot, Dwayne.

Anytime, Mullen, says Dwayne Klatz.

Mr. Weissman takes Mullen's hand and leads him out the door, down the hall. Dwayne Klatz and I glare at Randy Schloz.

He didn't have to throw up in my desk, says Randy.

Deke and I go to the credit union on a Friday after school. We walk down the street so that Deke doesn't have to drive the El Camino. Whatever its other merits, says Deke, combing his hair with a black comb, the El Camino carries with it a certain stigma. I'm not saying it's justified, I'm just saying. Junior high school kids sit on their skateboards on the steps of the Elks' Hall, smoking. They sit on their skateboards even though the sidewalks are all icy, the streets caked in ice from the rain.

Lou Ellis from Aldersyde stands in front of McClaghan's hardware store, chewing some tobacco. McClaghan has the awning pulled down to keep the rain off. The two of them play with the dial on the radio, trying to get the news. He waves to Deke. Good day for a walk, eh Howitz? Sure thing, Deke says, sure thing.

McClaghan's hardware store is right in the middle of town, so people like to stand around on his sidewalk and sound off. McClaghan will be sitting outside any time you walk by, smoking his Matinée Slims. If McClaghan's inside the store, selling two-by-fours or saw blades, you can sit on his curb and watch the cars from up the hill drive by, looking for parking spaces. The Russians like to sit in front of McClaghan's store and listen to his radio.

Howitz, you didn't come to McGentry's funeral, McClaghan says. He sits in one of the folding lawn chairs against the big picture window: shovels, rakes, a wheelbarrow. He coughs and spits in his jar.

Bert McGentry died? Deke asks.

Fell down the stairs at the Legion Hall, says McClaghan. He got bone fragments.

Bone fragments?

They roamed around internally, says McClaghan. Fucking with his vital organs. He spits in the jar.

Bert McGentry from Millarville?

Bert McGentry lived three blocks from here, says Lou Ellis, behind the public library.

Have a look, says McClaghan. New telephone. He holds up a phone receiver with no cord. Just a mouth and earpiece, and those touch-tone buttons, all one piece.

Deke whistles. How far away can you walk with that?

McClaghan shrugs. The main piece is back on the desk. Sometimes you have to put it back, to charge the battery.

And you can hear people talking all right? Deke asks.

Hear 'em fine.

Deke thinks for a second. Takes a deep breath. Well, he says, I've been thinking about the rent.

McClaghan's face shrinks a notch. Thinking about the rent, he says.

Yeah, says Deke. Thinking, you know, what with the increase ...

An increase reflecting a fair assessment of inflation.

Deke thinks some more. Well, he says, I'd been talking with Vaslav Kurskinov, a few doors down ...

If you ask about the hot-water tank, I'll evict you, says McClaghan. Your hot-water tank is fine.

Lou Ellis takes off his hat. Well goddamn, he says.

She comes up the sidewalk. A red scarf wrapped around her shoulder, hands in the pockets of her black pants. McClaghan spits in the jar. She walks up the sidewalk and stops in front of the hardware store. Reads the signs in the window: Fall Sale, and Authorized Dealer, the names of chainsaw companies and their logos. Lou Ellis scratches the top of his head.

I haven't got any more primer, says McClaghan. Next week at the soonest. He spits in his jar. Black flecks stick here and there in the waxy yellow layers.

I need a thermostat, she says. The boiler is old and none of the wiring matches up.

McClaghan takes another Matinée Slim out of his pocket. Lights a match off the aluminum siding. A boiler? You haven't got a boiler, he says. You've got a furnace.

I have a boiler, she says. Her voice is deep and careful, and the French in the h's and e's and o's makes every word really stick with you. Heats water with a gas element, she says. Steam piped up around the building, to the radiators. A boiler.

McClaghan smokes. I haven't got anything like that, he says.

Can you check? she asks. There's a scratchy, throaty sound to the voice, like it's coming over a radio.

I haven't got any thermostats, he says.

She does up a button on the cuff of her jacket. What about the electrician? Morley Fleer? Fleer doesn't do retail, says McClaghan. He spits in the jar. Deke and Lou Ellis both scratch their chins. McClaghan smokes.

I'll be back next week for that primer, she says. Late next week, says McClaghan. She stares at him. Her lips are narrow and she breathes through her nose. Next week, she says. She turns around and walks back up the sidewalk.

Goddamn, says Lou Ellis.

McClaghan squints. Once she's far enough away down the sidewalk he picks up his new telephone, punches the numbers. Fleer, he says. Right, damn cold. Hey. What? No, at work. Listen, have you got thermostats? An old one, I guess. For a boiler. What? You know, hot water and steam, piped all around to radiators. Yeah, there's a few different makes, I guess. I guess steam. They don't build gravity boilers anymore. 'Cause they're not safe. He holds the phone between his shoulder and cheek and smokes. Yeah? Just one? Look, put it under the counter. Don't sell it to anyone. What? Sure, I'll buy it eventually. But don't sell it to anybody. I don't know, it might be a while. Not to anybody. Right. What? Fleer, the RCMP can't curl for shit. Keep your money. No, the Elks. The

Nanton Elks will win that match. Don't sell that thermostat. Right.

He pushes a button and sets the phone down in his lap. Glares at Deke. Tell that fat Russian he's lucky not to live under a bridge, says McClaghan. Right, says Deke. A bridge.

At the credit union, the doors slide open automatically. We get in line in the roped aisles. People shift on their feet and pop their gum, some of them still soggy from the rain.

Now, you don't need to talk, Deke says to me. Just look respectable. Give them those big eyes, like when you found out that all the fish had died. Sure thing, Deke, I say. Davis, Deke says, Davis Howe. Right, Davis Howe.

The man ahead of us wears a wide-brimmed straw hat. Flat, stringy hair pokes out from underneath. He holds a thick black leather book under his arm. When the teller waves he takes two long steps and sets the book down heavily on the counter. I need $4,400 in cash, he says. Withdrawn from my account. Also, I need twenty-seven envelopes. The teller plays with her pen. Sir, we aren't authorized to give out that much. On the fourteenth of October, bellows the Hat Man, I stood in this line and watched you dispense $5,600 in cash to Glen Trottner from Black Diamond, a man whose credentials I could say a thing or two toward. I have the funds available in my account and I'm sure that the institution will remain solvent. He drums his fingers on the cover of the book. The teller backs up and whispers to another teller.

They bring him the envelopes and go off to whisper at a desk. The Hat Man takes a thick black marker out of his jacket, starts writing on the envelopes. I stand up on my tiptoes but can't see. Hey, Deke, I whisper, what's he writing? Davis, says Deke. What's he writing, Davis? People's names, says Deke. One name on each envelope.

Hello, I'd like to apply for a loan please, my name is Howe, Davis Howe. I've brought these forms. And here are some affidavits, and releases.

The teller scribbles on her white pad. How much do you need a loan for?

I need $400,000.

She coughs. She scrunches up her eyebrows real tight, like she practices scrunching them. We can't loan you $400,000.

This here, says Deke, is a signed testimonial to my credentials and character. Notice all the signatures.

We can't lend anyone $400,000. We haven't got the capital. We can't cover the liability.

I have these forms.

You might try in Calgary, says the teller, with a larger institution. Someone with a broader investment base.

Deke leans on the counter. How much money can you lend me?

It depends, she says, on what you need it for. Are you starting a business? Deke picks up his papers, taps them on the counter to make the edges all even.

I need to buy a submarine.

A what?

A submarine. A surplus Soviet diesel submarine, from the Black Sea fleet. Built in 1971. Its warhead payload already decommissioned and removed, so that's not an issue. I need $400,000, far below the actual value, to purchase it from a man in the USSR – I'll have to buy him a few drinks. I'll have to hire people for crew. I figure that won't cost so much, given that a lot of people over there need work. Not everybody knows about submarines, though. I'll have to pay a few people to turn their heads, in Turkey, and through the Suez. Avoid the proper authorities. I thought I might come back around the Horn. I thought that might be a good trip.

The grey in the teller's hair stands sharp under the fluorescent lights. At the next wicket the Hat Man scribbles on his envelopes. The ceiling is high, with the ducts and pipes exposed, painted black. The scribbling echoes.

Why do you need a submarine?

Deke waves his hand. I think it's fairly obvious why anyone might need a submarine. It's about as useful a machine as a person could possibly own.

We're very busy today, Mr. Howe, she says, And there are a lot of other customers with legitimate business to conduct here.

You're saying my business isn't legitimate?

Mr. Howe –

I'm not going to stand here all day explaining oceanography to you.

Mr. Howe, if you could please be on your way.

You're worried that I won't be able to pay off the loan, aren't you?

She folds her arms across her chest.

Deke reaches into his pocket, takes out some throat drops, the lemon kind. Unwraps one and puts it in his mouth. The smell of lemon and medicine fills the air. Well, he says, I could always go down to the Caribbean. There's a lot of those cruise ships down in the Caribbean, and yachts. If worse comes to worse and the legitimate aspects of the business don't work out, I might go down to the Caribbean and find one of those cruise ships. I figure we could get right up close to it, underwater, in the submarine, and then come up to the surface. Surprise it. And then my crew, we'd get in little boats, and we'd need ropes, with those hooks on them – what do you call those? Grappling hooks, I say. Right, says Deke. We'd all climb up onto the cruise ship, I guess we'd have to have guns, so that would be another start-up cost. That's what we're talking about, right? Start-up costs? We'd make everybody give us their wallets, and their wives' wedding rings and jewellery. We'd knock over the fancy statues and play the piano drunk. Then we'd slip back into the depths with our plunder, leaving the ship to sink. I figure we'd do it that way, not just in the Caribbean, mind. So what

I mean is, supposing my legitimate maritime business comes up short, there'll always be some way to pay back that loan, owning as useful a piece of equipment as a submarine. What do you think?

We have a seat on the steps outside so that Deke can light a cigarette. The rain comes down in a slow, icy wash. Not really big drops, just kind of this constant, cold wet. Water drips off his nose.

Well, I suppose that wasn't my finest moment, he says.

You ought to get them with the Milk Chicken Bomb, I tell him.

The what?

The Milk Chicken Bomb. It's the worst thing.

How do you make a Milk Chicken Bomb?

I shrug. I was hoping you'd know

Deke sighs and stands up. We should've just driven the damn El Camino.

At school today it's tricky, on account of the electric tiles. The black ones are all right, but all the white ones in the hallways have about sixty million volts in them. I have to hop from black to black, so as not to get all cooked up into a cinder. Makes it real slow, moving around, because sometimes the tiles alternate, like a checkerboard, but sometimes they spread out. Sometimes the floor will be all black, like an oil slick on television, and then it's easy going. But sometimes the floor just whites right up. I can't go down the hall to the gym at all, and in the hallway to the library there's just one row of black tiles right up against the wall; I have to shuffle sideways, with my arms up against the lockers, to keep from falling over.

At recess Mullen and I go over behind the gym to throw a tennis ball. We like to throw the tennis ball at the wall and catch it.

The way I figure, Mullen says, we can go down to the train bridge after school. Did you know there's a tunnel under the train bridge, goes right into the riverbank? He roots around in his bag, gets out a hard hat with a light on the front. Hands me a pair of goggles, like pilots wear. You can wear these, he says, and I've got some of my dad's gloves. The heavy kind he wears to smash ice.

Where'd you get that hard hat?

It was in our basement. In a box. My dad's got all sorts of crazy stuff down there, packed up in boxes. Wish I'd found this a long time ago, he says. He fiddles with the light and it blinks on. He points it into his face and blinks. Stares at it as long as he can manage then twists it off again.

Mullen, I probably shouldn't stay out. I mean, after staying out at Deke's all night and almost getting pneumonia. I might hear about it.

You might?

Well, you know. Eventually.

I hear about everything, says Mullen. My ears ought to be bigger. Anyway, I've got this scarf too. See, it's blue, you like blue, don't you?

I throw the ball at the wall, let it bounce before catching it. If you don't catch it you have to chase it before it rolls down the sidewalk onto the playground. Mullen throws the ball and I miss it. The ball rolls down the sidewalk. Rolls down the sidewalk and some kids come around the corner, one of them reaches down, picks up the ball. Aw hell, says Mullen. Aw hell.

These are some real Dead Kids, six feet down. Their hair all combed and pictures on their T-shirts, little surfboards, or skiers with sunglasses. Dave Steadman, his dad owns the pharmacy. Drinks a cola out of a can. Dave Steadman is two inches taller than me, he must weigh more than a hundred pounds. He plays hockey on a team where they're allowed to board check.

Hey, says Dave, it's the Feedlot kids. He tosses the ball up, catches it. Well, the Feedlot kid and the kid who wants to be just like him.

Take off, Steadman, says Mullen.

Steadman looks over at his friends. Throws one of them the tennis ball and walks right over to us.

Seriously, he says to me, what's the deal with hanging out downtown all the time with this loser and his gangster friends?

What the hell are you talking about? asks Mullen.

My dad says those Russians are criminals, says Steadman. That the RCMP take pictures of their house and one day they're all going to jail, for selling drugs and keeping dead people under their house. Other stuff too, way worse stuff.

Your dad sells drugs, says Mullen.

My dad's allowed to sell drugs, says Steadman. He's got a licence. It's hanging in his office.

It's a good thing your dad isn't a detective, says Mullen, or we'd have a lot more crime in town. People shooting each other in the street, everybody's car getting stolen all the time. Detective Steadman, everybody'd say, where's my car? And him just standing there all slack-jawed. Glassy-eyed. Thank your dad for me, Steadman, for not becoming a detective.

I'm going to beat the hell out of you, Mullen.

Mullen shrugs. I bet I can smoke more cigarettes than you, he says.

All the other kids go quiet. Steadman sticks his hands in his pockets. You don't smoke. The only kid in the fifth grade who smokes is Christine Sutz. And Jenny Tierney, but she doesn't count 'cause she should be in junior high by now. Mullen shrugs. He reaches into his pocket and pulls out a pack of cigarettes, Export A blue, Deke's brand, nearly full.

You probably haven't even got any matches, Steadman says, but nervous now. The other kids poke him in the back. Smoke a few, Dave, they say. Let's see him throw up. Mullen puts a cigarette in his mouth, lets it hang in the middle, the paper stuck to his lip, the way Deke does. He gets a pack of matches out of his pocket, the kind they give you at Red Rooster. A blue cover with a green tree. I bet I can smoke more cigarettes than you, Steadman, he says. He lights a match, sucks at it with the cigarette. He coughs, then takes a long drag. Makes a show of inhaling, waits a few seconds, then blows out a thick cloud.

Steadman takes a cigarette out of the pack. Turns it over a few times. Takes the matches. You're turning green already, he says. You can't even finish that. Mullen smokes. Are you a detective too, Steadman? Inheriting the family business? Steadman tries to light a match, can't. Tries again, can't. He puts the cigarette in his mouth, folds the cover of the matchbook back over a match, pulls it out. Lit. Then he coughs the match out trying to suck it into the cigarette.

Here, Mullen says, smoke this one. Gives Steadman his cigarette and lights another. Tobacco smoke hangs in a cloud. Smells like the inside of Deke's El Camino, like the curling rink after a garage sale in the spring. Steadman has a drag and coughs. Mullen coughs and has a drag. They smoke.

Pete Leakie comes around the corner. Stops and takes his time getting a good look at everything. Hey, Mrs. Lampman's coming, he says, any second. Everybody looks at everybody else. Over here? asks Steadman. Right this way, says Pete Leakie. Steadman drops the cigarette, crushes it with his running shoe.

Mullen has another drag. You're green and yellow, Mullen says. Steadman makes to hit Mullen in the face when Mrs. Lampman comes around the corner, eating a sandwich.

Mullen, you're smoking, she says. He drops the cigarette, stomps it out. Mrs. Lampman wraps her sandwich in a bit of cellophane. Everybody stands there not saying anything. She walks over and holds out her hand. Mullen gives her the cigarettes. He's got matches too, says Steadman. Mullen hands her the matches. A kid who tells on another kid is a Dead Kid, he says. Hey, she snaps, that's enough. She takes Mullen's hands and walks away with him.

You better run away now, Steadman says to me. His face still pretty green. Pete Leakie and I run away.

It keeps raining. The ice gets thicker. The Russians build a ramp in the street with plywood and a few old tires. They freeze it with the garden hose. Pavel and Solzhenitsyn roll old steel garbage cans out of the garage while Vaslav sits on the step, scribbling in his notebook. They tie on their skates and take turns skating down the street and over the ramp, over as many cans as they can. Pavel clears two, arms windmilling. Solly gets over three. Pavel catches his toe on the way over a fourth, goes heels over head onto his face. My eye! he shouts, lying on the ice. They both get down on their hands and knees to look for Pavel's glass eye. He keeps one hand over his face, like he's embarrassed by the hole.

Hey, Vaslav, I say, you ever been to Uzbekistan?

Vaslav taps his pencil on the side of his face. Makes this hollow knocking sound. Uzbekistan? Where the hell is that?

The Uzbek Soviet Socialist Republic, Vaslav. It's in Russia.

I'm from Petersburg, he says.

No, you're from Leningrad, says Solzhenitsyn.

And now that I'm not there, I don't have to call it that.

You never went to that big Uzbek desert? I asked.

When I was a kid, we went to the Ukraine, says Vaslav. For a field trip. They showed us an aluminum smelter. We all had to wear badges. Solly, he shouts, you know all about geography apparently. You ever heard of Uzbekistan? Solly doesn't say anything.

Hey, Vaslav, I say, you've lived on this street for a long time. Longer than anybody.

I have not, says Vaslav. Kreshick down there on the corner, he's lived here since before there was electricity in town. Look at that hedge of his. I'm not some old derelict.

You know that shop, I ask, across from the post office, with the windows papered over?

The windows aren't papered over anymore, Vaslav says. The Lévesque junk shop. Antique shop, he called it.

The what?

They sold, you know, china plates and old bed frames. Candlesticks. He had rocking chairs. You know, junk. It's got a basement, they say. Full to bursting.

Pavel sits up, grins. Brushes his eye off on his coat lapel, breathes on it. Stretches out his face and pops it back in. Vaslav writes something down in his notebook, then crosses it out. Full to bursting, he says.

When the wind gets too cold, we all go inside. Mullen's dad shows up with Mullen and a case of beer and the four grown-ups clank their bottles together around the table. We sit around the table and listen to the wind scrape along the ice. The frozen windows tug on their hinges. All over the house, patches of duct tape along the edges of the windows keep out the rain. Plastic bags stick out of cracks. Striped Hudson's Bay blankets hang in doorways.

Mullen's dad and Solzhenitsyn talk about politics, with a lot of big words I don't get, something about Russia. Vaslav writes in his notebook. Pages and pages. Chews his pencil. Solzhenitsyn brings out some chicken soup. Mullen and I slurp our soup and mostly they ignore us and talk about politics. We slurp pretty loud to see if they'll get edgy but sometimes they just don't care what we do.

Solzhenitsyn gets up and goes into the kitchen. They all watch him. Vaslav leans out over the table and whispers, Twenty bucks on the girl from the junior high school, that new art teacher.

What, all flaky-like?

Saw him help her out with her groceries the other day. Had the bottom go out of one of her bags, see. Cans and cartons all over the place.

I don't know, says Mullen's dad, it doesn't seem likely. I thought he was all for the pharmacist's wife.

Sure, goes without saying. But this art teacher …

Solzhenitsyn comes out of the kitchen with a bubbling pie plate. Oven mitts. Everyone shuts up and looks all innocent-like. Solly sets down the pie. The brown crust steams and bubbles, red juice runs out of cracks and hisses overtop of the crust.

What on earth is that?

It's a tomato-soup pie, says Solzhenitsyn. Everybody looks blank at him.

You know, tomato-soup pie. Cabbage, potatoes. Like I used to make when we lived above the taxidermist. He cuts into the crust. The pie bubbles like a vinegar volcano in science class.

I don't think I've ever heard of tomato-soup pie, says Vaslav.

We made tomato soup pie in Petersburg, when Brezhnev was in charge. Couldn't get anything fresh, just canned cabbage and tomato soup.

We lived in Edmonton when Brezhnev was in charge, says Pavel. You mean Andropov.

No, Andropov came later. I mean Brezhnev. You know, in the sixties. Pointy ears, jowls. I was in high school.

You mean Andropov, says Pavel. Andropov was first, then Brezhnev. We were in that place on Jasper Avenue. I never saw any tomato-soup pie.

They both look at Vaslav. He holds up his hands.

Don't ask me. I'm a conscientious objector.

The house rumbles. We all stop talking and look around. Solzhenitsyn stands back up, pulls off the oven mitts. Cocks his head.

The sink? asks Vaslav. Solzhenitsyn shakes his head. Mullen reaches out his fork for the pie and Solzhenitsyn holds his finger up to his lips.

A groan, like wood stretching, and a long rattle. Metallic and hollow. Solzhenitsyn walks over to the radiator. Squats down and puts his ear close to the heavy coiled pipes. It's that goddamn hot-water tank, says Vaslav. Solly turns the valve on the side of the radiator, just so. He stands up and goes into the kitchen. We all stay quiet, listen, watch the steam from the pie. He comes out of the kitchen with a ball-peen hammer. Goes into Vaslav's room. We hear a ping ping ping of soft hammering on iron.

There's a longer, slower groan, more of a sigh, which tapers off into a thin hiss out of the radiator. The hiss fades into a low hum. Solly comes back out, sets the hammer down on the window sill. Sits back down and starts to cut more wedges of the pie.

A house is under pressure, he says. Water, steam, gas, air, shit. More delicate than you think.

We hold out our plates and he dishes out hot red pie. Mullen reaches out across the table for the water jug and winces. His dad puts down his fork.

Let's see.

It's fine, Dad, come on, says Mullen. Blows on his pie.

Did the bandage come off?

Can I have the water, please? asks Mullen. His dad reaches over and pulls his sweater down over his shoulder. The tape has pulled off the top of his arm. Hot, puckered pink skin underneath. Mullen's dad pulls the white bandage back over and pushes down the gummy tape.

How'd that happen? asks Pavel.

My son has the good sense of a washtub. Took it into his tiny head to find horizontal fireworks and stand in front of them.

Schblaow, says Mullen. Holds his hands up, fingers spread. It was blue. Bluest thing I ever saw. Right close-like. He squirms away from his dad's hands, pulls his sweater back up. We all blow on our hot red pie.

At school we play kickball. Kids stand at the bases or sit on the bench, all wearing jackets and complaining about the rain. Can't we just say inside? ask all the kids. The rain is cold and gets right inside your jacket, inside your boots. It drips out of your hair. Mr. Weissman wears a yellow rain slicker. Blows his whistle and waves his arms. Come on, he says, you've got to keep moving. Keep that blood going! The pitcher rolls the big rubber kickball down the wet diamond, water spinning off in beads, and kids kick it off into the field. It splashes when it hits the wet, frozen grass.

Pete Leakie walks up to home plate. Takes his wet round glasses off, breathes on them. Rubs them on his shirt. Puts them back on and squints.

The pitcher rolls the ball down the icy diamond and Pete steps into it and misses. His boot flies off. He rubs his glasses and stands there on one foot while the pitcher walks out, picks up his boot. Throws it back to him. The pitcher bounces the ball while Pete puts his boot back on. He runs out toward the second pitch and misses again. Kids sit on the bench getting wet. Out in the field kids stamp in the wet grass.

The third pitch rolls down over the thin wet ice and Pete kicks the ball, it makes a solid thwopping sound and flies out between second and third base. Pete looks pretty surprised. He runs out to first base and kids yell and whistle. He runs out to first base and there's this big crack and all of a sudden I can't see. Everything turns black and white and I can't see, it's like when you close your eyes after staring into a bright light, and I can't see anything except Pete Leakie, a foot up in the air, not quite at first base. Up in the air with his arms and legs sticking straight out like a starfish, black against white.

There's a huge crack and crash and then we're all standing around, confused, kids screaming and crying. Kids stand around with their hands over their ears and Pete Leakie lies there on the ground. Mr. Weissman shoos all the kids away. Pete Leakie lies there and the ground is dry all around him, and you can see his lips moving, like he's talking to himself, steaming there on the ground.

Mullen's dad looks at his watch. The pitcher. The No Dogs Please sign. Us.

Come on, you guys. It's the middle of the day. What are you trying to pull? asks Mullen's dad.

School's closed.

He looks up into the sky. Not so cold, he says. Hardly any snow. What is it this time? Teachers' strike? Gas-line break?

Call the school, says Mullen.

What did you do this time? Did they send you home?

Just call the school, says Mullen. I don't want to talk about it.

Pete Leakie got struck by lightning, I say.

What?

You know, Pete Leakie, I say. Draws on the sidewalk, wears glasses. Lives a few blocks up the hill.

You can't get struck by lightning in October, says Mullen's dad. There's no cumulus clouds. No thunderstorms. You need the heat on the ground for the pressure difference, to make the static electricity.

Go call the school, says Mullen.

Mullen's dad goes inside. Later he comes back out.

We all walk downtown to watch them knock down the grain elevators. Old farmers with high-peaked hats and mouths full of chewing tobacco stand around watching. They spit on the ground. Mullen and I sit over on the curb watching all the old men. An RCMP constable gets out of his car and waves his arms to get everybody's attention. Talks to them for a while, pointing up at the elevators. The old men nod and they all take a few steps back.

Just like Deke said. Two Bobcats. Steel mesh over the windows. They drive the Bobcats into the wall. The wood splinters, cracks all the way up. The Alberta Wheat Pool logo cracks in half. One side caves in, broken lumber crashes on the steel roofs of the Bobcats. The elevator leans, you can hear it crack and break, all the wood. Is a grain elevator hollow? Are there stairs, drywall, light bulbs inside? The whole top half crashes down in one piece, topples over and crashes into the gravel. Can't see anything for the dust. Deke was right, saying it was like dry toast.

Workmen in hard hats walk through the wreck. Walls and parts of walls that didn't fall they hit with sledgehammers. The Bobcats push broken boards into a pile. Some of the old men flick their cigarettes at the wreck, turn away.

The rain turns to snow after school, around four o'clock, before the school buses even get out of town. Cars slide around in the slush; they stall in intersections, in front of Town Hall, at the railroad tracks. Somebody tips over a shopping cart in front of the Alberta Liquor Control Board. School buses drive slow up the hill, their back halves at wrong angles, take up the whole street. In the windows kids scrape at the frost.

Mullen stomps his feet, looks into the sky. Slaps his hands on his hips. You see that? The real thing, he says. Look at those clouds. Look how low they are. Mullen picks up some soggy snow and packs it into a ball. Tosses it up and down. We'll have to wax the toboggan, he says. We'll keep snowballs under the porch. He runs and slides in the slush, arms held out.

We head down to the river to throw some rocks. The water's too fast to skip rocks, but we like to throw them anyway. We like to sit down by the old rowboat we pulled up from the bottom last summer. Mullen gets a big chunk of concrete and heaves it into the river. I find some flat rocks and throw them at trees on the far bank. The snow comes down wet and steady. All the rocks around the river are slick with ice and covered in snow. We walk carefully on the slick rocks, arms out for balance, trying not to fall over.

If we had a pickup truck we could rob McClaghan's store, Mullen says. Go late at night, park in the back alley. I bet we could get that door open with a file. We could get all the fireworks we wanted and fill up the truck and drive away before anybody even heard. Nobody would say anything 'cause nobody likes McClaghan anyway.

We can't drive, Mullen.

Lots of people know how to drive, he says, and nobody likes McClaghan, they all talk about what an old jerk he is and how he's always raising the rent.

I bet you couldn't get his back door open even with a file, I say.

Mullen throws some rocks in the river. Nobody likes McClaghan so much, we could throw a rock through his front window, says Mullen, break his front window and people would hear and not care. All the fireworks we wanted.

Hey, you hear that sound? asks Mullen. We listen. It sounds like somebody digging, I say. It does, Mullen says, it does.

A little bit up the river, Deke, digging a hole. Wearing just jeans and a T-shirt, even though it's cold and snowing. His mesh Skoal hat. All covered in sweat. Deke is digging a hole about ten feet up from the river, where the bank is shored up with big grey rocks. All around, the brush and shrubs have been hacked down. There's a wheelbarrow, with a pickaxe and hedge trimmers.

Hey, Deke, what are you doing? Deke looks up, wipes his forehead with the back of his hand. Get out of here, you kids. What are you digging, Deke? asks Mullen. A hole? A trench? Deke leans his shovel against the wall of the hole, already about four feet deep. You kids are going to get me found out. Step off. He sits down, drinks out of his water bottle.

I stay at Mullen's house for a while. We sit in the kitchen and read comic books while Mullen's dad makes us macaroni and cheese. Across the street Deke comes home, pushing his wheelbarrow, with all his muddy shovels.

In gym class we play dodgeball. Everybody runs around throwing balls at each other. Dodgeball isn't much fun because Dead Kids like to come right up to you and throw the ball as hard as they can at the top of your head or your stomach. We all run around and Mr. Weissman waves his arms. It's about reflexes, he shouts, not brutality. Be considerate. I'm pretty much the slowest – the slowest except for Pete Leakie maybe. But Pete Leakie still isn't back at school, so mostly I get hit with the ball. Mullen likes dodgeball but isn't allowed to come to gym class these days, on account of his detention backlog.

Dave Steadman walks up to Jenny Tierney while everybody is playing dodgeball. Leans in and whispers something in her ear. She turns a colour. Everybody stops. The ball, mid-throw, slaps against the wall and rolls into the corner. She stands there, that colour that Jenny Tierney has never turned before, and then she walks out of the gym. Dodgeball, says Mr. Weissman. Let's not forget about dodgeball!

After school the country kids wait for their buses. Town kids stand around in the rain, muttering. Every kid knows what's coming. Steadman and his friends stand around by the blue dumpster, waiting. Looking nervous, for Dead Kids. It's too bad Mullen's in detention, Dwayne Klatz says to me, I bet he'd appreciate seeing Steadman get murdered. I tug on my mitts. Yep. He'd sure like to see that, I say.

Dwayne points at the front door. Here she comes, he whispers. Figure she'll murder him right now? Guess so, Dwayne, I say. We sit down on our lunch boxes. Dwayne draws in the snow with his finger.

Jenny has her keys on a bit of shoelace. Spins them around, the way Mullen's dad does. Steadman and his friends stand up and puff out their chests. Girls from the sixth grade huddle by the gym doors, whisper and point.

I'm going to murder you, Dave Steadman.

Steadman puts his hands in his pockets. Takes them out. I'd like to see that, he says. Some real tough girl. He folds his arms across his chest. Go on, he says, I'd like to see that. I'd like to see you try. He juts out his chin.

She presses the point of her keys into her palm. Now? Of course I'm not going to murder you now. How would that be fun? She reaches out, casual-like, and grabs one of Steadman's friends. Twists his arm up behind his back. He yelps. Falls down on one knee. Steadman sticks his chin out further. You don't get it, Steadman, she says. You still think life will turn out all right.

She holds the Dead Kid like that, one knee in the snow, sniffling. Staring at Steadman. With her free hand she gets out her cigarettes, shakes one out and puts it in her mouth. She pulls out a yellow plastic lighter. Light my cigarette, she says. Steadman blinks at her. She twists the arm a bit, the Dead Kid whimpers. I'm not going to light your cigarette, Steadman says. The kid in the snow starts to say something but she gives him another twist and he chokes up. I'm going to murder you if you light my cigarette or not, she says. You don't get any more choices, Dave. Things are pretty much finished.

Steadman takes the lighter. Cuffs his hands around her cigarette. Everybody holds their breath. The insides of Dave's hands flicker. He has to flick the lighter a few times before Jenny can get a puff. Then she blows out a thick cloud.

Jenny lets go of the whimpering kid. He just lies there in the slush, moaning. Steadman puts his hands back in his pockets. Jenny smokes. Remember, Dave, she says. Murder. Like in the Bible. Any day now. She blows smoke off to the side and walks away. We all stand still and don't talk, just watch her walk away across the playground, smoking.

Too bad Mullen couldn't have seen that, says Dwayne Klatz. Too bad, I say. Nobody goes anywhere. I don't know why, but I cup my hands around my mouth and shout, Some kind of real prizefighter, Steadman.

Nobody goes anywhere until Jenny Tierney is out of sight. The country kids take their backpacks and get on their buses. Steadman and his friends stand around, like they don't know what to do.

Dwayne Klatz kicks the snow. Spits. Hey, Dwayne, I say, aren't you going to catch your bus? Dwayne watches Jenny Tierney disappear over the hill, the last puff like a cartoon train behind her. Yeah, he says, the bus. What about you? You just walking home?

Well, Mullen won't get out of detention for another twenty minutes, I say.

Right, says Dwayne. Looks back to where Jenny vanished. Well, I guess I'll see you around then. He hitches up his backpack and gets on his bus.

Mullen's dad gives us ten dollars. Go to the IGA, he says, Get some laundry soap. The kind without bleach. He writes No Bleach on the back of a crumpled receipt. Can we get popsicles? Mullen asks. Mullen's dad flips through the newspaper, not really reading. Don't get popsicles, he says, get Christmas oranges. Wouldn't you rather have some Christmas oranges? They don't have those yet, Dad. It's only October. Mullen's dad rustles the pages. See if they sell them individually, he says. So that you don't have to get a whole box.

We do up our jackets and pull our toques down over our ears. We run and slide on the frozen sidewalk, like curlers, arms out. Mullen runs and slides into a light post. Staggers away, rubs his nose. We get wet, our toques get soggy and drip.

At the IGA they've got a picture of town, blown up as big as a tabletop, taken from an airplane. Must be a few years old. There's only one rink at the recreation centre. And three grain elevators still, down by the railroad tracks. Must've been taken in the summer – you can see tiny hay bales in the square fields around town. Marvin sure looks funny, all made of roofs sticking out of those brown and green squares.

We get a shopping cart and push it through the aisles. It's fun to push the cart fast and then hop up on the back bar, but they'll make you leave if they catch you, the teenagers who work there. I hope we'll have enough space, says Mullen. He grabs a box of cereal, one of the marshmallow kinds neither of us is allowed to eat. I'll stop here, he says. You go to the butcher aisle. He puts a brown bag of oatmeal in the cart. Brown rice in a sack.

They sure have a lot of meat. Things I've never heard of, sliding in blood on Styrofoam trays. I get a pork tenderloin, some flank sirloins, ham hocks. The packages are real cold; I have to stack them up on my forearms. You can get wrapped chunks of what might have been heads, faces. I get a fish, Chinook Salmon, says the tag. Its big eye not quite staring at me. I have to balance the stack with the bottom of my chin.

Hey, Mullen, I got us a Chinook Salmon. Mullen puts some canned ham in the cart. Fantastic, he says. He prods the fish eye with the tip of his finger, it presses into the soft head. We stuff the bottom rack of the cart with cans of split-pea soup and dried pinto beans. You know anything about pinto beans, Mullen? Mullen grabs some more cans. Feel how heavy these are, he says. I bet pinto-bean cans are heavier than any other sort of bean cans. We push the cart around and it lurches, the wheels get turned sometimes and it makes like it might fall over.

At the till Mullen gets out the bank receipt. We need laundry detergent, he says, without any bleach. And a box of popsicles, I say, the sort where you get all the different colours. The teenager at the till looks at our cart: mop heads, cat litter, light bulbs. Are you going to need a hand out with that? It isn't ours, Mullen says. We found it by the milk cooler. What we need is laundry detergent without any bleach. Where do we find that?

Out in the parking lot, Vaslav sets two paper grocery bags on the hood of his truck. Takes a credit card out of his wallet and scrapes ice off his windshield.

Hey, you got some groceries? asks Mullen. Vaslav puts his wallet away and opens the door. Get in, kids, he says. Snow. Time to make mustard. Mustard? I ask. We get in the truck and scoot up against the passenger door so Vaslav has room to shift the stick. He starts up the truck, grinds the gears and coughs and backs up out of the IGA lot.

Mustard, says Vaslav. Have to make mustard when it snows.

Inside the Russians' house we all take off our boots and put them on the little shelf beside the door. We shuffle in our socks across the wooden floor. Vaslav sets his brown paper bags on the counter in the kitchen, pulls out bottles of white vinegar, jars of spices, cloves of garlic. Solzhenitsyn sits in his chair by the window, reading the newspaper. Folds it up so he can hold it in one hand and drink beer with the other. We sit in the wooden chairs and rock – none of the legs are quite the same length. Our feet don't reach the ground.

Summertime mustard is bad for the digestion, says Vaslav, and rain mustard gives you bad dreams.

I dreamed I had a beard, says Mullen. A big beard, all bushy, I could keep stuff in it. Pencils and matches and a harmonica. Do you know how to play the harmonica?

Rain mustard gives you mildew dreams, says Vaslav. Mould and rot and centipedes. He bends down and gets some steel mixing bowls out of a cupboard, a dented pot, a wooden spoon. In Petersburg we always made mustard on the first snowfall because that makes it the luckiest. First-snow mustard makes your kids grow up strong and smart, and melts women's hearts. There's no women in this town to melt, says Solzhenitsyn. He folds up a paper airplane and throws it over Mullen's head. Lands in a potted plant on the window sill. Vaslav coughs. Go chase a skirt, he says. Go down to the post office and buy some stamps. Right, says Solzhenitsyn, looking at us. Stamps.

Vaslav gets a mortar and pestle out of a cupboard, like on Steadman's Drugstore's sign. Pours in yellow mustard seeds and crushes them up. Sour yellow dust rises up in the air. Mullen kicks me with his damp sock under the table and I kick him back. Solzhenitsyn gets a beer out of the fridge and sits back down. Picks his paper back up, moves his finger along the hockey scores, counting to himself. Vaslav grinds up the mustard seeds and shakes the yellow powder into a steel bowl. Opens a white paper bag tied up with a string.

Pours in more yellow, more yellow dust rises. Napa Valley, he says. I have to get this through the mail. A goddamn headache getting it over the border. Solly coughs.

He stirs all the powders and sets the bowl on top of the toaster oven. Chops up garlic cloves, two, four, six. Smashes them with the blade of his big knife. The air gets thick. Sprinkles salt on the garlic and mashes it down flat into the cutting board. He turns on the gas stove and narrows his eyes at the flame, turns the knob slowly right, then left, right again, until the flame is the right size. He sticks his finger in the butter dish above the stove, drops a yellow smudge in the pan. When Brezhnev was in charge we couldn't get butter and had to save soap shavings, for fat, he says. You're full of it, says Solly. Vaslav drops in the garlic and it sputters and stinks. Brown sugar and salt, and ginger and cinnamon, and other spices, I don't know what they are and he doesn't say.

The most important part of mustard, says Vaslav, is vodka.

Russian vodka, I say, 'Cause it's the best, right?

You can't get good vodka even if you drive to Calgary, says Vaslav. He stands on his tiptoes and cranes up into the top shelf. Grunts. Good vodka, I mean Russian or Polish vodka, is repeatedly distilled, smooth, doesn't have any crap in it. But good vodka doesn't make good mustard. He grunts and gets the bottle down, puffs. Lloydminster's Finest Polar Vodka, says the label. Has a picture of a moustachioed man in a fur hat, with lightning bolts in the background. This isn't good vodka? asks Mullen. Vaslav laughs. This will take enamel off the side of a bathtub, he says.

The pan spits and stinks and steams and he opens the vodka bottle and turns it upside down over the pan and a big cloud goes up and sizzles. He stands with the bottle upside down and glugs the whole thing into the pan.

Lord, says Vaslav, Lord, the earth is hard. We dig in the cold earth and always, underneath, harder and colder. The stone heart of the earth will freeze the lungs and burst the chest. We cough ice, we gasp and die, harder and colder, mouths full of snow and with picks and shovels left helpless. Lord warm my fingers, Jesus warm my toes, and I'll dig in your frozen heart no longer.

Have you heard the pipes making any more fuss? asks Solly.

Vaslav stirs the pan. I'm a busy guy, he says, I don't just sit around listening to the plumbing all day.

Sorry, I forgot, says Solly. Unfolds the newspaper, turns a page. Folds it back up. A very busy guy.

We need to get McClaghan to look at our hot-water tank, says Vaslav. When was the last time that thing got any attention? When did you last see a repairman? It's the water we cook our food in. The water we brush our teeth with. He picks up the steaming pan, moves it onto the back burner. Picks up the steel bowl with the mustard powder and pours in a stream of cold water. Stirs it into a thick paste.

Our water tank is fine, says Solly. It's the pipes, the pipes up this whole street. All these houses of McClaghan's. I don't trust any of it. At least he could move to central heating in most of them. In the places that aren't straight write-offs. A furnace, you just clean the filter. No need to panic. But these boilers, I don't know.

We have a boiler?

Don't you pay attention? Haven't you noticed the radiators?

I've got things on my mind, says Vaslav.

Someday, says Solzhenitsyn, I'm going to buy this place. He wouldn't refuse a reasonable offer. I bet I could get Jarvis Lester to cosign a loan for me. He's always on about how his packing plant is a family, how he's there to help us out. Not even McClaghan would refuse a reasonable offer. We'd tear out all those cranky pipes and radiators and get the sturdiest, least exciting furnace around.

Then what? asks Vaslav. You'd be bored to death. You'd turn up at the neighbours to listen to their pipes.

The point is, our hot-water tank is fine. Not that I'm advocating McClaghan profiting more off our backs.

McClaghan wants us all to get rickets and die in the cold, says Vaslav. He wraps a checkered cloth around the handle of the hot pan and starts to pour it, slowly, into the mustard paste. Stirs with his other hand. I want a cold wind to blow him into hell.

You should get him with the Milk Chicken Bomb, I say.

The what?

Don't you guys know how to make a Milk Chicken Bomb?

Whatever that is, kid, it sounds disgusting, says Vaslav.

I sit on the curb in front of the post office and watch her, in the window of the junk shop. She sits in the middle of the floor and changes the bits in a screwdriver. Pieces of cardboard boxes and Styrofoam packing blocks scattered all around on the floor. She builds a shelf, a piece at a time. Screwing brackets into tall wooden sides.

I want to stop everything and go in there. See what she's up to. Stop everything like in the school Christmas play, when the angel shows up to give her speech: all the kids in the shepherds' bathrobe costumes freeze, their mouths wide open, their arms up and their hands all spread. Those bathrobe shepherds are pretty good at holding still – they stretch out so it's really hard, and one of them, he's probably the best shepherd, he stands on one foot. I want to stop everything like that. Run across the street while she's frozen there putting a new bit in her screwdriver. I want to look in all her drawers, in her desk, under her table. I want to run up the stairs: does she sleep up there? Is there a little bedroom, up above the junk shop? Is she settled in, or is that all in pieces too, like the main floor? Is there furniture, a toothbrush on a shelf, a reading light, clothes hanging in the closet?

She looks up from her shelf at me. I duck under my comic book. After a while I peek up and she's still watching me. She sits there across the street, watching me, and after a while I put my comic book into my backpack and walk away down the street. She watches me go.

In the winter you can stay inside at lunch so long as you go to the library. Mullen and I always go outside at recess, especially when there's snow, but days he has to stay in detention all lunch I don't mind the library. Not all the books are school-type books.

The library used to be a courtyard. I remember in the first grade it was concrete tiles, weeds poking up out of the cracks, and old picnic tables. The inside classrooms had windows that looked out on the courtyard. I was in the second grade when they covered up all the windows with newspapers. We'd sit in math class or language arts class and listen to them hammering, listen to them sawing and digging. Kids who sat in the back row could maybe catch a look through the gaps in the newspaper and see the workers in their hard hats, sawing and hammering. They built a roof out of ribbed steel over the old courtyard. Like the inside of cardboard, on red steel beams. They poured a flat grey concrete floor. Any time I'm in the library I keep an eye out for weeds coming up through the concrete. They must be down there somewhere, the old courtyard weeds, growing and growing. All white and soft in the dark, like some big weedy octopus trapped under the concrete and carpet, listening to kids whisper and turn pages. The soft heels of their inside shoes. Waiting for the right day to push off all the concrete and climb out.

The librarian sits behind her desk. Flips pages in a catalogue. Licks a thick finger. I walk up and put my elbows on her desk.

Hello, I say, I'd like to find some books about Uzbekistan, please.

She looks over her glasses at me. Pardon me?

Uzbekistan, I say. It's in Russia.

The Union of Soviet Socialist Republics, she says.

No, I say, the Uzbek Soviet Socialist Republic. In Russia, the country. Some of my friends used to live there. One of my Russian friends is a writer but he doesn't know too much about geography. But people have written books about everywhere else, so someone must have written one about the Uzbek Soviet Socialist Republic. In Russia.

You can use the card catalogue, she says. Look under Subject. How is it spelled?

It's got a zed in it, I say. There's a desert, except it's very cold.

I find a heavy book in a plastic jacket, *The USSR in Pictures*. I flip the thick pages. Soldiers march past banners. A spaceman, all alone in a rocket, stars reflected in his round helmet. Pruney-faced women with handkerchiefs, like the Hutterites who live outside Cayley and sell potatoes at the Millarville farmer's market. I flip to the index and find nothing about the Uzbek Soviet Socialist Republic.

Dwayne Klatz and some of his friends hunch low around a big library table, books propped up in front of them. Dwayne waves me over to the table. How do you spell goddammit? he asks. I think about it for a while.

It's got two D's, I say. Pete showed me in one of his books once. Two D's and two M's. Goddamme it. No, says another kid, it's got a B at the end. What? says Dwayne Klatz. Say it slow, says the kid. God D A M B I T. The librarian shoots a look over at us and we all make like we're reading.

Dwayne opens his lunch box, orange plastic, a decal with a Viking. A helmet, with wings. He looks inside and makes a face. Anybody want to trade for a granola bar? he asks.

A granola bar? says another kid. You're nuts.

A kid unscrews his Thermos lid, turns it over like a cup. Pours his hot soup, it splatters a bit on the table. He blows on the steam. Lifts it and touches it with his puckered lips. Too hot, he says and sets it back down.

Come on, says Dwayne, it's got chocolate chips. It might as well be a candy bar.

I've got yogourt, I say, and a doughnut.

Dwayne peels the plastic wrap off his sandwich. Lunch meat and brown bread. He lifts the top slice to peek inside. Macaroni-and-cheese loaf, he says.

I tug at the plastic around my sandwich. What's that? asks a kid.

It's a pizza sub, I say.

Everybody's eyes get big. Like, from the store? asks Dwayne.

Yeah, I say, from the store. I pull at the plastic. Everybody stares. Dwayne holds his sandwich, not really near his mouth, stares at me trying to open the stupid sandwich.

Hey, Dwayne, I say, I'll trade you sandwiches.

You want to trade a pizza sub from the store for my macaroni-and-cheese loaf?

Sure, I say. Dwayne looks at everybody else, then holds his sandwich out to me. I give him the fat sub, locked in its plastic. The ingredients printed on the side label.

The bread is pretty soft. Mustard and butter and salty meat. I chew and chew. Your mom sure makes good sandwiches, Dwayne, I say. Dwayne tries to open the tough wrapper. Tears at the plastic with his teeth. He finally gets the sub out and takes a big bite. Red meat sauce squeezes out the side. He chews and smiles.

Do you think Jenny Tierney wears a bra? he asks.

Keep your voice down, I say.

She isn't anywhere around, he says. She's probably out in the parking lot smoking.

Well, you never know, I say.

She always wears those baggy sweaters, or those black shirts with guitar players. You can't ever get a good look.

Who wants to get a good look? I ask. I bet she gouges out the eyes of any kid looks at her boobs. Jesus, why not just go play on the highway, if you're sick of life.

I bet she wears a bra, says Dwayne, staring out the window. I mean, if any girl does, it'd be her. She ought to be in junior high.

So go to the junior high if you want to look at boobs, I say.

It snows and snows. We wear our snow-pants at the lemonade stand. All up the street people come out and unplug their cars, wrap the long orange extension cords up around their elbows. People sit in their cars and jog the engines, they chug and gasp and start eventually. We have to keep brushing the snow off the lemonade counter. We have to keep stirring the lemonade to keep it from freezing. But at least we don't need any ice.

We go down the hill behind Mullen's house on black garbage bags. The hill under the junior high school is good for tobogganing, because it's longer, but the hill behind Mullen's house is only big enough for bags. We sit in garbage bags and slide down the hill. Crash into the fence at the bottom. Mullen goes down face first, his head gets buried in the snow when he crashes into the fence. It's cold! he hollers. I'm burning up!

We walk up the street pulling our bags behind us and catch up to Deke, pushing his wheelbarrow full of shovels. He looks up at the sky, a shovel over his shoulder, at the snow falling. He looks worried.

Hey, Deke, how's all the digging going?

What digging? asks Deke.

Come on, Deke, Mullen says, you can tell us about it. What's going on? You've been digging for days. Where are you headed? How far are you going?

Deke turns around and groans and sighs. Stops pushing his wheelbarrow. An RCMP car pulls around the corner. Drives up alongside of us and stops. The window rolls down.

Howitz, says Constable Stullus, leaning out the window.

Evening, Constable, Deke says.

Why are you digging up public property, Howitz? asks Stullus.

Deke looks down at his wheelbarrow. The shovels are caked with mud. His shirt, covered in mud. Scratches under his cap. I'm not digging up public property.

You've been down there all day hammer and tongs, Stullus says. On municipality land.

Pick and shovel, says Deke, not hammer and tongs. So what? So I'm digging a hole in a lot of muck. Don't see much issue with some hole.

Stullus pulls a pill bottle out of his pocket, a plastic bottle like from the drugstore. Pops off the top and takes out a toothpick. You know what I heard, Howitz? I heard you plan to divert the river into the basement of the credit union.

That's a funny thing to have heard.

Yeah, says Stullus, I hear you drove out to the Black Diamond Hotel last week. Got real drunk and ran your mouth off about diverting the river into the basement of the credit union. How it'd serve them right, getting washed out to Saskatchewan. I also hear you punched Glen Trottner in the nose and broke the pistachio machine.

I never said I was going to divert anything anywhere, Deke says. Just thought I'd dig a hole. I wanted to show these kids here the rock stratum. You know how keen these kids are on finding stuff out. The riverbank there, it's a wealth. All them different layers of sediment and rocks. Isn't that right?

We want to be archaeologists, Mullen says. Digging up old skulls and stuff.

Stullus stands up, puts his pen in his shirt pocket. Don't dig holes on municipality land, Howitz. And leave these kids alone. They're growing up warped on account of you. He waves and walks over to his car. Drives away real slow.

Archaeologists, says Deke.

A silver minivan drives up to the main doors. A woman gets out of the driver's seat, walks around to the other side. She opens the door and there's Pete Leakie, sunk down into the seat. She says something to him and he shakes his head. Looks up over top of his round glasses at the sky and shrinks further into the seat. She talks to him and strokes his hair. She rubs his cheek. Eventually she undoes his seatbelt. He nods and takes her hand. The two of them run from the minivan to the school door, Pete holding his backpack over top of his head.

At recess I find a dry spot outside behind the dumpster and read comic books. The Under Queen gets more than she bargains for when she frees the Tomorrow Nazis from their prison on the moon. Seems pretty stupid, thinking that the Tomorrow Nazis would do whatever you asked them to out of gratitude. They smash open the dome of her city and the water floods in and all the Under People scream and run and drown. The issue ends with just black panels. I fold up the comic and stick it back in my bag. I really doubt the Under Queen drowns. She always comes back. I bet she'll be back in five issues at the longest.

Pete Leakie stands in the doorway by the second-grade hall, leans on the door frame. Holds his hand over his eyes and watches the grey sky.

In comic books, when kids get struck by lightning they get superpowers: X-ray bolts or bampfing through walls or lifting dumptrucks over their heads. Pete Leakie stands against the door frame and looks at the sky with his hand over his eyes. If he's got any superpowers, he sure isn't letting on about them. The bell rings and all us kids line up to go back inside. Mullen and I always line up last, or at least we do when Mullen is allowed to go outside for recess. We all line up behind Pete Leakie, hunched in the doorway, drumming his fingers on the door. The teacher opens it and he runs inside.

In Uzbekistan I've got it made. I live by myself in this old train car in the desert. A caboose, I guess, or a dining car. Wallpaper on the inside and empty light fixtures. I've got a hole dug in the sand, in the shade, down to where there's water. In the morning I fill a bucket, down in the hole. Sit at my table, in front of the train car, in the shade, the bucket covered with an old trashcan lid. Sure is hot, here in Uzbekistan.

They come on a ship, sailing in the sand. With masts and rigging. I watch it come out of the distance, churning up the sand. The ship leans in the sand. They climb down on ladders. Russians in tall hats and thick jackets, patches on their shoulders. Old men with goggles and scarves, Arabs with mirrored sunglasses. On the deck of the ship are their biplanes, tied down with cables. They line up, holding tin cups. I get them water out of the bucket with a ladle.

The sailors swap me everything I need for the water that I get out of the hole. Aviator sunglasses and heavy leather boots too big for my feet – I have to wrap and rewrap the laces around my ankles. Mirrors in brass frames I stack in the corner. They bring me railroad ties, a wheelbarrow, steam kettles that whistle. They bring a cardboard box full of rubber balls, all different colours; I like to sit on top of the train car at night and throw the balls out into the desert. If the moon is bright you can pick them out in the white sand.

In the desert, the sailors shoot rockets into the sky. Up a hill, where the sand is all packed and hard, we drag the rocket down off the ship on old logs, with ropes. It's the sort of rocket that's fat in the middle, with red stripes, and fins. You'd expect a rocket to be shiny and clean, so you could see your face in the side. But their rocket is tarnished and riveted, you can see where it's been welded, where it's been hammered into shape. We build the bleachers out of wood and wire, we sit there in the desert night drinking water out of tin cups.

I ask the sailors if any of them know how to build the Milk Chicken Bomb. They all shrug. None of them have even heard of it. They pull the rocket upright with ropes, grunting. They run a fuse to a plunge box. An old man in a welder's mask stares at his watch. The rocket fires and we all cheer, hands over our ears. Bang! it fires, steam and sand and everybody coughs, the rocket off into the sky, we crane our heads and watch it shoot off into the desert, where it'll crash, out there somewhere.

Hey, Solly, can we get popsicles?

Kid, it's winter. Look around.

Hey, Mullen, I ask Mullen, you want a popsicle?

Yeah, he says, but one of those ice cream ones. With the orange outside. That frozen orange kind. Hey, Solly, let's get popsicles.

Solly claps his hands together. Look, kids. Road salt on parked cars. Dead leaves in piles. Frost on power lines. Winter, you see that?

Please, Solzhenitsyn. Come on.

Well, I've got to go see McClaghan. I guess the Red Rooster is down that way.

Solly drives us in his little red hatchback. One of his windows is knocked out and covered with a taped-on garbage bag. In the Red Rooster there's mud tracked all over the floor. Mullen scratches in the mud with the tip of his boot. We get up on tiptoes to look in the popsicle cooler. What flavour you want, kid? Solly asks. You want grape? I want the frozen orange kind, with the ice cream, Mullen says. Me too, I want that one too, Solly. Solly gets us some popsicles. He gets a grape one for himself, just the plain kind, without ice cream or fudge or anything. Pays the teenager behind the counter with a taped-together two-dollar bill.

Hey, Solly, are you Russians going to beat the Pentecostals tomorrow?

The Golden Oldies. We don't play the Pentecostals for a while.

Yeah yeah, says Mullen, are you going to win, though?

Solly scratches the back of his head. Well, Pavel's been throwing his draws something fierce. Pulling in tight spots like he's parking a sports car. And so long as Vaslav doesn't drink so much he can still sweep.

How's the new second? I ask.

Solly thinks about it. The new second is all right, he says. More patient than the last one. Does what he's told.

Mullen sticks his tongue out. Hey, is my tongue orange?

That stuff doesn't come off, you know, Solly says. It'll stay that colour. When you grow up and try to kiss girls they'll run away the second they see that thing. Orange.

Mullen curls his tongue around the popsicle. Maybe I ought to get a different colour next week, he says. Maybe next week I'll have a purple tongue. Or blue.

Hey, Solly, I say, are you the skip now because Vaslav drinks too much?

Solly sucks on his popsicle. I'm the skip now because Vaslav calls shots like a choirboy even when he's sober. Always hedging. Never figuring the other guy can put the rock where he wants. The guy can put the rock where you want if you want it in the right spot.

Do you know where the right spot is, Solly?

Solly laughs. He's got a purple tongue now.

At the hardware store all the old men stand around watching McClaghan's new television. It sits on a little rack up in the back corner, above the bike locks and the Keys Cut sign. McClaghan sits on his stool behind the counter and flips channels with the remote control.

We got four stations out of Calgary, he says, flipping through the news anchors and furniture ads.

So what, says Lou Ellis, I get forty stations on my satellite dish.

It's a hardware store, says McClaghan.

The CBC sure doesn't come in so well, says Morley Fleer. You're not going to be able to watch the Maple Leafs games.

What is this, a nightclub? Walk down to the Short Stack if you want to watch hockey, this is a hardware store. He flips to the CTV news. An ad for lawnmowers.

Hey, that woman came into my office the other day, says Fleer.

What?

That French woman.

What French woman?

You know, Lévesque's daughter, or granddaughter, or whatever.

McClaghan glares at him. How do you know she's French?

We're talking about the same woman, right? You have heard her speak? Besides, she's Honoré Lévesque's granddaughter, says Fleer. Stands to reason. She inherited the junk shop. She's some Montreal fancy-ass type.

So what? says McClaghan.

She asked about thermostats, says Fleer.

She wouldn't even have been born when he came west to open that rat trap, says Lou Ellis. I'd just graduated high school. I remember hearing that accent for the first time, never heard anyone speak like that. He didn't say much, but when he did he didn't much care who was around. Always complaining about the noise.

He was a miserable crank, says McClaghan. He complained about everything. What noise could possibly have bothered him around here?

No, it was his hearing, says Ellis. His ears rang. You must have known about his ears.

I don't care about his ears.

They were always ringing. The slightest sound was a chore for him, with all that clatter in his head. You opened a door, he made a face. Trucks changing gears, electric fans. I remember him staring into the sky, his hands clapped on the sides of his head.

It was the pressure difference, I imagine, says McClaghan. The altitude change. Quebec is right there at sea level.

He wasn't from Quebec. He was from New Brunswick. An Acadian. One of those French-Canadian Maritimers.

Is Acadia at sea level? asks McClaghan.

Of course it is.

So there you go.

He always said it started at home, says Ellis. Came out here to find some quiet, he'd tell me. I don't recall if it was any quieter back then.

McClaghan watches announcements run by on the television screen: Tomorrow night, the Calgary Flames versus the Hartford Whalers. Her name is Hélène, says McClaghan. Hélène Lévesque. Don't sell her that thermostat. Don't even show it to her.

McClaghan, why are you such a son of a bitch? asks Solzhenitsyn.

McClaghan thinks about it. Force of habit, I suppose. I try to get most of my son-of-a-bitchedness out of the way before Thursday, so that I can be more, what do you call it, on the weekends.

Relaxed?

No, you know, my good deeds and all.

Benevolent.

That's the word. What do you want anyway?

Solly reaches inside his jacket, pulls out a long white envelope. Here's November then, he says. How's hardware?

McClaghan nods and takes the envelope. I brought in this mitre saw, he says. Jarvis Lester was on about taking up a hobby and, I don't know why, I thought, I bet he'll want a mitre saw. But now I hear he's building a ship in a bottle. Sometimes you're just plain wrong.

I'm sure someone else will want a mitre saw.

McClaghan leans in close. You think Jarvis is going to make it? Every time I drive by, the lot of that new Meatco plant is crammed full, trucks coming and going from every which way. Feedlots all the way to Brooks, all the way to Lethbridge. How is Jarvis going to get any kind of comparable price?

Solzhenitsyn shrugs. All this competition makes my stomach hurt. Sure, the Meatco plant is big and expensive. Us, we render meat in open vats. But Jarvis Lester is a fair and admirable man. Goes a long way.

He's too small, says McClaghan. They'll buy him out and then what? He coughs into his fist. Say, you're in plumbing and heating, aren't you?

And gauges. And valves. I mainly do refrigeration. Somebody has to keep all that meat frozen.

McClaghan snaps his fingers. I knew it. I knew that one of you guys did that job at the plant. Can I get you to take a look at something?

Sure.

We follow McClaghan down the aisle to the back of the store. He pulls out a set of keys and opens the door in the back. Don't touch anything, he says to Mullen and me. Pulls the door open and flicks a light switch. We follow him in.

Something smells, really bad. We stand in McClaghan's little office: a black-and-white checkered floor, and a desk covered in paper. Stacks of cardboard boxes with pictures of nails and screws stamped on the side. Against one wall there's a little counter, with a sink, and an old avocado-green refrigerator. Mullen and I both pinch our noses.

Solzhenitsyn opens the fridge door; the smell gets way worse. I don't know when it blinked out, says McClaghan. I had some chicken in the freezer, though, and it went off. Scrubbed the whole thing out but that stench just isn't going away. Anyway, I can't for the life of me get the stupid thing to work. Solly closes the door. Reaches around and pulls the whole thing forward with a grunt. He peeks around behind. Here, says McClaghan, I'll get you a flashlight.

Grab me a set of screwdrivers too.

McClaghan brings him tools. The two of them pull the fridge out even further. Behind it there's all kinds of dust and gunk, coils of wire. Solly squats down and starts to poke around with screwdrivers. Here, he says to me, hold the flashlight. I shine the light where he's working, try to get it so that his shadow doesn't get in the way.

Where'd you learn all this?

Used to do odd jobs for the Labour Collective Council in our neighbourhood back in Leningrad. Fixed stoves and heaters in the apartment blocks all up our street. Some of these things had grime and gunk under the tops that would ask you about the tsar's health. Everything was barely held together. Made quite a good living, keeping those appliances up and running.

I tell you what. You get this thing working, I'll reseal your windows. Put some of that plastic sheeting, you know, over the panes. Cut down on your heating bill.

Right benevolent of you. Solly sticks his tongue out of the side of his mouth. Twists something. Twists it again, and then the whole fridge rattles, starts to hum.

I'll be damned, says McClaghan.

Sorry I can't help with the smell, says Solzhenitsyn. Stands up and hands McClaghan the screwdriver. Opens the door again, reaches into the back and turns the dial underneath the light. Try not to fill it up too full. The air needs to circulate freely for everything to work properly.

Right, right.

And next week's probably a good time to come by and do those windows.

Sure, says McClaghan. Next week.

I sit on Mullen's step and yawn. Rub my hands together. Inside I hear the taps come on, which means somebody will be out soon. Some days when I'm up too early I have to wait forever, out here on the step, for Mullen to get up so we can sell lemonade. I sit on the step, in the dark, yawning, wishing I'd been able to sleep last night. Nights you can't sleep, there isn't much else you can do except get up early, so here I am, waiting.

The door opens and Mullen comes outside, zipping up his coat. Yawns.

Every morning the pounding sound comes out of Deke's house from seven-thirty, when the mailman comes by, until Mullen and I call last call for lemonade and go to school. And it's not just one kind of sound. Sometimes it's hammering, but not hammering like a nail into wood. Rings more, rings and clangs. Or sometimes duller and deeper. Every morning at seven-thirty Deke peeks out the window of his door. Deke never used to get up at seven-thirty: he used to say he wished he'd never see the sun rise again.

Constable Stullus sits in his car outside Deke's house. He shows up every morning right after we set up the lemonade stand. Pulls up and shuts off his car, sits there reading the newspaper and drinking coffee. Sometimes he turns the car back on for a few minutes at a time, when he gets cold I guess. Sometimes, when the hammering and banging inside Deke's house gets loud, he turns up his radio.

Hey, Officer, Mullen shouts, you could use some lemonade. Get the blood flowing. Get your detective skills up to snuff.

He rolls down his window. You kids should be in school.

School doesn't start for half an hour, I say. Plenty of time to sell some lemonade.

Yeah, Mullen says. It's not like we're causing public mischief or anything.

Officer Stullus prods his chin with a toothpick. When I was in Alert, he says, we made hot lemonade. Boiled water with a kettle and stirred in a can of that concentrate. You know, the cardboard can with the metal cap.

Mullen flips a quarter. Where's Alert?

North, says Stullus.

North like Edmonton?

You don't know north, kid. He rolls up his window. His windows fog up but you can still make him out, leaning on the steering wheel, staring at Deke's house.

It's too cold, Mullen says. Look, all the ice cubes are frozen together. I can't get them apart. All up the street, smoke puffs out of metal chimneys on the roofs. Look, Mullen says, chipping at the ice with his closed tongs, It's like a stupid rock.

Deke comes outside for a cigarette. Hey, Deke, Vaslav shouts from the chair on his porch, committed any crimes lately? Stullus rolls down his window. Blew up the legislature in Edmonton, Deke says. It was hard work, I had to rent a truck. You sure are hardboiled, says Vaslav. Stullus rolls his window back up.

I bring a cup of lemonade over to Deke. We sit down on his porch and he shows me his new submarine magazine. Flips the pages and points to pictures. Look at this, he says, the Kilo. Diesel electric. Gets up to sixteen knots underwater. And these big sons of bitches, the Typhoons. Biggest submarines anybody ever built. They can get down to 1,300 feet, on account of their titanium hulls.

What do they do down there, Deke?

Well, there's lots of stuff they've got to do. Maintain radio silence, for instance. And you've got to make sure you don't have any radiation leaks. He flips through the pictures. Narrow hallways, lights in cages, sailors in undershirts leaning on metal walls. Ladders and hammocks. Black metal and black water. Technical drawings of submarines cut in half, arrows point out the engine room, the fuel tanks. The top tower of a submarine alone in a wide, empty blue sea. The water still, barely a wake behind. He folds up the magazine. Stands up and glares at Stullus in his car. Gives me the plastic cup and heads back inside.

Mrs. Lampman draws a Red River cart on the chalkboard: tall wheels with spokes. They made so much noise, she says, because they couldn't oil the axles. People called them Squealers, because you could hear them coming before you even saw them. Kids write notes on their lined paper: Red River, Squealers. Mrs. Lampman tells us about David Thompson, the Athabasca River, the Kootenay River, the Columbia River. We all write the words on our lined paper. The bell rings and we pack up everything for recess.

Hey, Mullen, you're through with your detentions now, aren't you?

For a while, says Mullen. Yep. For a while.

We lie on our bellies in the snow, looking at the grey sky. I can feel old leaves under the snow: sticks and tough bark, and soft mouldy leaves. We look at the grey sky. Mullen points out where people might be staring at us through periscopes, up in the black tree branches. Turns out there's a lot of spots.

Some Dead Kids look at hockey cards. Sometimes they look over at us and we back up real slow-like on our elbows. We talk under our breath and stare straight ahead. Sometimes they shake their heads and sometimes they watch us awhile. Mostly they ignore us.

I unwrap my sandwich. Mullen cranes his neck to see.

What did Dwayne Klatz's mom make today?

Ham and cheese, I say. She slices the ham real thin. I like the mustard a lot.

Those must be some sandwiches, says Mullen.

Did you finish your outline? I ask Mullen. For your social studies report?

Outline? Hell, I started to write the report. That'll shake them up some, me getting my report done early. I may not be the smartest kid ever, says Mullen, but I figure David Thompson was the best ever in Canada for history.

David Thompson just made a bunch of maps, I say, just like all the rest of those explorers. Who can keep them all straight?

When we moved from Winnipeg, my dad and I got stuck, Mullen says. I mean stuck. We drove right off the road into the ditch. That was the coldest I ever felt, when we were sitting in the ditch beside my dad's car because we were waiting for it to get fixed. Sometimes my dad isn't the best driver. David Thompson was that cold all the time, not just when he had to wait for something, but he had to eat dinner and brush his teeth when it was that cold too.

Way down at the little hill some kids have blue plastic carpets. They slide down on the blue sheets, rattling on bumps. The thin, hard snow scrapes at the bottoms. A lot of kids have fancy three-runnered Canadian Tire sleds, they've got crisp, waxy toboggans. We watch them zoom down the little hill.

Those fancy sleds are wasted on those kids, says Mullen. They're hardly even doing anything. If you went off a snow bump with one of those, you'd get right up in the air. You could build as big a ramp as you wanted and just shoot right off it.

You should ask for one of those Canadian Tire sleds, I say, for Christmas.

Mullen looks at me. Yeah, he says, easy for you to say.

No, really. You should ask for one. I bet your dad –

My dad can't afford one of those sleds, says Mullen. Just 'cause some kids get everything.

Oh yeah, I say, everything.

Well, Mullen glares at me, some of us are never getting stuff, whether we ask or not. There's a big difference between never asking 'cause you won't and never asking 'cause you can't. So just don't even talk about it, okay? He sits there, legs out like scissors, hands slouched on the ground.

I get up and point at the school. The bell rang, I say. Mullen, slouched and scissored, stares ahead. I've had it, he says.

Kids start to line up against the ribbed aluminum portable walls. Mrs. Bea, one of the sixth-grade teachers, leans one skinny hand on the black railing. Just a sweater around her thin shoulders, even though it's real cold. I've got two pairs of socks on. Kids start to line up. A few kids walk back from the swings. Some kids are still running around.

The bell rang, I say. Get up. He stares.

Mullen, come on.

Nah, he says, I'm really through. I think I'll just sit here. Why not?

Kids stop running and get into line. They shuffle around and Mrs. Bea looks them up and down and they all get real still and quiet.

Mullen, come on. Everybody's back. Sure are, says Mullen, those kids sure are back. They sure stand still good. Mullen, come on. I mean, he says, you figure you can stand still that good, you ought to go show them. Get in on that serious-type good fun. Serious-type, I say. Real serious-type. That's great.

She looks out at us. She raises her head and sees me, standing and looking back and forth, and Mullen, sitting in the snow. Not just sitting but sprawled. Like on a sofa. She raises her head and crosses her arms and just keeps looking.

Okay, she sees us, I say. I look back and forth and realize I'm looking back and forth real fast and snap my head back to Mullen and try not to move it.

Mullen sticks his tongue out and tries to cross his eyes to look at it.

Boys, calls Mrs. Bea.

Hey, did you ever look at your tongue? asks Mullen. Well, I'm not really looking at it, 'cause it's all out of focus and double. But have you ever tried and thought, if I could just relax my eyes right, I'd be able to see it right square?

We have to go right now, I say.

Mullen uncrosses his eyes and looks at me. The last two kids walk to the back of the line and Mullen sighs and stands up. Walks past me with his hands in his pockets. We walk to the back of the line.

I pull my elbows up on the counter at the Red Rooster.

Hey, I say to the teenager behind the counter. Hey.

He sets down his rock-and-roll magazine and leans over. Yeah. What?

I need a Greyhound ticket, I say.

The teenager leans down over the counter.

You're what. Eight years old?

What does it matter how old I am? I need to go to the Yukon.

The Yukon. Right. The teenager flips open his magazine. Leans back against the cigarette rack.

Hey, I say.

He licks his finger. Flips a page.

Hey. How long does it take, anyway? The bus to the Yukon? I've got a pillow in my backpack, so –

Get out of here, barks the teenager. I sigh and get down off my tiptoes. Head out the door.

It's dark now, dark and only six o'clock, white street lights and snow. I sit on the bench outside the Red Rooster, kicking snow. Cars drive slow up and down Main Street. Everybody who works in Calgary coming home. A lot of people are lawyers and real-estate agents and land surveyors, but around here we only need one of everything so everybody else drives to the city. Red station wagons and long sedans, big jeeps with ski racks drive up Main Street, then turn, up the hill, to the houses up there where all the lawyers and real-estate agents and land surveyors live. Down here on Mullen's street it's just meat packers and labourers and Russians, and Kreshick, he's lived on this street longer than anybody.

The white Christmas lights shine all the way down Main Street.

The lights are on at the Elks' Hall. Mormons stand under the awning and drink juice out of paper cups. The Mormons are all young, with short hair and dark suits. They nod and sip their juice, and inside, Mormon kids in thick sweaters play in the coat racks, running through the jackets. I guess they're Mormons, on account of their suits, and none of them smoke cigarettes or spit on the ground.

The lights are out at Steadman's, the long lines of fluorescent lights above the rows of toothpaste and paper towel. Up the street the lights go out at Yee's Breakfast All Day Western Noodle. Someone opens the door, pulls the wooden bench inside. Turns the Open sign around. Goes from table to table picking up all the napkin dispensers and soy-sauce jars. I can see the red glow of a cigarette cherry. I watch the Mormons drink their juice, laugh and gesture, dark suits on long arms. I stand under the street light and lean against the cold metal. Inside, kids hide between overcoats and long scarves. I can smell the potluck, the roast beef and gravy and hot potatoes.

Pavel walks down the street, on the other side. He stops at the intersection, looks around, sees me leaning on the street light. He walks diagonally across the street.

Just waiting around in the cold, eh, kid?

I guess so, I say.

Hold on a second, he says. He goes into the convenience store. Comes back out a minute later with a Styrofoam cup of coffee.

Can't you make coffee at home?

Pavel's eye looks up to the Greyhound sign in the Red Rooster window and the bus schedule up above the bench. Pavel's other eye, the not-real one, always looks a little past you, up and to the left. Almost the same colour of brown as his real eye, almost. A little shinier. I like the Red Rooster coffee, he says. The Styrofoam makes it taste right. And the walk.

Across the street the Mormons finish their juice, and someone gathers up all the plastic cups, stacks them one inside the other. They hold open the door and the sound of laughing kids comes out of the yellow hot light into the street.

Heading out someplace?

He won't sell me a bus ticket, I say.

Kid, why do you need a bus ticket?

Yeah, well. Sometimes you just need to get out.

Pavel nods. Sips some coffee. You know what'll cheer you up, kid? asks Pavel. Kreshick's going to lose.

I jump up off the bench. I stamp my feet. Tonight's the checkers? Pavel, you have to take me to see the checkers. Please take me to see the checkers, please, I promise I won't make any noise and I'll sit still and won't bother anybody and I won't tell anybody tomorrow or any other time.

You don't want to watch a bunch of old men cough and fill ashtrays. Go home. Read a book. When I was your age, I was always watching cartoons. You know, Winnie Pooh, he says. He pronounces it Vinny Poo-ehh.

Please take me to see the checkers, please. Is Vaslav going?

Vaslav's home, going over cover samples. He says none of the illustrators can do a bodice right.

I tug on his arm. Please please please. Pavel walks down the street, sips his Styrofoam cup. I tell you, kid, it's the opposite of exciting. Bad for the health, the habits of old men.

But Kreshick's going to lose tonight. Kreshick never loses. That's pretty exciting.

Pavel stops. Sips his coffee and looks up and down the dark street. Then he looks down at me and grins. Yes, it is. He grins and his eye looks out way to the right. He slaps me on the shoulder and we walk up the street.

All the lights are out in McClaghan's big windows. Just the red glow from the exit sign on the edges of the wheelbarrows and table saws. Red on the TV screen in the corner. But the shuttered windows on the second floor are all lit up, yellow and open, you can hear talking and laughing inside. Sometimes a hand reaches out the window to ash a cigarette. The ash floats along with the snow.

Pavel rings a doorbell beside a dark door, left of the hardware store door. I stand on my tiptoes but don't hear any bell. Pavel pulls the heavy hat off his head, holds it against his chest, puts it back on his head. Tugs it down his forehead almost over his eye. We puff under the white light bulb.

The door rattles, locks unlocking, one, two, three locks. We stand back and the door opens and McClaghan pokes his head out.

Come for the fleecing?

Brought the shears, says Pavel.

McClaghan looks at Pavel, looks down at me. What is this, a daycare? Get him out of here.

Pavel pats the top of my head. I have to take him home later. He isn't going to make any noise, righ,t kid? I lean back on my heels. I'll be real quiet. Won't say a word.

McClaghan coughs. Can't have kids. Ruins the whatsit, the camaraderie.

Pavel takes his wallet out of his pocket. Holds it open under McClaghan's face. I could always take the shears home, says Pavel. McClaghan's eyes get big. He holds the door open. Teach the virtues of patience, I suppose, he says, looking down at me. Scowls. Not a word. I shake my head. They look at each other and laugh.

We climb a narrow staircase, lights in brass fixtures stuck in the sides of the walls, not the ceiling. McClaghan coughs while he walks and Pavel takes off his hat, shakes out the snow. At the top is a hallway, plaster, wallpaper yellow at the edges along the rim of the ceiling. McClaghan opens a door and there's light and smoke and noise. Lou Ellis, and Morley Fleer, and a lot of other old men. They drink cans of beer and smoke cigarettes and laugh, on stools and in chairs, around a big, heavy table. A red-and-black checkerboard the only thing on the table, aside from some dirty ashtrays. At the end of the table sits Kreshick, not talking or laughing, drinking a heavy glass of whisky in little sips.

Kreshick is the oldest guy in town. He makes the best ice for curling and he always wins at checkers. He's thin, like Mullen's dad, like Solzhenitsyn, with thick brown spots on his cheeks, his neck and hands. An old bolo tie loose around his skinny neck. He drinks his whisky and sees me and whistles.

What is this, a hostage-taking? How much are you worth, kid?

All the old men laugh. Pavel pulls a seat up to the table, and McClaghan shuts the door. I lean up against the wall. McClaghan stamps his feet and waves his arms. Shut up, shut up, he shouts. No more stragglers, let's get started. Judd Fischer isn't here, somebody says. Bad night to be Judd Fischer, says McClaghan. Everybody laughs and he waves his arms again. He stands behind a heavy man in a checked shirt, bald on top, with a moustache. Claps him on the shoulders.

This is Gord Miggins, Lethbridge checker champion. Won the big checker games far south as Salt Lake City. Those big Latter-day Saints checkers, right?

Everyone takes out their wallets, pulls out thick bundles of ten- and twenty-dollar bills. McClaghan gathers everyone's money around the room. Lou Ellis makes ticks on a chalkboard. He makes a scrawl of two-letter initials down the left side. Across the top it's EK/GM. McClaghan brings him the money, held in separate clumps between his fingers, and points around the room, while Lou takes the bunches of bills and makes ticks beside the rows of initials.

No, says Pavel, I'm for Lethbridge here. He takes out one, two, three, five, ten twenty-dollar bills. People whistle, take off their glasses and shine them on their sleeves. When all the money is counted up on the chalkboard, everybody gets real quiet and leans forward around the table.

You flip a coin round here? asks Miggins.

Allowing the foreigner rights to start, that's the custom, says Kreshick, every word slow and brittle.

Miggins moves a checker, pushes it with a finger. His head leaned a little back. Kreshick flicks his tongue against the inside of his mouth.

They push checkers, real slow and careful-like. All the men in the room sit as still as they can, crane their necks for a better view of Miggins and Kreshick frowning and pushing checkers. As the checkers get closer and closer together, they take longer and longer to move them.

McClaghan sits with his legs wide apart and one big fist around his jar, rested on his knee. Spits in it from time to time. Thick pasty spit. He rocks it back and forth and none of the bottom bands move at all, settled in the bottom like layers of glue.

Who do you like in the Okotoks bonspiel? someone asks. Kreshick snorts. They don't keep the ice for shit in Okotoks. That's where all you pick up such bad habits. Their filthy ice and your filthy knees. All you fat men who put your knees down on the ice beside the hack when you clean off the bottoms of your rocks. Do you know how long it takes to fix the holes you melt in the ice with your fat knees? I can recognize the filthy kneeprint of every fat curler in the district. He glares at Pavel. That fat Russian is the worst, your friend with the beard. I have to melt all the ice around the hack with a blowtorch. The filth works its way down into the ice, see, in sediments. I can date the ice to the weekend, depending on the knee.

No snoozing, kid, McClaghan says to me. Snoring is bad for the competitive atmosphere.

I'm not tired, I say. Miggins frowns at the checkerboard.

How's Howitz's big dig coming along? McClaghan asks me. Everybody has a big laugh. Let's hope he called the municipality first, says Lou Ellis, asked for the right excavation information. I'd hate for him to dig into a gas line.

Or a water main, says McClaghan. It'd be awful if he flooded himself out before he gets the chance to do his flooding out. Everybody has a big laugh.

So he's doing a bit of digging, I say. Don't see why everybody's so bent out of shape over a bit of digging.

Kreshick gives me a funny look. Then he grins with all his crooked teeth. Course not, kid. Intrusion into the ground is the abiding concern around here. All over the foothills. Whole region's prosperity is dependent on what men have dug up out from the earth.

And when that prosperity's through, you can always dig yourself back under the earth, says Lou Ellis. Everybody has a laugh.

See, Kreshick says to me, your friend there is just keeping up with what we've always done around here. Escaping downward, as opposed to laterally.

Take Dobb Jensen, says McClaghan. You remember Dobb Jensen, Kreshick?

Sure. A big geology aficionado. Always looking at the ground for what do you call them, ore veins and trilobites.

Right. So Dobb decides he needs the mechanical advantage if he's going to get a good look at the real live geology. Starts heading to Calgary on weekends to buy up decommissioned steamship parts. All those big boats from the Kootenay Lakes. He buys up the drive screws and steam boilers, and he builds himself his very own steam excavator.

I remember it clearly, says Kreshick, Dobb there, bowler hat, bowtie. Sitting up on top of this big drill, hands on the levers, grinning. Like a giant post-hole digger. He even had a gas mask, with a hose. To feed him his air as he went drilling down into the ground.

Way my dad told the story, you could hear the explosion several towns over, says McClaghan.

It's true, says Kreshick. It rained wingnuts, rubber fanbelt scraps, fingers and kneecaps far away as Nanton.

Everybody's quiet. Gord Miggins holds a finger overtop of a checker.

You two are completely full of shit, says Morley Fleer.

McClaghan and Kreshick bust out laughing, like kids. Kreshick tries to move a checker and has to stop, wait until his chest stops shaking. He takes a deep breath. Gives me a look. Of course, he says, if we're going to talk about famous Marvin geologists, we certainly couldn't ignore your best friend's illustrious father.

Everybody gets a little funny. Morley Fleer and Lou Ellis both finish their beers and set them down loudly. Fleer opens two cans of beer at once.

Let's play checkers, says Pavel. His voice is a little high.

Yeah, I say, Mullen's dad is a geologist. He used to find oil, back before he moved out here to work at the meat-packing plant.

Everybody stares at me. Lou Ellis chokes a bit on his beer.

Kreshick wipes his mouth with his sleeve. In 1981 –

Don't tell him this story, says Pavel.

Kreshick rolls a little in his chair, sour and gleaming. In 1981 Marc Lalonde declared the National Energy Program and looted all the money out of Alberta. In Calgary the streets were empty and all the windows boarded up and office towers leaned and fell over like those old grain elevators. No one cared.

Don't, says Pavel.

Gord Miggins, Lethbridge checker champion, puts two fingers on a red checker and pushes it across a square. Kreshick taps a yellow fingernail on a black checker.

So this big-shot geologist from Manitoba shows up in Turner Valley. Bad time all over those towns, not like growing grain was doing anybody any good, then the oil industry collapses. The whole southern foothills were drunk for a few years. This Winnipegger pulls into town with a black portfolio and a station wagon full of surverying equipment.

Makes himself real obvious, out on the side of the road, photographing and looking through the, what, the theodolite. Writing in his little notebook. Turns up at the municipal hall one day and gets himself a meeting with the resource department. Hours and hours. Now, people have been talking for days: is it natural gas? Some kind of petro-tar? What's he found? What's he found?

Kreshick pushes a black checker. Coughs.

Comes out of that meeting with a licence to excavate ten miles out of Turner Valley for coal. Coal. Says he's found the biggest stake of coal in Alberta since goddamn Turtle Mountain.

Kreshick hops a red checker at the left front, pulls it off. Shows his teeth. Hey, anybody from Turner Valley in here tonight? He looks around the room. Where's Sigmann? You're from Turner Valley, aren't you?

A man in the back with a big red beard coughs. Turner Valley all right.

You invest in that Winnipegger's coal mine?

Sigmann just glares. Everybody with a beer has a long drink.

Even I can see the path Kreshick has left for Miggins. One, two, three black checkers, in a neat zig-zag, all ready to jump. Miggins narrows his eyes. Tries not to stare at the route. Looks from face to face. Kreshick's lips pull further back, black lines above his teeth, black veins and yellow cracks.

Lethbridge checker champ, he says.

Nobody says anything. Miggins jumps the first, the second, the third. Stacks the three black checkers and pulls them off the board. His front red checker now deep on Kreshick's side, nothing behind it, a sitting duck. Kreshick doesn't jump it, though. Moves a black from the side into the middle of the board.

A lot of people wondered how a geologist from Winnipeg would know the first thing about coal in Turner Valley.

They've had geologists in Turner Valley for seventy-odd years now. You'd think they'd have come across a seam as big as this son of a bitch was talking about. Most people in town just figured he'd taken them for suckers and cooked the whole thing up. That's most people, mind. Sorry, Sigmann.

Yeah, well. That's how it is sometimes.

Miggins has been staring at the board. Suddenly, anywhere he might move, there's a black checker in front and a gap behind. His front red trapped against Kreshick's back row, to be jumped any time.

Kreshick stares at me. Fingers wrapped around his glass. McClaghan stares at me, leaned back in his chair, his hands rested on his belly. Gord Miggins takes his eyes off the checker game he's about to lose to stare at me.

Did he find any coal? I ask.

Kreshick laughs. A big gut full of ghua-gha-gha-HA-ha. He coughs and sputters and laughs and drinks whisky and chokes and spits it out on the checkerboard and laughs. McClaghan throws his hat on the ground and laughs. Stands up and wipes his eyes and sits down and thumps his hand on the table. Lou Ellis and Morley Fleer clap each other on the shoulders, hug each other tight and laugh.

Did he find any coal!

They laugh and laugh. Kreshick takes all of Gord Miggins's checkers in a few turns and Pavel throws up his arms. Lethbridge checker champ, he mutters. He pushes out of his stool, kicks the table leg. Lou Ellis's stack of bills knocks over onto the floor. Everybody still laughing too hard to even pick up the money. Did he find any coal! Kreshick has to struggle for breath.

On Fridays they open up the Snack Shack at lunch. Kids line up in front of the little counter at the far end of the gym to buy little bags of potato chips, spicy beef-jerky sticks, chocolate milk. Kids line up right down the hall. Everybody wants them to open the Snack Shack every day, but the teachers say that eating junk food every day is bad for you. They're always going on about junk food and the Canada Food Guide and the Nutrition Pyramid.

We open up our lunch boxes, standing in the long line for the Snack Shack. Dwayne Klatz's mom made egg salad. Egg salad is usually pretty gross, but not when Dwayne Klatz's mom makes it. Dwayne's gotten pretty good now at getting the wrapper off my pizza sub. Hey, Dwayne, says another kid, You want to trade that pizza sub for my Hershey bar? Dwayne snorts. You've got to be kidding, he says. Do you know how good these things are?

Mullen rubs his quarters together. I wish they sold pop, he says. I wish they sold root beer. I can drink more root beer than anybody.

Drinking root beer is easy, says Dwayne Klatz. Drinking any kind of pop is easy, half of it's gas. What's hard about that?

I can drink more root beer than you can, says Mullen.

I can drink more milk than anybody, says Dwayne.

Milk? says Mullen.

Drinking milk is hard. If you drink too much milk you throw up. Milk hasn't got any gas in it at all.

We get to the front of the line. Dwayne and Mullen spread out all their change on the countertop. The Snack Shack lady leans down and listens to them. Shrugs and picks up all the quarters. She brings out four half-litre cartons of milk.

That's not so much milk, says Mullen. I bet I could drink that much milk.

Dwayne and Mullen each drink a half-litre of milk, a glug at a time, staring at each other overtop of the cartons. Keep glugging away, raise the cartons higher and higher until they're both empty. Klatz wipes milk off the top of his lip with the back of his hand. Other kids stand around and watch, munching on their potato chips.

Man, says Dwayne Klatz, I could just drink milk all day. They open the second cartons, they drink milk, smack their lips, drink milk. Mullen sticks out his tongue and lets the last drops drip from the carton mouth.

We all get back in the Snack Shack line.

Sorry, says the Snack Shack lady, I haven't got any more milk. We all stand at the counter and look at each other.

What do you mean? asks Klatz.

I haven't got any more milk, she says, that's what I mean. Those were the last four cartons.

But we can drink way more, says Mullen.

You'll throw up if you drink too much milk, she says. She wipes the counter with a cloth.

We sit down in the hallway by the library. Kids in gym shorts head into the gym for intramural floor hockey. You can hear the rubber balls slapping against the walls inside.

Hey, I bet I could eat that plant over there, says Dwayne.

Forget it, Klatz, says Mullen.

Come on, he says. That big spider plant. I'll even eat the dirt.

Forget it.

The Glue Men come down out of the sky in their yellow parachutes. Legs out wide, hooting and hollering. Uh-oh. That's the last thing I need today: the Glue Men. They land on Main Street and their parachutes blow up behind them in the wind; they pull the cords and their parachutes blow off. Like sails, disappearing up into the sky. The Glue Men hoot and laugh and drip their thick yellow glue everywhere. They go to take a step and they can't, 'cause their gluey feet are stuck to the pavement, and they all howl and laugh and strain and then pull chunks of asphalt right up out of the street. Now we're in trouble. Everybody in town runs away shouting, confused, while the Glue Men stomp around town on their new asphalt shoes. They stick to everything. They stick to stop signs and drag them along behind. They stick to car doors, yapping dogs, teenagers on mountain bikes. They stomp around dragging everything that gets caught in the sticky glue. Laughing and slobbering – everything sure is funny to the Glue Men.

The only good thing about the Glue Men is that you've just got to wait it out. Eventually each of them has so many tires and mailboxes and bowling trophies and garage-sale fliers stuck all over that they can't even move. The overloaded Glue Men struggle to take that one last step, then fall over and sit in the street. They keep laughing for a while, but it doesn't sound so funny anymore, and pretty soon the streets are full of sobbing Glue Men, and all the scared, crying kids and little old ladies stuck to their sides. Yep, the Glue Men are the last thing anybody needs.

This time we do it right, says Mullen. Right, I say. Right.

Curlers carry their gym bags into the recreation centre, brooms over their shoulders, every broom with a little bag over the bristles. Mullen and I get to carry the Russians' brooms, which is pretty fun, although you've got to be careful. You wouldn't want anything to happen on the day of a big match like today.

We watch the Pentecostals warm up in the next rink, stretching and sliding up and down the ice. The reverend takes a minute to talk to each of the players. He'll whisper something close to them, then the two of them will grab each other's hands, close their eyes and move their lips.

Do you have to play them today? I ask.

Today we play the Golden Oldies, says Solzhenitsyn. And it's a good goddamn thing too. The Pentecostals really made a mess of us last year, in the big Okotoks bonspiel. Just a complete disaster. We'd cleaned up all the other rinks, here in Marvin, and in High River too. Then we go to Okotoks and these holy rollers here just cream us. That minister there, he's inhuman. You'd think he was some kind of hydraulic curling robot. Every movement the man makes, it's uncanny. Like he's not even real.

Well, God chooses his instruments, or something like that, says Vaslav.

Maybe God should go join some bigger league, says Solzhenitsyn. Give the rest of us a sporting chance.

Come on. You don't want to get soft, do you?

It's rubbing off on you. That Prairie Protestant zeal.

I'll see you in Hell, says Vaslav.

You're going to spend a lot of time in Hell, says Solzhenitsyn. Seeing all these people.

Come on, Mullen says, we need to find a can.

The second-graders play their marble game just like always, their duffle bags full of swimsuits and towels piled up against the wall. Some of them have already had their swimming lessons; their eyes are red and their wet hair sticks to their foreheads. Marbles clack into each other.

A Dead Kid from our grade winds up and throws his giant king cobb steelie. The biggest marble ever. He pitches it underhand like a bowling ball. Rolls over marbles and scoops them into his purple whisky bag. The kids watch the big steel marble roll around with hungry eyes, they flinch every time it smashes one of theirs. His purple marble bag strains at the seams.

We watch them play marbles. Mullen uncaps his pen, writes OLDIES/RUSSIANS on the pad. Four to one on the Russians, says Mullen. They've got those old-timers cold.

You don't know anything about curling, says the kid with the marbles. He's tall and has hair down in his face. Pulls chocolate-covered peanuts out of a bag and pops them into his mouth. You're full of it.

I'm telling you, says Mullen, no one on the Golden Oldies rink has any shot at all. The skip, he calls shots like a choirboy. Yeah, I say, a choirboy.

You're that Mullen, whose dad works at the shithouse.

You're that Ed Carter, who's going to be doing community service, like the last kid who said that.

Hockey players, says Ed Carter. You think a bunch of downtown deadbeats are going to beat hockey players at anything? Come on.

Mullen shrugs. Put you down for what, fifty cents? Seventy-five? You can get one of those roller hot dogs when you win.

How much are you putting in?

Mullen reaches into his pocket. Pulls out a handful of quarters. Pushes them around in his palm. I've got three ... nope, four dollars. Feeling pretty good here. I think I might put the whole thing down.

Four dollars on deadbeat Russians against hockey players.

Mullen pours all the quarters out into his tin can. Lets each one ring.

Here, says one of the second-graders, I've got fifty cents. Is that enough?

Sure thing, says Mullen. We take all comers.

I've got a dollar, says another kid. They all dig in their pockets, pull out dimes and quarters. Ed wrinkles his nose, then pulls two two-dollar bills out of his pocket. Drops them in the can.

Hockey players, he says.

Sure thing, Ed. Sure thing.

The Golden Oldies throw some pretty good rocks. They puff along with their brooms, sweeping when their skip tells them to, stopping when he tells them to. They get rocks right inside the eight-foot line. Their second even puts a guard rock up, just outside the house. The second-graders all point. What's happening? asks a kid. Is that good? Yeah, says another kid, that means we're winning.

Vaslav smirks. He holds Anna Petrovna out with both hands and kisses her right in the yellow bristles. Heaves himself down into the hack – he looks like he could fall over any time. At the other end of the rink, Solly stands beside the cluster of rocks in the house. Swings his broom above them like a baseball bat, points to the back of the room. Then he walks up a little further and puts his broom near the guard rock. Raises an arm for the turn he wants.

Vaslav creaks back, his rock comes right up off the ice, and he pushes out of the hack. The rock curls gently down the ice. Pavel and the second shuffle along sideways just in front of it, sweeping when Solly tells them to. Kids get right up close to the glass. The rock passes by the guard, nearly touches it. Sweep! we hear Solly shout, as loud as he can. Pavel and the second lean into their brooms and sweep as hard as they can. The rock curls right inside, like they're drawing it along with their brooms, and crash, knocks right through both the Golden Oldie rocks, sends them spinning out against the boards.

Hey, he hit all of our rocks, says one of the second-graders. Is he allowed to do that? Ed Carter puffs out his cheeks.

After a few more ends the Russians are way out in front. Every time the Oldies get a few carefully inside, Vaslav lumbers into the hack and knocks them all out. Every time he does it Ed Carter swears under his breath.

Hey, Ed, Mullen says, rattling the tin can. They're about to get going on that next rink there. Who do you like, the Chamber of Commerce or the Pentecostals?

Haven't got any money left, dickhead.

That's too bad, 'cause I figure the Pentecostals will make a real mess of the Chamber. Throw them around.

You're full of it, Shithouse Boy. Mullen shrugs, rattles the can.

You could bet your marbles, one of the other kids says. The other kids are up or down a quarter maybe, or a dollar, but the can is full of Ed's bills. Ed throws some more chocolate into his mouth. He opens the drawstring and pours a handful of cat's eyes, a giant creamy, into his palm.

Mullen looks at me. What do you figure?

I figure those aren't worth shit.

He's right, says one of the second-graders, those aren't worth shit.

Mullen rattles the can. Come on, they're about to start. In or out?

The king cobb steelie clangs in the can. Almost knocks it out of Mullen's hand. Churches can't curl, says Ed.

Yeah, says Mullen, churches.

The Pentecostals curl like robots, like someone built them in a factory just to win at curling. They curl better than the Russians. Other curlers, their matches finished, stand around not talking, leaning on their brooms. The Chamber of Commerce curlers shut their eyes at every crash. They turn away when the Pentecostals throw. They cover their faces when the Pentecostals sweep. Out here on our side of the glass, all you can hear is the muffled bang of rocks knocking into one another, the Pentecostal skip barking, hand held up rigidly, finger pointed in the air.

Your dad works at the shithouse, Mullen.

Yeah, well, look at all the money in this can here, Ed. You see that? Here, listen to it rattle. You hear that? A shithouse. Next time I'll take your goddamn running shoes. You can walk home barefoot.

Mullen goes to the concession, buys a pack of chocolate cigarettes. Peels off some of the paper, pops one in his mouth.

In the second-floor lounge the curlers laugh and shout at each other, and smoke cigarettes and drink beer. The air is clogged with cigarette smoke, and if you sit inside too long you smell like a wet ashtray, but it's fun to sit at the big windows and watch them curling down on the ice. Mullen and Pete Leakie and I sit on the carpet by the window and pull at the loose threads around cigarette-burn holes.

Hey, hey! shouts Vaslav. Hey, everybody, give me a second. One! somebody shouts. Everybody laughs. Vaslav waves his arms. The crowd quiets down and he picks up his plastic cup, splashes a bit of beer foam over the side.

My friends, says Vaslav in his loudest voice, my excellent good friends. Today I am a very happy guy. Everybody claps and whistles. He holds his hands up. Very happy! Firstly, and not least because myself and my prodigious friends are one step closer today to being the best curlers, not just in this town, but across the region. Everybody hoots and claps and people knock their plastic cups together and slosh beer. The whole room smells like beer, that doughy, wheaty smell.

Vaslav raises his hands again. Yes, today would have been a good enough day for all of that. But, my friends, today I am doubly blessed. Now, I don't often talk about my work. But as a few of you know, I am an author of books. People whistle. Although I've never liked to use that term, author, says Vaslav, because it's usually affixed to writers who have actually had their work published, which does not describe me. Everybody laughs. It's okay, somebody shouts, we'd still call you a curler even if you didn't win.

Vaslav's smile takes up his whole red face. He spreads his arms open wide. Today I heard from Toronto. From the publisher in Toronto. And they said yes! A tentative yes!

People stamp, slap their hands on the tables. More beer splashes everywhere.

So here's to next month in Okotoks, when we cross brooms with Their Holinesses. We can only hope that the Good Lord is otherwise occupied that day.

The door opens and Jarvis Lester comes in. Everybody quiets down a bit to watch him hobble across the room, his steel cane thumping heavily on the floor. Solzhenitsyn gets up and pulls over a couple of chairs.

Much obliged, says Jarvis. Grunts and settles himself down in the chair, then reaches down and pulls his leg up onto the other chair. Jarvis Lester is the only black man in High River, and when he comes to Marvin, he's the only black man here too. Wears a white shirt and blue tie, his pants pulled up over the wooden leg to the middle of his thigh. The leg is ashy, a steel joint in the knee, more steel at the ankle disappearing into his sock. Hard to Kill is written down the front of his calf in woodburnt letters, like on a baseball bat.

Somebody get me a drink, he says.

Who is that? whispers Pete Leakie. That's my dad's boss, says Mullen. He owns the meat-packing plant. What happened to his leg? asks Pete. The hide-ripping machine, says Mullen. Pete makes a face. What's a hide-ripping machine? I don't know, says Mullen, but that's what it did.

Here you go, boss, says Solzhenitsyn. Hands Jarvis a plastic cup of beer. Why, thank you. Jarvis has a long drink, then sets the cup down on the flat top of his leg, like it's a table.

Well, we're one step closer to our new career as professional curlers, says Vaslav. You'll have to find yourself a new pipe-twister. We're going to take him away from you.

Solly laughs. I wouldn't worry too much about it, boss. That's the least of your worries, I imagine.

Jarvis's face gets really serious, really hard. Closes his eyes and rubs his forehead. The least of my worries, he says.

Everybody standing around gets quiet. Jarvis has another long drink of beer. The Russians all lean in a little closer.

What do I have to do to keep you hicks from dismembering yourselves? asks Jarvis. We make meat. We kill animals and chop them up. We chop them up and square them and steak them and rib them. We freeze and boil them. It's not the post office. You have to pay attention.

What's going on, Jarvis? Come on, spill it.

Jarvis sighs, a really heavy sigh. Milo Foreman fell in the rendering vat, he says.

Nobody says anything for a long time.

What do you mean, fell in the –

I mean, fell in the rendering vat, says Jarvis. This afternoon, the weekend shift. Slipped on the flyover, went right through the railing, you know how heavy he is. Plop, into the rendering vat.

You can't fall into the rendering vat from the flyover, says Solzhenitsyn, it doesn't even go overtop.

Plop, says Jarvis. He finishes off his beer in one more long drink. Holds up the empty cup. Somebody takes it from him. Somebody hands him a new one.

Did you see him?

I saw him, says Jarvis. Makes a whistling sound. Splash. And you couldn't –

You know how high the sides of that vat are, someone says. Everybody thinks about it. Everybody gives Jarvis's wooden leg a long look. People slurp down their beer. At the counter the bartender is already setting out cups and cups full of beer.

Last week, Milo comes into my office, says Jarvis.

Solzhenitsyn holds up his hands, shaking his head. You can't fall into that vat, he says. The flyover doesn't go anywhere near over the top of it. You just couldn't.

You'd have to take a run at it, says someone in the back of the crowd.

A run? You'd have to climb into the rafters, shimmy out jungle-gym style above the air intake, walk along the duct and then drop straight down, says Solzhenitsyn.

Let me just say, Jarvis points a long finger at all of them, that I will stand on the roof and pour hot pitch on the heads of the first sons of bitches that talk union. This is a freakish, aberrant incident. I'll brick up the doors. The merest mention of any three-letter acronyms will be met with gunfire.

So, Milo comes into your office.

I recall every detail, says Jarvis. Sharp, like it had happened to me. You know when someone tells a story, and it sticks? The details? This thing happened to a friend, you always start out. And as the years go by you start to change this or that, because this detail makes it funnier, a better story like so. And eventually you don't start with This thing happened to a friend, because by then it's happened to you.

Milo comes into my office and says, Jarvis, I have this dream.

We should get these kids out of here, says Pavel. They don't want to hear this.

We can stay, says Mullen. We don't mind.

Vaslav slaps Solzhenitsyn on the shoulder. Solly leans

forward, elbows on his knees, fists out in front of him, clenched tight. Eyes wide, not blinking. We'll take the kids home, says Vaslav. Solzhenitsyn nods. Jarvis turns in his seat and waves to the bartender. We're going to need a lot of beer here, he says. The bartender nods.

I dunno, I say. That snow is pretty heavy. I think we'll get stuck.

Mullen thumps the bottom of the old toboggan on the ground, knocks snow out of the seams. Don't worry, I greased it up good. He runs a thumb over the wood, it comes off shiny. Mullen's Secret Toboggan Grease, he says. It's the best ever. One coat makes it all new, like it'd never ridden over any gravel or ice or spent time in a garage. I figure I'll make up a few buckets and sell them to McClaghan. He could have a display, you know, a cardboard sign next to the sleds.

McClaghan will just rip you off. Don't you pay attention? McClaghan sticks it to everybody, 'cause he owns everything. He already owns your house, you want him to get his hands on your toboggan grease?

My toboggan grease is pretty fantastic, says Mullen.

The snow is too heavy. We'll get stuck halfway.

Mullen sits in the front and wraps the yellow rope in loose loops around his fists. Take a running start, he says.

Lift your arms, I need room to get my legs under there.

I cough on my mitt and sniffle. Some kids try to slide down the hill on plastic carpets and get stuck halfway down in the heavy snow. Sit there dug into a drift. I take a deep breath and run at the sled.

I hit Mullen's back with both arms outstretched, his head whips back and he whoops. The sled pushes over the lip of the hill. I keep pushing, expecting the sled to bog in the snow, but it shoots away, I have to jump forward to catch up. I land on top of the toboggan, stick out my legs, and Mullen grabs one and gets it around under his armpit in his lap. The other drags out in the snow and the sled veers to the right.

Jesus! shouts Mullen.

I get my other leg on top of him; the rope catches my foot. Mullen hauls us in to the left. We don't slow down. We go faster and faster and bump on all the bumps and shoot off a drift. I can't see anything, all the snow in my face. We start to lean over to the right, to the left, to the right again.

I can't see! I shout. I let go of his shoulder to wipe my face, and we crash down on the far edge, spin at a right angle, then sideways down toward a girl at the bottom of the hill, her back to us.

Mullen opens his mouth to yell and it fills with snow. Jenny Tierney, her cigarette just lit, turns around, her eyes open wide, and we crash into her.

We all sit up and stare at each other. The toboggan upside down in the middle. Mullen's face, all covered in snow, coughs, his mouth full of snow. A neat cone of snow on his head. Jenny Tierney's hair full of snow. Her cigarette, bent, drips.

That does it, she says.

I lost a boot.

I'm going to tear you limb from limb, says Jenny Tierney. Put your heads on stakes on my lawn.

I lost a boot, says Mullen. Anybody see a boot?

We all get up and shake. Mullen's Secret Toboggan Grease, he says, grinning. Jenny Tierney shakes snow out of her hair. Looks to us like she's deciding who to hit first. Mullen stands on one foot, his sock wet, half off his foot. Holds up his hands.

We'll help you get Dave Steadman.

Stakes, she says.

It was an accident. We'll get you cigarettes.

She takes a step forward. And you'll get me lemonade too, sure.

Are you going to the roman-candle fight tomorrow night? asks Mullen.

She stops. What?

The skaters at the junior high, he says. The Tuesday-night roman-candle fight.

You made that up.

It's the best thing. He waves his arms and makes a big bursting sound. Fireworks everywhere. Sparks and fire and pickup trucks.

You made that up.

He takes off a glove, rolls up a sleeve. Shows her the flash burn on his shoulder. I went out last month and watched and got this. Just winged me. I had to go to the High River hospital. She grabs his arm and yanks him forward. Leans down to look at the raw pink skin.

Did you cry?

Goddamn right I cried. Look at that, it was all blistered.

Fireworks?

We'll take you.

She thinks for a while. You have to give me a hostage.

What?

A hostage. Give me your bag.

I need to find my boot, says Mullen.

Jenny reaches out and shoves Mullen over. Then she shoves me over into the snow too. She picks up Mullen's knapsack out of the snow, shakes it dry. Unzips the top and looks inside. She pulls out a red duotang, crumpled corners. Opens it up and reads the first page.

Report on David Thompson and His River Exploring, she says. Flips a few pages. What's this here, she asks, points to a pencil-crayon map, British Columbia? Look, you labelled all the rivers. Mullen sits in the snow, his soggy sock, half off his foot, sticks out in the air. Watches her flip pages. David Thompson wanted to find the Columbia River for the North West Company, she reads, because nobody had ever found the Columbia River and it was very important for the fur trade which is what the North West Company did. This is due tomorrow, right? she asks.

Tomorrow, says Mullen.

And these junior high boys shoot fireworks at each other tomorrow night?

Mullen nods.

Well, I'll give this back to you after you take me to see junior high boys shoot fireworks at each other. She curls the duotang up and sticks it in her jacket. She opens her cigarette pack; snow drips out. She sighs and puts them back in her pocket. What time?

Six, says Mullen.

Six o'clock. At the Red Rooster parking lot. You can take me out, show me around, then I'll give this back. See you tomorrow, she says.

Yeah.

We watch her walk away.

If you get sent up one more time, I say.

Mullen digs around in the snow. Won't much matter, if my head's on a stake on her lawn.

Mrs. Lampman said if you were late with your social studies report you'd be in detention until after Christmas.

Discapitating, that's what they call it. Kid Discapitated, all over the newspapers. They'll have a picture of my head on the stake. I need to find my boot.

We sell lemonade in the morning. Mitts and boots and two pairs of socks and the snow falls all over. Mullen sits with his arms crossed, doesn't say anything. Cars drive by, windshields scraped, the side windows with wet melts in the white frost. No one buys any lemonade.

We fold up the tablecloth, lean the planks against the side of the garage. Mullen picks up a cinder block to take inside. Here, I say. He stops at the garage door. I unzip the top of my backpack and pull out a duotang. I changed the title page, I tell him. Look, it's your name. I figure I get sent up a lot less, so I'll do less time. When Jenny Tierney gives back your report, I can hand it in.

Shut up, says Mullen. Remember when we had to hand in our outlines? I got six out of ten for not using enough capital letters. Your report's about Father Lacombe, and mine's about David Thompson, and the teacher already knows that.

Come on. I wave the report at him. Look, I used white-out to change the name.

Shut up. He tugs his mittens down on their strings. Tugs and tugs. So I get sent up for a while. That's nothing new. I'll just do something else anyway, even if I don't get sent up for this. I'll just run my mouth off or something and it'll all be just the same. He tugs his mittens and bangs on the garage door. Dad! he shouts, hands cupped around his mouth. Dad, we're going to school now and I can't open the garage door so we're leaving everything here.

It's a real good report, I say. Father Lacombe and the Blackfeet. They had treaties. Look, I numbered all the pages. And there's your name.

Father Lacombe isn't David Thompson, though, is he? Just 'cause you never hear about it for anything doesn't mean the rest of us won't. Hey, Dad! Mullen's dad comes out, takes a second to fit the zipper on his jacket together. Look how shaky I am, he says, fumbling with the zipper. You should wear your jean jacket, says Mullen, with the buttons. Too cold, says his dad. Fumbles and then zips up the jacket. Too cold. He looks at the plank, the blocks. You guys go to school, he says. I have to warm up the truck. Go to school and I'll put that stuff away. Thanks, Dad, says Mullen.

Mullen's dad gets down on his knees, zips Mullen's jacket all the way up. You come right home after school, all right?

Dad, I have stuff to do.

Sure, you have a lot of stuff to do. But I want you to come right home. Your teachers say you never have anything done on time. Right? You need to start coming home earlier, to get everything done.

You never come home on time either. Solzhenitsyn never even knows where you are.

Well, I don't always have everything done on time either. Not far from the tree.

From the what?

Just go to school.

Don't forget to change back that name, Mullen says to me.

At school all the kids pull off their boots in the dark hallway. It's hard to see after all the bright snow. Kids hang up their jackets on their hooks, pull off boots and stack them by the wall, try not to step in wet puddles of melting snow while they slip on their running shoes. The hall smells damp and hot. Kids file down the dark hallway to class, yapping and laughing.

In class all the kids line up in front of Mrs. Lampman's desk. She sits in her chair holding her hot coffee mug under her chin in two cupped hands, and kids line up and lay their reports on her desk in a pile. Duotangs and manila folders, and some kids even have clear plastic sleeves. Title pages, the date and a kid's name and a title: The North West Mounted Police, The Riel Uprising, Mackenzie and the Northwest Passage. I put my folder on the pile, and Jenny Tierney puts hers on the pile: Fort Whoop-Up, by Jenny Tierney. She doesn't have a folder, or the date. Stapled in the corner twice, because the first staple didn't go through all the pages. Mullen stays in his chair.

Mrs. Lampman sips her coffee and all the kids sit down, rattling their chair legs against the sides of their desks.

Mullen?

Mullen looks over at Jenny Tierney. She raises an eyebrow. He takes a deep breath and stands up. Didn't do it, he says. David Thompson isn't so important I guess. Besides, the library is full of books about David Thompson. Dozens of them: what he did and where he went, which rivers he fell in, how many canoes he built, how many jackets he wore. I figure the world knows enough about David Thompson and doesn't need some dumb kid going on and on.

Mrs. Lampman sips her coffee. Hunches her shoulders and lifts both cupped hands right up to her face. Nods. Mullen stands behind his desk. Mrs. Lampman nods and doesn't say anything. Everybody waits.

Every year at Christmas I get my husband a subscription to *National Geographic*. I think he likes the maps. I think he looks at the articles: tidal changes in the Solomon Islands, or the secrets of the Mayan calendar. They pile up around the house, all these facts. But does he read them? She sips some coffee and stares down at her desk, not really at anything. Everybody waits. Some of the front-row girls hold their pencils, ready to take notes. Mullen stands behind his desk, confused, like he doesn't know if he should sit down or not.

I could –

I don't want your report on David Thompson, says Mrs. Lampman. You're right. Who cares? What do you know? Do whatever you like. David Thompson isn't good for young people to be learning about anyway. Nearly spoiled his vision by staring into a candle. If he'd just shut his eye, he'd have seen fine into old age, but he wonders, What would happen? What else is there to see? Not much of a role model. The exploring itself is mostly bloody-minded macho work fantasy. Imagine a glorified trucking company, whose dispatch records get taught centuries later in university literature classes. But the eloquent, almost effeminate care with which these drunk brigands dragged themselves back and forth across the continent with their oily rodent carcasses in hand for some reason inspires the male imagination today still in this country. You're right: now's as good a time as any to break the chain. Sit down. She sips some coffee. Stands up.

One of the front-row girls puts up her hand. How do you spell ... ev – eminate? she asks. Never mind, says Mrs. Lampman. Have we talked about Simon Fraser yet? The front-row girls nod. Who haven't we talked about? The front-row girls shrug. Mrs. Lampman taps her chalk on the blackboard. Little white ticks. What about Louis Riel? We talked about Louis Riel last week, someone says. She nods. I always like the Louis Riel part, she says. Such a good story. Why do we glorify cranky geographers who don't even get to the mouth of the river first, and hang Louis Riel? You want to hear about the Red River Rebellion? Doesn't that sound exciting? We learned about Louis Riel last week, someone says. Right, says Mrs. Lampman. Taps the chalk. Last week.

Jenny Tierney sits under the pay phone at the Red Rooster. Her knees tucked up against her chest, her chin on her knees. She doesn't wear a toque, no gloves, pink cold fingers wrapped around her ankles. Pink ears.

Wait a minute, I tell Mullen. He rolls his wrists, makes his mitts swing in circles at the ends of their string. What? he says. We'll be late. She'll tear up David Thompson. Just wait a minute, I say.

Jenny Tierney is tall but skinny. Her arms seem too long, longer than she knows what to do with. She folds and unfolds and taps her knuckles on the concrete. Rubs the back of her neck. People park their cars, blue station wagons, half-tons with dirty bed covers. People park and go into the Red Rooster, buy cigarette cartons or a litre of milk, plastic bottles of pop. They lean over the counter and rub nickles over scratch-and-win lottery tickets. Some of them leave their engines idling. Jenny blows on her hands.

Hey, Mullen.

What?

What's a rendering vat?

I asked my dad. He didn't want to tell me at first.

So what is it?

He says it's this great big vat, full of boiling fat. They take all the leftover meat, all the parts they can't use, and they boil it.

Oh.

Yeah.

It doesn't have a lid?

I guess theirs doesn't, no.

Jenny puts a cigarette in her mouth, rummages through her black purse. One of the straps frayed, held there with a safety pin. Rummages. A man in grey cowboy boots gets out of a grey truck.

Hey, mister, you got a lighter?

The man looks down at her. Walks past her into the Red Rooster.

How tall do you think she is?

She'll see us, says Mullen.

Yeah, but how tall do you think she is?

She puts the cigarette back in her mouth. Rummages in her purse some more. Then she looks up, across the parking lot, at us, leaning against the credit union wall.

Are you going to stand there and stare at me all night? she shouts. Jesus, don't they teach you any manners in Sunday school?

We rush over. She sits under the pay phone, looks up at us. Frowning. Mullen digs in his pockets. Let's get candy, he says. I've got forty cents.

Fireworks, says Jenny Tierney. Mullen swings his mitts. Schablaow, he says. She leans forward and stands up, careful not to bump against the pay phone. Tugs down her black T-shirt. Leaves her short black jacket unzipped. A faded print on the shirt, someone with messy hair and a guitar. Johnny Thunders, it says. Not really black anymore, like it's been washed too much.

We walk around behind the Red Rooster, down the alley. It's not really an alley like in movies, with walls on either side and clothes hung on lines and men in hats lurking and smoking. It's just a road behind the buildings, with potholes and washboard, weeds and frost and thistles. Just sort of where the town stops. On the other side of the alley the weeds grow up into bushes along the river. Okotoks has a river and High River has a river, and they're both deep and fast, but the Marvin river is just like everything else here, it just sort of slugs along. You could probably swim across it no trouble if grown-ups weren't always yelling at you not to.

You have to think pretty hard to imagine Main Street from the other side, to remember which back doors and parking lots and blank brick walls go with which buildings. Behind McClaghan's are heaps of cardboard boxes, some of them broken down flat, but some of them stacked into one another. Some of them big enough to sit inside. Mullen and I slow down to stare at the boxes, but Jenny Tierney shoves us both between the shoulders and we stumble and keep walking.

Jenny Tierney whistles while she walks. When she isn't smoking. Not a round whistle, not loud like Lou Ellis, whistling along to McClaghan's radio. Lou Ellis can whistle the *Hockey Night in Canada* song, and all the country-and-western songs on the *Top Six at Six*. Jenny Tierney has a skinny between-the-teeth kind of whistle, real quiet. I don't think she whistles any songs, just sort of up-and-down scales.

Icicles hang off the footbridge, down toward the river, the snow shovelled just enough to walk single file. Jenny Tierney whistles and shoves us when we slow down and nobody says anything on the walk up the little hill to the junior high school.

The prairie comes right up to the junior high school, you can follow the snowdrifts, against fence posts, how the wind comes down all the way from the mountains, drifting snow across the parking lot, up against the long yellow brick walls, the squat windows. Sometimes we come to the junior high for a science fair, or a play in the auditorium, but I've never been to the junior high parking lot at night.

They sit in the boxes, up on the box rails and wheel wells of the trucks, or lean standing against the back windshields. Floppy toques, black hoods pulled over their faces, ball caps with mesh backs. Held together here and there with duct tape. Roman candles laid across their laps. Clouds of truck exhaust drift out into the snowy pastures.

Teenagers talk and laugh; some of them smoke, some of them drink slurpees. All of them tall, some pimpled and too skinny. Junior high girls share a slurpee cup and giggle, their thick neon coats open, their legs long, hair teased up, high bangs. They talk and laugh and some of them look over at Jenny Tierney and whisper to each other. They flick their cigarette ash on the ground. They don't wave. Jenny stands next to us, real quiet, not even whistling. Stares straight ahead.

Paul Grand sits on his creaky skateboard on the sidewalk, rolls side to side. He sees us and waves us over. We walk through all the teenagers, they stare at us but no one says anything. They stare at Jenny Tierney.

How's your shoulder? Paul asks Mullen.

All better, Mullen says. Pulls his jacket open, tugs down his shirt to the pink mark on his shoulder. Paul whistles. You sure did have us panicked when you took that. Straight on, bang, he says. But all better now, right? All better, says Mullen. Zips his coat back up.

Hey, Paul, I say.

Paul stands up, picks up his skateboard. In a minute, kid.

I just wanted to ask –

We've got to get started, says Paul. He puts both his index fingers in the sides of his mouth and whistles. Loudest whistle I ever heard. All the teenagers stop talking and turn around. Paul gives us the thumbs-up, then jumps into the back of a truck. We stand under a light post. Jenny Tierney still doesn't say anything, but her eyes are real wide.

Paul puts his hands on the roof of the truck, then huffs and pulls himself up. Stands on the roof. All the teenagers stop what they're doing; they whistle and clap. Paul waves.

Well, he says, just watch out for people's faces I guess. No shooting at anybody's head. And if somebody shoots at your head, then duck. Okay? Keep the music off, and no jumping out of moving trucks. Unless they're on fire.

They rev the engines, flick their windshield wipers on and off, grinding against the icy glass. A teenager in an old Chevrolet, rust-pocked, road salt on his running boards, sticks his head out the window, scrapes at the ice with his fingers. Paul scrambles back down into the box, pounds on the roof of the truck with his flat open palm. Everybody screams as loud as they can.

They rev their engines and throw out their clutches and the tires screech on the ice. None of them move for a second, back ends all drift out, right, left. Then they lurch and jump forward, all right at each other. I think they'll all crash head-on, but they jerk out of each other's way, veer out, zoom past each other. Engines grunt from gear to gear and the kids white-knuckled in the boxes all yell and lean into the cold wind.

Jenny Tierney claps slowly, her cold, pink hands quiet.

The trucks shoot out to the sides of the parking lot and then pull around, seven pickup trucks in a circle around the snowy edges. Sometimes they slide on patches of snow, buckle from side to side on black ice. The kids all toss around in the boxes. They lap the parking lot, one after the other, some of them flashing their lights. Lights swing all over, throw the walls of the junior high on and off, the yellow bricks blinking.

Then someone honks their horn, a red Dodge, the ram on the hood bent and staring off to one side. All the kids in the box duck low, grip the sides tighter, and then the truck's wheels lock. It pitches sideways with a grind, buckles. Kids fall from one side to the other, and the truck takes off, right up the middle of the lot. At the far end of the tarmac, another truck peels around, the snow behind it red from brake lights, swerves out of the lap and up the middle.

Mullen claps, cuffs his mitts around his mouth and shouts, Kaboom! Kablam!

In either box a kid stands up, leans forward against the cab. They raise the roman-candle tubes and all the kids duck down against the truck beds, disappear.

Then green and red, bang! Fire and sparks blow up all over the fronts of the trucks, fire on the hoods, sparks and smoke on the windshields. Horns honk and we all shout and cheer, the trucks peel out, drive through the smoke and green and red afterflares, like Christmas. Teenagers stand up on the truck beds, roar and wave their arms, they all stand awhile until the trucks turn again and they fall down, hooting.

We clap and shout while the fireworks blow up all over the trucks. The fireworks leave hot white spots on the backs of my eyes. I watch the trucks circle and buckle and I close my eyes and stare at the drifting colours, the hot white that fades into blue, into green. I move my eyes, closed tight, and listen to the clutches and engines and the white spots fade blue, they dart around, never quite where I'm looking, eyes scrunched up behind my eyelids.

Aw hell, says Mullen. I open my eyes, the blue spots fade green. The trucks circle around, and out at the back of the parking lot the snow flashes red and blue, red and blue in long, quick sweeps.

The RCMP car drives slow-like across the parking lot.

Jenny Tierney walks along the side of the junior high. Calm, runs her hands along the bottom of each window. Mullen and I follow, duck when the RCMP blast their horn. Chases the pickup trucks in slow circles around the parking lot, careful on the ice. Some of the skaters ball up snowballs, throw them at the windshield. The wipers flick the snow away.

Jenny stops at a window. Grins at us. She hooks her fingers under the sash and lifts. Ice cracks around the bottom. She lifts up the window and presses in at the mesh screen inside. Pushes in the corners and bends one inside. She pushes her head, her shoulders through the window. Pulls her skinny body up, lifts herself up and kicks her legs. Mullen and I each grab a black boot and push her up, inside. She falls down heavy inside. Mullen looks at me, his eyes all lit up. The police lights pan, blue and red, across the dark brick walls, across us. Slow circles around the parking lot.

I fall in through the window onto the floor. Pick myself up and look around a dark classroom, the walls all covered in junior high serious stuff, maps and charts, a big grid full of funny-looking letters. The dark shapes of empty aquariums. I pull Mullen in through the window, kicking and grunting. We hear Jenny Tierney, laughing. Running, far away down the hall.

We run in the dark. Tall metal lockers snap past. We run down the dark halls lit up exit-sign red. Damp and spilled, the clean white floors squeak when we slide, our wet boot bottoms. In the stairwells our feet ring louder and louder. The steel banisters bang and echo.

At the end of the hallway a cart, mops and brooms, with a long dark shadow. Jenny Tierney runs ahead of us, her long legs, her heavy black boots stamping, half as many stamps as our short, panting footsteps. I hear Mullen yelling and laughing. Jenny Tierney runs ahead of us, sometimes she looks back. She laughs and laughs.

Hélène pushes open the Red Rooster door. I wait a few seconds before I follow her inside. Try to scrape the snow off my boots quietly while she roots in her purse. She walks up to the counter and points to her cigarette brand. She picks up a bottle of aspirin from the countertop display. Reads the label.

Do you have anything stronger than this?

The teenager holds out her cigarettes. Stronger? You'd have to go to the pharmacy.

Are they still open?

They close at nine.

She looks at her watch. Sighs and sets down the aspirin bottle. It'll be fine, she says.

Hey, the teenager shouts at me, put down the comic book. You always crease up the pages. Get out of here.

I put the comic back on the rack. What time does the bus come? I ask him.

Get out.

Hélène watches me. Puts the aspirin into her purse.

Are those for your ears?

She stops. Excuse me?

For the ringing in your ears, I ask. Do those help?

Get out of here! shouts the teenager. He starts to come around the counter. I run out the door. Hélène stands there, hand in her purse, watching me.

I run up the street, sliding in the snow. Sometimes I stop and scoop up a handful of snow to throw at a sign. The street-lights glow white with all the frost in the air. Across the lot where the grain elevators used to be it's dark, just white drifts on the black ground, the rutted gravel. Behind the black lot, snow drifts on the railroad tracks, on the dirt service road, in the skinny trees beside the riverbank. Marvin, Alberta, is pretty small when you stop and look around: the businesses on either side of Main Street, the quiet houses with the narrow roofs in the street behind.

It's dark out there, along the river, but you know that if you made the mistake of walking over there you'd find the real dark. The real black heavy dark that doesn't let you get away. You can't see it but it's out there, breathing, in and out, thick and heavy, and wet. As long as you don't wander out over there you're probably okay. I mean, it's never come over yet, hungry, creeping through town, covering everything in thick, sticky, wet dark. Pulling everything inside. It hasn't yet. I run and slide in the snow. Shuffle a little faster on the slippery sidewalk.

I turn up Mullen's street and there's Pavel again, hands in his pockets, walking home. He sees me and waves.

Why is it always just the two of us out this late? he asks. I pack up a snowball and throw it down the street. Yeah, I guess so, I say.

He looks at me for quite a while, like he wants to say something. That look that grown-ups get when they're all concerned. He looks at me that way for a while, then takes a deep breath and shakes his head.

Tell you what, kid. We'll get my truck and I'll give you a lift home. Spare you the walk. It's a bit of a walk up there, isn't it?

Well, it's not too bad.

Either way, kid, either way. We walk up the sidewalk, stamping in the fuzzy, light snow. Pavel fidgets in his pocket. Just got to get the truck keys out of the house, he says. Won't take a second.

He puts his key in the door, opens it. Then he gags. A thick cloud of stinging, stinking smoke pours out. All sour and nasty, like plastic, like when you leave the lid of the margarine tub on top of the toaster oven. We both gag and hold our hands over our mouths. What the, Pavel chokes. What the hell is going on?

Inside we hear a thump, a crash. Hey, shouts a voice from inside, it sounds like Solzhenitsyn. Hey, is someone home? What the hell is going on? Pavel hollers into the house. Don't come in, Solly yells, I'll be right up. Don't come in!

Pavel shuts the door. We both stand on the porch and cough. He spits on the porch and I do the same. The door opens and Solzhenitsyn comes out in another nasty cloud of smoke. Slams the door behind him.

What the hell is going on? Pavel asks again.

It's the boiler, says Solzhenitsyn. The boiler's blown.

What do you mean? What's that awful smoke?

We've, Solly says and then starts to cough. Coughs into his black work gloves. Something's ruptured in the boiler. And the glycol that's in there, the boiler is all full of glycol, see, well, it's pissing all over the place. It's pissing out and straight onto the burner, which is fired up all the way, and it's burning.

Fired up all the way? Pissing all over the place?

I shut it off. I shut off the gas.

That's our heat. It's freezing out. Can't you fix it?

I can't even breathe down there right now. I need to wait for the air to clear. But the whole house is going to freeze in the meantime.

Pavel leans over, looks in his window. Presses his face up against the glass. Solzhenitsyn coughs and spits, a really awful, thick cough. There's no way we can stay in there?, says Pavel. Solzhenitsyn leans over and coughs.

We stand there coughing on the porch and some head-lights come up the street. Mullen's dad's truck rattles to a stop in front of his house. He and Vaslav climb out. They see us and stop.

Getting a little air? asks Vaslav.

The boiler exploded, says Solzhenitsyn.

What do you mean the boiler exploded?

We've got glycol burning, apparently, says Pavel. It doesn't smell like it's anything you'd want to breathe.

It's moving through the pipes, that smoke, says Solzhenitsyn. It's getting distributed. It'll need a few days to clear through.

Wait, says Valsav, is there heat?

No. And there won't be, not for a few days.

So call the gas company.

It's the middle of the night, says Solzhenitsyn. I'll call the gas company in the morning. Look, he says, tomorrow I'll get everything fixed and it will be fine. In the meantime it's midnight and it's cold and we've got the kid here and I just want to go to sleep.

Mullen's dad sighs. Come on, he says. I'll pull out the couch.

Solzhenitsyn goes back inside their house. Holds his breath and opens the door. A white cloud puffs out. Vaslav pokes his head inside and jerks it back out, coughing and sputtering. Dear god, he says. Dear sweet god, what the hell is that?

Solly comes back out a minute later, coughing. Has a mug full of toothbrushes, razors. A stack of towels under his arm. Pavel stands on the porch with his arms wrapped around his shoulders, lost. Vaslav starts to brush his teeth on the porch. Stops with his toothbrush in his mouth and looks down at me.

What are you doing here anyway? he asks. It's the middle of the night.

Sometimes you just need to get out of the house.

Vaslav gives me a sideways look. Then he spits his toothpaste over the porch. We all follow Mullen's dad inside. Mullen's in the living room in his flannel pyjamas, rubbing his eyes. What's going on? he asks. I heard a lot of shouting. It woke me up. His dad rubs his hair, he squints.

The Russians stand in the kitchen and brush their teeth. Mullen's dad looks around the living room: his one sofa, his recliner. He opens the closet, gets out some fuzzy blankets, a few old pillows. Lays a few on the floor and a few on the couch. Pavel comes out of the kitchen with a glass of water and a salt shaker. Sprinkles in some salt, then tilts back his head, slowly twists his glass eye and pops it out. Drops it in the glass.

Solly stares out the window at his house. How long does it have to cook like that before the seal breaks? he says to himself. I should have heard that. An airlock. I should have at least heard it.

Mullen's dad brings me an old flannel shirt to wear and a pair of wool slippers. I guess you two can sleep in Mullen's room, he says.

You're sleeping over? Mullen asks.

Yeah, I guess so.

Mullen's room is small and narrow. His clothes are in a basket in the corner. A plastic tub full of Lego blocks, a pile of comics on the dresser. There's a picture of a woman above his bed, a picture in a little wooden frame. Black hair and glasses, and a pearl-buttoned country-and-western shirt, red roses stitched on either side of her chest.

Mullen's dad comes in with a sleeping bag, some blankets. Lays the blankets on the floor, the sleeping bag on top. Mullen sits on his bed and pulls his socks off. His dad waits until we're both under the covers, Mullen on his bed and me on the floor, then he shuts off the light.

Mullen sits up after a while. Sits up with his hands on his knees. Pretty late, huh?

Yeah, I say, pretty late.

Mullen lies down, turns over. Squirms for a while to get the blankets right.

I listen to the Russians grumble and mutter, then gradually they're quiet. Mullen's dad makes a phone call, hushed.

Then another. I can't make out what he says. After a while all the lights go out.

My arms feel too long. I try the arm up and under my head but my shoulder starts to pull. Turn over, both hands under my chest. I try to breathe steady. My hands start to tingle. I try not to move and they tingle and tingle.

What if I never get to sleep again? I guess I'll go crazy. Like old men in alleys in the city, like the little old grannies who yell at the waiters at Yee's Breakfast All Day Western Noodle. Like the Hat Man at the credit union. But kids don't go crazy, I don't think.

Over on my other side with my arm behind and it falls asleep right away. I can't feel it. I try to turn myself over and can't feel my arm. Reach around behind with my other hand and try to grab my shoulder but it's too far. I sort of flop forward, push my forehead into the mattress. I lever myself up with my head and reach underneath and pull the arm out and collapse. Whew.

When I'm crazy I hope I still get to have fun. I don't know if crazy people read comics or go down hills or try to drink the most milk. I try not to look at the clock. If I see the time, I get all anxious because I can't sleep and soon it'll be morning and I won't have slept and I'll go crazy. I'll get short of breath and have to roll over and I'll be awake forever. Do you have to go to school if you're crazy? Learn about Louis Riel and do sit-ups?

Tomorrow will be Monday: school and inside shoes and the dim lights in the hallways, desks and foolscap and going outside at lunch. Compasses and protractors and the Northwest Passage. And all I ever do is wait around. Wait around for after school, for Friday, for Christmas. But what am I going to do? Wake up Mullen and try to tell him? Wake up Solzhenitsyn and Mullen's dad, and tell them that I can't sleep? How come it's always my job to tell people when something's wrong anyway?

Mullen snorts and breathes heavy. He inhales through his nose and exhales through his mouth. His foot pushes up and down, up and down under the blanket. Like he was hopping up and down. When I'm crazy I hope me and Mullen still get along. I hope we still sell lemonade. I guess I'd understand if he didn't want to sell lemonade with a crazy kid. If I go crazy, he'll probably make the lemonade too sweet.

Mr. Hyslop draws notes on the music-room chalkboard. Has this block of wood with five pieces of chalk all held together, draws five parallel lines across the board. Whole notes and quarter notes. He counts with his hand, back and forth and up and down, and we all sing songs, except most of the boys don't sing, just open our mouths along with the words. I do my best not to yawn too much. Sometimes my eyes droop and my head bobs forward and I almost fall asleep. Pete Leakie nudges me every time my head starts to bob and I wake up and keep opening my mouth to the words.

After school I go to see how the Russians are doing. Pavel and Vaslav sit on the porch in their parkas.

Did Solzhenitsyn fix the boiler yet?

Look inside, says Vaslav, there's frost in the sink. An icicle hanging out of the faucet. My goddamn home.

He's at the hardware store buying tools, says Pavel.

He was whistling, says Vaslav, making a sour face. Practically giddy. Like it's the best thing that's happened all year. It's appalling.

He says it will take a few more days to air out, says Pavel, before he can turn everything back on.

But he can fix it, I say, right? He can fix anything.

He can fix anything, says Pavel. Vaslav coughs.

You should stay at Deke's house until he does, I say. Vaslav coughs and spits on the porch. That miserable son of a bitch won't open the door. Says he'll shoot anybody tries to come inside. He thinks we've got that cop with us and we're all out to bust up whatever loony scheme he's cooking up in there.

I heard at the Short Stack last night that he's counterfeiting, says Pavel. He's got a metal press, making his own quarters by the roll. Planning to flood the whole municipality with counterfeit coins.

Fleer figures he's building an aqueduct, says Vaslav.

A what?

You know, like the Romans used. Fleer says he saw that El Camino go by late one night full of scrap sheet metal. Figures Howitz is building an aqueduct piece by piece, to flood the credit union over land.

Shouldn't you be working on your novel? I ask Vaslav. He balls up his fist and coughs. He coughs for a long time. Sometimes he stops coughing and tries to catch his breath, then wheezes and chokes and doubles over and coughs again. Pavel hits him on the back and he coughs heavy and wet into his hand. He takes a deep breath. Opens his hand and makes a face, holds his damp, sticky hand away. Pats his pockets with his dry hand. Pavel unfolds his cloth handkerchief and hands it over.

Who can write when there's no heat? When you can't go inside? He coughs, clutches at his chest. The proofs are out. In the mail. I'm on vacation, he says.

I pull off my inside shoes to go out for recess and Pete Leakie says, Hey. I put my inside shoes on the shelf. Hey, are you going outside? asks Pete. He squints beside the door, his face pulled back into the dark. Squints at the bright white sky. It sure is a lot of snow, says Pete. He scuffs his shoe on the black doormat.

It's not that much snow, Pete, I say. I pull on a boot. Why don't you come outside? I figure I'll go sit in the gully awhile. Pete watches the sky.

Mullen in detention? he asks. I nod. Pete tugs at the neck of his sweater.

You reading any of those books you like, Pete?

Pete looks down at the book in his hand. Horses and swords and pointy white mountains. Well, I read all these books, he says, and they're all kind of the same. There's a country without a king, and a kid who doesn't have parents, and then a stranger, with a ring, or else it's a kid from somewhere else, like England, who gets lost, and ends up in this place with wizards and badgers. And everybody wants things how they used to be, except things changed, and now there's a dark lord in a tower, or a witch in a tunnel. So the elves or wizards or badgers or whatever give the kid a sword that makes him a king, a ring that makes him hold his breath, or a hat that makes him hear the sleeping queen when she's breathing.

Pete turns away from the white sky. Sounds great, Pete, I say.

Yeah, well, you have a good time sitting in the gully, says Pete. He backs away from the door, neck a little bent, eyes narrow. It's awfully big, isn't it? he says.

It's the sky, Pete.

Sure it is. Sure it's the sky.

Out in the field Dead Kids play ball hockey in the hard-packed snow. Kids wind up for big slapshots and whack other kids in the chest. Whenever Dave Steadman winds up for a slapshot, all the kids take one hand off their sticks and cover their crotches.

Dwayne Klatz stands near the monkey bars. Looks all over the playground. He hops from one foot to the other. Dwayne takes a deep breath and slaps himself across the face. He shakes his head and slaps himself. Shakes his shoulders, like he's going to run a race.

Dwayne steps in front of Jenny Tierney, on her way toward the school. She almost walks right overtop of him. Get out of my way, she says.

He reaches into the chest pocket of his overalls. Unfolds a piece of paper, holds it out in front of his face. Clears his throat. Then he reads out loud.

> *Jenny, all I ever do*
> *Is think of spending time with you,*
> *And how you are the prettiest girl*
> *I ever saw in the whole world.*

He coughs into his mitt.

Jenny's eyes get about as wide as I've ever seen them. Not a face like in gym class, the dodgeball hitting the wall and her leaving the room. Her eyes get wide and her eyebrows raise up and her mouth sort of hangs open. Dwayne stands there. Scratches the back of his head.

Uh, do you want to keep the poem?

Jenny stares at him. She balls up her fist, raises it a little, waits.

Some front-row girls near the swing set whisper to each other. They point and whisper, point at Jenny and Dwayne and giggle. Jenny looks at them, she looks at Dwayne and then she looks at her fist.

Uhm, says Dwayne.

Jenny Tierney puts her hands in her pockets and walks away, toward the school. Dwayne looks at me, real pale. I shrug. The front-row girls by the swing set laugh and laugh.

The hardest part about November is the night. The nights get bigger and bigger. In November you walk out of the double front doors of the school and the sun is already low on the horizon and the air is grey and before you know it, it's nighttime. And it's cold and it's dark.

The thing to do is get all the fireworks you can carry and bundle them all together, and tie them onto your backpack. You can tape them on with duct tape, that'll hold them good. You have to make sure that they're all facing the right way. Then all you need to do is make sure that your backpack is strapped on real good, and light a match. And then bang, you're flying away. You're shooting off into the sky on the front of the brightest, loudest explosion ever. The trick is to get enough fireworks that you can keep going, zooming through the air, the wind stretching your face, like you were standing up in the back of a racing truck. If you've got enough fireworks you can keep up with the day, firing off west, chasing the sun.

Pavel comes out of the frozen house with his arms full of clothes: black overcoats and white shirts. Mullen and I sit at the table flicking pennies at each other while the grown-ups go into the bathroom, one at a time. Solzhenitsyn and Pavel both squeeze white shaving foam out of metal tubes. Mullen's dad just lathers up a white bar of soap, spreads it on his bristly cheeks. Vaslav doesn't shave at all. They all brush their teeth and comb their hair with black plastic combs. They put their white shirts on over their white undershirts. Then they line up and Pavel ties all their neckties. Mullen's dad and Solzhenitsyn have thin black ties. Vaslav has a wide red-and-white striped tie. They hold their chins up and Pavel loops the ties around and ties the knots, folds their collars back down. He has a good look at them all, then nods.

I'll start the car, says Solzhenitsyn.

Mullen's dad nods. He looks at us. Chews on his lip. I don't think we should bring the kids, he says.

Solly shrugs. So don't bring the kids.

Yeah, but I don't want to leave them alone either.

So send them to the rec centre. Lock them in the living room. You leave them alone all the time.

That's exactly the point. I leave him alone all the time, and look at the results. If I let this miscreant out of my sight for a second, he's liable to burn my house down. I've had it with school principals calling me a jerk and a bum.

Every kid needs to go to a wake, says Vaslav. There's living and there's dying and you've got to see it all.

So bring them along, says Solly. It's just the Short Stack. Not like we're taking them to the casino in Calgary.

He glares at us. Mullen holds up his scribbler. I'll bring my homework, he says. Won't bother you at all. Long division, I'll be in the corner. Yeah, I say, I've got a book report. We'll sit in the corner and won't even look up from our books. Heck, we'll be so busy we won't even know where we are.

Absolutely not. Absolutely no way am I taking my already disreputable, hell-bound child to the town trough.

Jarvis said – hell, how did he put it? Solly tugs on an ear-flap. Said that failure to attend would constitute sedition. You know how it is when he talks all *Reader's Digest* style – means he's in a right flap.

Send them over to that teacher lives across the street, says Pavel. She can look after them.

She has a low enough opinion of me already. Take the kids, I have to go to the bar? Can't do.

Howitz, says Vaslav.

Mullen's dad raps his knuckles on his knee. Chews his lip. Get your car, he says to Solzhenitsyn. Stares at us. You sit in the corner, he says. You don't talk to anybody.

The corner, Dad. Right.

You sit in the corner, you don't talk to anybody, you don't get up from the table.

Long division, with a remainder. Right, Dad.

We wait for Solzhenitsyn's hatchback to warm up. He gets a roll of duct tape out of the glovebox, puts a few new strips around the garbage bag over his window. Scrapes the frost off his windshield. Mullen's dad paces on the porch. Mullen puts his scribbler and his math textbook in a plastic IGA bag. Drops in a handful of stubby pencils.

The hatchback putters down Main Street, Mullen's dad and Solzhenitsyn up in the front, too tall, heads hunched over the dashboard, past the IGA and the Red Rooster, past houses, where the street narrows down and the sidewalks stop. Vaslav and Pavel follow behind us in the pickup truck. The road curves out into scrubby poplar trees along the river, and the railroad tracks run right up beside it, and Solly drives around the curve and there's the Short Stack. A few old trucks in the parking lot, dirty, one of them snowed right over like it hasn't moved in weeks. Red neon blinks in the dark, SHO T ACK, blinks on and off, makes all the snow red, then dark, then red.

It's been a long wait, says Mullen's dad. Feels like a long wait. Funerals usually happen a lot sooner.

Well, says Solzhenitsyn, it's not like there was a body.

Mullen's dad shudders. No, he says, I guess not.

We park and get out of the car. Mullen's dad walks up the wooden porch, a few plastic chairs still outside, covered in snow. Stamps off his boots, opens the heavy door.

Inside it smells like old towels, like the sink in Deke's kitchen when he rinses out his beer bottles for the depot. Red and blue light from neon beer signs, posters with women in bikinis, on sailboats, or in car garages, with toolbelts around their hips. Men in denim shirts and corduroy ball caps sit at the bar, their legs spread wide on their stools, their bellies resting against the dark wood. Big fists around their bottles. Ashtrays full of crushed butts.

The men from Lester's Meats stand around the pool tables, all of them in their best black coats, clean blue jeans. Some of them wear big black cowboy hats with fancy bands. They stand around the pool tables, each of them with a bottle or a glass, talking. They look serious and sad and a little drunk, all of them. Jarvis Lester sits in one chair, leg up on another, drinks something pale out of a small glass. Everybody waves when we come in.

The bartender stacks glasses: short glasses, fat glasses with flat sides, tiny glasses with stems, shot glasses. Water from his soggy hands drips on the row of wineglasses, leaves streaks through the dust. He picks up two pint glasses, holds his arms out to either end of the long row of beer taps. Flips down the handles with either forefinger, the pints loose in his hands. Gold beer fills the tilted glasses. He straightens them as they fill, closes the taps with his thumbs.

Mullen's dad looks for a dry spot on the wood, leans on his elbows. I'll get four Labatt 50s and – what do you kids want? You want lemon-lime? Root beer? Ginger ale, says Mullen. Yeah, I say, we want ginger ale.

The bartender leans over to look at us. Christ, he says, you can't bring kids in here. It's not the goddamn dinner theatre.

Babysitting, says Mullen's dad. We'll keep them under strict parental supervision.

No minors. I'll get shut down.

What, says Mullen's dad, the Alberta Gaming and Liquor Commission is going to shut you down for a couple of kids drinking root beer?

Ginger ale, says Mullen. We want ginger ale.

It's not like we're out for a night on the town, says Vaslav. It's a wake.

The AGLC is everywhere, says the bartender. Leans close and hushes his voice. They've got spies. Secret sting operations. They send in seventeen-year-olds, undercover, dress them up as college students.

When I was a bartender in Edmonton we got AGLC stings, says Solzhenitsyn, but they get too into character. You can spot them because they always order fancy import beer. Anybody asks for something made by monks in Belgium is an AGLC spook. He looks down the bar at all the old men. How about those 50s?

The bartender pops the caps off four brown bottles. Keep them away from the bar, he says, fills two plastic glasses with ginger ale out of the soda gun. And keep them away from the pool table. Keep them away from everybody.

Mullen here has long division, says Mullen's dad. And you, he says to me, where's your book report?

I didn't bring it.

You didn't bring it. He takes his beer from the bartender. You got anything this kid can read?

The bartender pulls a plastic tub from under the cash register. Corkscrews, a box of chalk, stretches of wire, a television remote control. He finds a skinny book. *Old Trafalgar's Finest Cocktail and Bartending Guide.* A picture of Queen Victoria on the cover. I mean it, he says, I don't want them talking to anybody.

How's homelessness? Jarvis asks Vaslav.

Vaslav thumps his chest. A little adversity never hurt anybody. Keeps a man alert, dealing with less than ideal circumstances.

I've been running space heaters, says Solzhenitsyn. To keep the pipes from freezing. Guy from the gas company is coming tomorrow and we're going to turn it all back on. I think we've got the blockage clear; ought to be drying our socks on the radiators tomorrow night.

Listen to him, says Jarvis, he's never had such a good time. Massive heating emergency in his own home. Finally gives him something to do.

I flip through the bartending book. Look, I say to Mullen, pointing to the pictures, fancy brown drinks in stemmed glasses, cherries and plastic swords, limes and umbrellas.

What's triple sec? asks Mullen. He strains his head to see the shelves of bottles behind the bar. Which drink do you think uses the most of those bottles?

A manhattan has three drops of bitters, I read. And an amaretto wash.

What's amaretto? What does it wash?

Somebody holds up their bottle. Everybody gets quiet and does the same. The men with the cowboy hats all take them off. Jarvis gets his cane and hoists himself up. Holds up his pale glass of something.

I want to first thank everybody for coming to work last week. I know we're all rattled. I wouldn't have been surprised had no one darkened the plant door on Monday. But I think we all know, a small outfit like ours, well, losing a day or two and we'd be through. So thanks, everyone.

Everybody nods and has a drink.

Think the bartender would make us one of these mint juleps? asks Mullen. It looks pretty harmless. I bet it uses a lot of those bottles. Mullen's dad glares at us.

We've been an accident-free operation for a long time, says Jarvis, barring the obvious. He knocks the side of his leg with his cane. Everybody has a little laugh. Otherwise it's been six months since Little Joe put that boning knife into Henry's arm out on the line.

He really shouldn't have reached in front of me like that, says a short little man. Everybody has another laugh.

But this, well, this is something else. We've all lost a friend, we've lost a teammate. It's happened where we work and I don't imagine many of us feel very good about it. I know I sure don't.

Something crashes into the bar door, hammers on the door, pushes and pushes. Pull! shouts the bartender. The door pulls open and in stumbles Deke Howitz. People turn, a few at a time, while Deke walks across the room, slow, has to stop now and then to lean on chairs. Makes it to the jukebox. Nobody in the bar says anything, they just hold their drinks close to their mouths and watch Deke. He digs in his pockets. Spills lemon throat drops and dimes out onto the wooden floor. He puts a few quarters into the jukebox, leans right down against the glass, reading. Pokes the buttons with a slow finger. He turns around and leans, head back against the jukebox, and a piano starts to play over the speakers. Deke takes a deep breath and sings along.

> *When you're alone, and life is making you lonely,*
> *You can always go*
> *Downtown.*

Go to hell, somebody shouts. Everybody shouts and Deke sings along for a while then sort of trails off. People throw pennies and peanut shells. Deke rolls around, falls back against the jukebox. Looks all over. He takes a deep breath and pushes himself up. Takes slow, careful steps across the floor. Shit, says Mullen's dad. Deke walks past the bar, to the pool table.

He opens his mouth to talk and Mullen's dad cuts him off. Deke, the grown-ups here need to have a conversation. Please.

Deke shuts his red eyes, opens them. Deke's eyes are pretty red most of the time, but never this red. He takes off his jean jacket. Deke used to be really skinny, but he's not so skinny anymore. His arms and chest are bigger. You can see the shapes of his muscles, like he was a comic-book character. You never used to be able to see any muscles at all on Deke.

You've got a real chip on your shoulder, says Deke. His voice is pretty slurred. I may be a deluded welfare bum, but I've never brought a child to a bar. He winks at us. No sense studying in the bar, kids, he says. Take a night off for once.

Jesus Christ, Howitz, says Mullen's dad, you're a grown man. Don't you have any friends who aren't ten years old?

Everybody in the bar is real quiet. Someone snickers over by the window.

It's all right, Dad, Mullen says. We all –

Quiet, says Mullen's dad.

Deke has turned real pale. Stares at Mullen's dad. Somebody else snickers and Deke shuts his eyes and takes a deep breath. 'Downtown' keeps playing on the jukebox. After a while he opens his red, red eyes.

The bartender comes out and stands behind Deke. Slips his arms under Deke's armpits. Around his chest. Deke doesn't really notice, just staring, pale. He looks like he might say something, then looks down at the arms. Looks at Mullen's dad. He sighs and slumps backward against the bartender. His heels drag on the floor as the bartender walks him backward to the door.

Mullen and I watch each other and don't say anything. Jarvis and everybody else from Lester's Meats tell stories about Milo Foreman and I don't pay attention because I really want to go. Mullen flips through the bartending book. Other workers from the meat-packing plant show up, they come and shake Jarvis's hand. They all talk real quiet and serious, they all take off their hats. There's a sad serious woman that everyone hugs and speaks to quietly, and she nods and tries to smile but doesn't do a good job. I want to go.

An airlock, eh? asks the man from the gas company.

That's what I figure, says Solzhenitsyn. He's got his grey coveralls on, and his toolbelt. He looks extra skinny in the baggy coveralls. Screwdrivers and wrenches hanging from the leather loops, pulling down off his skinny hips. I figure there was an airlock somewhere in the line, he says, so the hot water never made the full circuit through all the pipes. When that happens, the boiler thinks it isn't actually running, so it fires itself up full-bore to overcompensate. It runs too hot like that for too long, fries out the seal, that's when you get the glycol leak.

The man from the gas company rubs the little black beard around his mouth. Takes a pen out of the chest pocket of his coveralls, puts it behind his ear. This is why I never work on gravity systems. They're a goddamn nightmare. You know, in Calgary, they won't even sell you a house with a gravity system. Nobody will insure it. 'Cause of this sort of thing. You should tell your landlord to put in central heating.

Vaslav makes a harrumphing sound, arms crossed across his chest. Slumped in his lawn chair, extra round from layers of sweaters and jackets. He looks like a pile of laundry.

Well, everything in there must be worked through by now. That smoke isn't getting distributed anymore at least. Let's go down there and turn it on.

Yes, says Solzhenitsyn, let's do that. The two of them go inside the house. Vaslav makes another snorting sound and sinks deeper inside his clothes.

How's school? asks Pavel.

It's not too bad, I say. It's the Christmas play soon, so we spend all our time cutting snowflakes out of construction paper.

That's educational? Construction-paper snowflakes?

Well, it's not the only thing we're doing. There's lots of geometry and Canadian history too. The other day we learned about John Franklin, and the Northwest Passage.

John Franklin found the Northwest Passage?

I don't know, I say, we haven't got that far yet.

That's when the shouting starts inside the house. We all look up at each other. Inside there's some crashing sounds, like heavy stuff getting thrown around, and a lot of shouting. Pavel half-stands up out of his chair.

What the hell?

We stand there and listen: banging and shouting and swearing. Then the whole house gives a big shake, and there's this really awful groaning, rattling sound.

Pavel stands all the way up. Vaslav holds his hand up. Let the good doctors do their work, he says. We'll just get in their way.

It sounds like –

Yeah, yeah it does.

The man from the gas company comes upstairs. The bottoms of his pant legs are soaked grey. He pats his pockets. Makes a face. Any of you guys got a cigarette?

What the hell happened down there?

Well, we turned the boiler back on and it started flooding. You really do keep too much shit in your basement.

Flooding?

Yep. All the water from the pipes, just gushing straight out the bottom. Most of it went straight into the ground, but when it thaws, it's going to stink something fierce. You ought to get a dehumidifier. They sell them at the hardware store.

What about the airlock? Can you fix the airlock?

Fix it? Hell, I don't work on gravity systems, they're a goddamn nightmare. He writes in his tiny coil notebook. I'll order a new boiler, but it will take about three weeks.

Three weeks?

They have to build it in Ontario, he says. Near Sault Ste. Marie, I think. Nobody out here makes them anymore.

Three weeks, says Vaslav, I'm going to sleep in the back of my pickup truck? Should I get a tent?

Downstairs Solzhenitsyn is still yelling. He's taking this pretty personally, says the gas man. Like some kind of personal affront.

It always listened to him in the past, see.

The gas man shrugs. Talk to your landlord. We'll want to get that order in soon, especially with the Christmas season coming up.

The Christmas season, says Vaslav.

You should really change over to central heating, says the gas man. Tear out all those radiator pipes and get a furnace. Talk to your landlord about it. He gets in his big pickup truck and drives away. Downstairs, Solzhenitsyn shouts a lot less. Less often and less loudly.

Vaslav puts his hand over his mouth and goes inside the frozen house. He comes out with a plant pot. He brings out all their plants, sets them down on the porch. Clay pots and plain orange plastic pots, and a white plant pot with blue ducks printed all around the rim. Every pot filled with sticky, gooey dead green. That's what happens when plants freeze I guess. They melt down into this gooey green mess, like frozen spinach.

I pour myself some lemonade. Just a little, in a cup.

Sweet. Gritty sweet, each little bit of sugar. I can feel the sugar between my teeth, on my gums. I spit the lemonade on the ground.

Mullen, what the hell is wrong with you?

Mullen chips at the ice with the tongs. What do you mean?

Why'd you have to go and ruin the lemonade? 'Cause you sure ruined it.

He chips ice. Don't know what you're talking about.

I pick up the pitcher. Walk out into the street and pour it out onto the snow. Mullen sticks his hands in his pockets. Lemonade makes puddles in the dirty snow.

Now that was a hell of a thing to do, says Mullen. Wasting money like that.

You shouldn't have ruined the lemonade.

Mullen opens our money shoebox. Takes out a quarter and throws it at me. While we're at it, we might as well get rid of everything, he says. Throws a nickel, it whizzes past my ear.

You're a real piece of work.

He throws a dime and hits me in the shoulder. So the lemonade's too sweet. So what?

Sweet lemonade is for Dead Kids.

Oh right, I forgot, it's just for rich kids who live up the hill, kids whose parents work in Calgary and make lots of money and get their kids anything they want. Right, Dead Kids. Kids like you.

I drop the pitcher and run into him. We roll around on the ground. We get on top of each other and rub snow in each other's faces. I guess we must be pretty loud because Mullen's dad comes out of the house and picks us up. Carries us to the porch, one of us under each arm. Drops us on the porch, our faces all wet and pink and cold.

Go to school, Mullen's dad says. Smarten the hell up and go to school. Both of us sniffle and don't say anything. Mullen's dad goes down and gets the shoebox, picks the pitcher up off the ground. He takes down the sign, pulls the plank up off the cinder blocks and takes everything into the garage. We sniffle and don't say anything.

Go to school, he says. He goes back inside.

Halfway up the hill, Mullen isn't around anymore.

At school we sing Christmas songs. Mr. Hyslop taps his little plastic stick on the music stand and whips it back and forth, while all the front-row girls sing 'Away in a Manger' and 'Joy to the World.' Swings his stick, his fingers pinched just so. Dwayne Klatz and Pete Leakie and I stand in the back and mouth the words without really singing. Mr. Hyslop writes notes on the chalkboard, half notes and quarter notes. Dwayne Klatz pulls a handful of elastic bands out of the pocket of his overalls. Nudges me in the chest. I look at his elastic bands and shake my head. I'm not really into elastic bands today. We mouth the words to 'Joy to the World' again.

Mrs. Lampman draws a sod house on the chalkboard. The pioneers had to make houses out of dirt because there wasn't enough wood on the prairies. I don't know why people stopped to live on the stupid prairies when the mountains are so close.

At lunch we trade sandwiches. Today it's tuna salad. Dwayne's mom chops up celery real tiny in her tuna salad, and it's just salty enough. Just messy enough.

Slipping out of the library at lunch hour is pretty easy. Days I don't feel like sitting in the stairwell I just wander around the halls. I sit in the hall around from the office and get all the cars out of my pocket. A red Firebird, like teenagers drive. I have a little blue police truck and a yellow bulldozer, with a little shovel that moves up and down. I guess there isn't much they do. You can push them around like in a chase for a while, and crash them together. Sometimes I like to see how far I can shoot them down the hall, but their little wheels always get caught on specks of dirt and they flip over.

I shoot the Firebird down the hall. Mullen's dad comes around the corner and the Firebird gets caught on some dirt and flips upside down. He looks down at the little red car and then up the hallway to where I'm sitting.

There you are.

I was just on my way to the library, I say.

He bends down and picks up the car. Walks down the hall and hands it to me. Put them in your pocket, he says. I put all the cars in my pocket. He holds out his hand. Come on, he says.

I was going to the library.

Come on.

We walk around the corner to the office. The principal leans against the doorway. He sees me and Mullen's dad and they shake hands. He gives me a look. Mullen's dad, too, the same look.

I was on my way to the library, I say.

Just wait out here, says Mullen's dad. They go into the office.

I sit on the bench and swing my feet. I spin the wheels of the little cars inside my pocket.

Does Mullen have more detentions now? I ask Mullen's dad when he comes back outside. I know he didn't come to school today, because of our fight. You should tell the principal that it's my fault, Mullen not being here. He shouldn't get any more detentions.

Mullen doesn't have any more detentions, says his dad.

So he can come out for recess again?

No. No he can't.

But if he isn't in detention ...

He isn't going to be here at all. Not for a while.

I look at Mullen's dad. Inside the office, the principal sits at his desk, looks through a stack of paper. Makes notes on typed sheets. Puts typed sheets into a brown file folder.

Go outside, says Mullen's dad. You shouldn't be in here.

Right, I say. Outside.

$\mathbf{M}$cClaghan comes out of the Russians' house, coughing. Coughs and hacks, spits on the ground. The Russians stamp their feet and blow on their hands.

Well shit, says McClaghan. Just blown all to hell.

You must have been class president at landlord school, says Vaslav.

I'll call the gas company, get them back out here. That other guy never should have left like that. They ought to have somebody who can work out whatever's in the pipes. How hard can a boiler be to fix?

Fix? asks Vaslav. Are you nuts? Fix it and wait for it to blow up all over again? Why don't we just kick out the windows and cut holes in the ceiling while we're at it?

Wouldn't be a chore to install a furnace, says Solzhenitsyn. Think of it as an investment. Long-term improvement to the building.

Do you know how much it would cost to pull out all those radiators? Put in ductwork? Have to pull up all the floors, tear all the walls open. Better off knocking it flat and starting over. No, a new boiler should be fine. With better care and attention. I admit, I'm occasionally inattentive.

Vaslav chews on the inside of his cheek.

McClaghan runs a gloved hand over the door frame. Looks around the porch. I used to rent this house out for two hundred dollars a month. Two hundred, the whole house. I had this young couple, with a young kid, must have been fifteen years ago. He was a labour foreman for a big general contractor out of Calgary. She had some university degree. They came out here to save some money.

They moved into one of your houses to save money, says Pavel.

Damn, you men are disagreeable. They were good tenants. She grew a vegetable garden in the summer. They put on the present coat of paint. Sure looked good back then.

And you evicted them why? asks Vaslav.

McClaghan knocks on the wall, knock knock knock. Pushes his hand down on the window sill. The eave fell down during a thunderstorm, he says. So what, an eave falls down? He told me, I'll fix that presently, McClaghan. Presently. I didn't think much of it. But he was awful busy, whatever job it was, they were pouring footings on a downtown high-rise. Round-the-clock kind of work. There's all sorts of things that are liable to distract a man. And meanwhile it rained and rained.

Well, it took that kid coming down with some kind of allergic fever before he went down into that basement. I think he'd forgotten about the eave, and you know how undeveloped the basement is, no call to go down there. Six inches of water. Mould, climbing right up the walls. The most awful scum floating in that cold, cold water. McClaghan makes a face. Worst mess I ever saw. Took a ferocious amount of pumping. Fumigating. I can still remember that smell, that stale, spoiled, still-water smell. They moved out the next week. God knows how long I spent, rooting in that basement, fans, blankets. Scraping away at the mould on the walls.

Solzhenitsyn sits on the railing of the porch. Arms wrapped tight around his sides, not really looking at anything. Better off knocking it flat and starting over, he says.

We'll get the boiler fixed, says McClaghan. Zips his jacket up to the bottom of his chin. Just requires a little more attention, that's all. It can be my New Year's resolution. He pulls the flaps of his hat down over his ears, waves, heads down the stairs.

Vaslav spits over the porch, onto the frozen ground.

Mullen's dad comes home after it gets dark. Pulls his heavy orange extension cord out from under the seat of his truck. The plug hangs out from under the hood, like a pronged yellow tongue. He walks slow toward the house, lets the cord unloop down onto the ground. He stands on the porch and waves to us.

You want to play some cards? hollers Vaslav. Mullen's dad shakes his head and goes inside. The lights come on a few at a time, in the front room, the kitchen. The windows fog up. Mullen comes to stand at the kitchen window for a minute. He blurs away into a white smudge.

Vaslav bends down in his yard, scoops up a handful of snow and rubs it into his red, bearded face. Pavel sits under a pile of blankets, stares straight ahead, his toothbrush sticking out of his mouth. The black shapes of boot bottoms press against the good window of Solzhenitsyn's hatchback. I hitch up my backpack and wave.

Sometimes when I've had it with everything, I like to get away. So I pinch my nose like I'm going to dive underwater, and take a deep breath, and start sucking. I take a deep, deep breath and suck in and in, and my eyes bug out, and my chest gets bigger and bigger, and when it seems like I'm going to pop, there's this big sucking sound, and then I turn inside out to nothing. First my fingers suck up inside my hands, then my hands suck up inside my arms, and then all of me just, pop, turns right inside out. It's a good trick for bad days at school, when the Dead Kids are stomping around in a big stampede, back and forth up and down the hallways. I just suck myself inside out to nothing and get right away. Then they can stomp around all they want, and it doesn't matter to me, 'cause I'm not even there.

It's even better, though, to do it outside on a windy day. On a windy day if you turn yourself inside out to nothing, a good stiff breeze can come along and blow you clear out of town. Heck, it'll blow you clear out of the province on a windy enough day. You're like the thinnest leaf, blowing up into the grey, grey sky, spinning out over the snowy prairie. And who knows where you'll end up. If you're lucky, you'll blow all the way over the mountains, over British Columbia, and out over the ocean. You can spin and blow, up over the endless grey ocean, tossing around in the wind. The only problem is, you don't get to pick where you're going; it's all up to the wind. But on inside-out-to-nothing days, anywhere at all is pretty good.

Kid, like, what are you doing out here?

The teenager leans out the window of a big black station wagon. Inside, other faces press up against frosty glass, trying to get a look at what's going on. Fingers leave little melted holes in the glass. The wind whips around, blows tough white drifts up out of the ditch, turns the barbed-wire fences into thick, fuzzy white lines, like pipe cleaners strung out across the prairie. I pull my damp scarf down from around my mouth, try to catch my breath in the cold. I'm going to the Aldersyde truck stop, I shout. I have to be loud because a big semi is rumbling up out of the valley.

Get in, kid, shouts the teenager. You're going to get run over out here.

It takes a really long time to walk to the truck stop; this time I've hardly made it anywhere. Not even to the Welcome to Marvin sign, so I guess that means I'm still in town, even though the sidewalks have all stopped and there's just the gravelly shoulder. Behind me the last few house lights flicker in the blowing snow. I guess I couldn't have picked a much worse night, but what are you going to do.

They open the back door and I climb in. The station wagon is full of teenagers. Their eyes are all red and glassy, they start to say things and then trail off. A teenage girl in a thin grey flannel jacket puts her arm around me, pulls me in close. She stares out the window, the white snow reflecting in her shiny, wide-open eyes. There's a funny smell in the car, something sweet and smoky.

One of the teenagers in the front seat turns around. Gives me a big grin. Hey, kid, you in a rush? The girl giggles and clamps a hand over her mouth.

Like, say we had to stop and do a few things before we get to Aldersyde, says the driver. Looking at me in the rear-view mirror. The snow flies in the headlights in long white lines; it makes you dizzy to look at after a while.

Uh ... sure.

They all giggle.

This one here, says someone beside me, pointing to a farmhouse at the end of a short driveway. A low garage and cars parked outside, all covered in snow. White Christmas lights, and a Christmas wreath on the door.

The headlights blink out. We drive up slowly in the dark, snow crunching under the tires. The teenager beside me reaches inside his jacket, pulls out a can of lighter fluid, like McClaghan sells.

The teenagers open the station wagon doors really carefully, like they don't want anybody to hear. The girl beside me grabs my shoulder. She grins and holds a finger up to her lips. We creep out of the car and up to the front, crouching down, looking over the hood.

Two of the teenagers walk up to the front door. One of them crouches up against the wall. He waves his arm up and down toward the other teenager. The other teenager rings the doorbell. We all wait.

A light comes on and the door opens. A woman in a big black sweater, a towel wrapped around her head, opens the door. Pokes her head out the door a crack. Yes? she says.

And then I don't know what happens, but all of a sudden the teenager is on fire. Hot yellow flames burst out all over him, his jacket, his arms. He waves his arms and the woman screams, I've never heard anybody scream so loud. The teenager jumps up and down, on fire, waving his arms, and the door slams shut, and then he jumps over into a snowbank, rolls around, squashing out the fire in the snow. Inside she's still screaming and screaming. The two teenagers run back to the car and we all jump inside. The one kid is covered in snow and stinks like lighter fluid. The driver turns the car on and we charge backward up the driveway, skidding left and right in the snow, then back out onto the highway. And the teenagers all laugh and laugh, they laugh so hard they're crying. The girl has her eyes clenched tight, face pressed against the frosty glass, and her wet, crying face makes sticky streaks in the frost.

We drive into the zooming white snow. And the driver turns around and grins, and says, Okay, kid. Aldersyde, right?

Hoyle the waitress stops, the coffee pot tilted in her hand, when she sees me.

Kid.

I pull myself up on a stool. Hi, Hoyle, I say.

You can't just turn up here in the middle of the night.

It's not that late. Probably, what, nine o'clock? Ten? Not that late.

It's nasty out there. Were you hitchhiking?

Well, I was walking, and some teenagers picked me up. I didn't ask them to, though. They just stopped.

She starts to say something and stops. She picks up a dishtowel and twists it in her fists and then throws it down on the counter.

Kid, she says, you can't just turn up here. Okay? You're a long way from home and it's late and that's no good.

That's what everybody keeps telling me, I say.

Kid – She stops. She sighs and picks the dishtowel back up. Then she leans over the counter. She has a black apron on over her red and grey Petro-Canada shirt. A pen behind either ear. Leans right over, hands on the napkin box. Her chest on the counter.

I get off work in two hours. You live in Marvin, right?

Yeah.

Okay. I'm going to get off work in two hours, and then I'm going to drive you back to Marvin. You can sit here in the meantime. They've got some magazines in the convenience store. And comic books. You like comic books?

Yeah.

Okay. Go grab some comic books. I'll get you something to drink. Okay?

Okay.

The doorbell chimes and the man with the wide-brimmed straw hat walks in. Sets his big black book down on the counter, muttering to himself. Starts to take things out of his pocket and arrange them: some coins, a ballpoint pen, some foam earplugs, a pile of paper clips. He arranges them all in front of him, then scoops them all back up and puts them back in his pocket.

What did you do with all the money the bank gave you? I ask him. The Hat Man starts a bit. Looks down at me. Drums his fingers on his heavy book. Mutters to himself and rustles his napkin. A milkshake, please, he says when Hoyle looks up at him. He jerks his head at the milkshake machine. Vanilla.

Hoyle rolls up her sleeve and opens up the little freezer. Leans down inside, roots around, then reaches over for the ice-cream scoop. You can see her breath. She grunts and digs in the freezer, grits her teeth. Eventually stands back up with a scoop of ice cream. She pushes the milkshake cup up into the machine, digs the long mixer spindle in and props the cup on the ledge, starts to blend the ice cream. Pours in a little milk. The Hat Man stares. She pours in a little more milk. The cup gets frostier.

What's your book about?

He keeps staring at her, pulling the cup off the machine. Pouring the milkshake into a tall glass. White milkshake drips off the end of the blender. She pops a straw into the glass and sets it down in front of him.

The Hat Man takes a long slurp of milkshake. Then he looks over at me. Jesus is four hundred feet tall, he says. Has another slurp through the straw. That's forty storeys. No one knows how heavy Jesus is. Some speculate He'd weigh the same as any person, expanded to that scale. Others hold that while the reincarnated Christ may occupy space, to claim a mass for Him is blasphemous. Mass, they say, implies the prevelance of force, namely gravity, and to assert the dominance of any force over any part of the Trinity is a sin. Flies in the face of reason.

He watches me for a while. Slurps on his milkshake. Then he leans a little closer.

After the resurrection, Jesus becomes an infinite series of anecessary possibilities. The divine privilege, however, is the maintenance of identity in spite of a simultaneous infinite progression across infinite dimensions.

Infinity, I say. Like going on forever.

He claps. Hoyle jumps, spills a bit of her ginger ale. On forever! he hollers. Slaps his thigh. Then he gets serious. Leans over, all secret-like.

My .... I am the four-hundred-foot Jesus. I see Him. If I keep the four-hundred-foot Jesus – His massive feet, His arms, how high He can reach – if I keep all these things at the forefront, all the time ... Alone on the prairies, the highway's tiny lines. He steps over valleys. I have to think, all the time, about the four-hundred-foot Jesus. To keep the place in the series, you see. A marker.

Like a bookmark.

He looks at me. Then he slaps his thigh again. Analogy is the key to philosophy, boy. A bookmark in an infinite book.

Do you know how to make the Milk Chicken Bomb? I ask the Hat Man. Hoyle stops wiping the counter and looks at me. The Hat Man coughs. No one will tell me, I say. I'm not even going to make one. I just want to know.

We find the world stranger as we leave than as we arrive, says the Hat Man. He slurps his milkshake in long, thick slurps, his cheeks sucked in. I'm through, he says. Through!

You owe me a buck twenty-five, says Hoyle. He snorts. Throws a pile of change onto the counter. Looks at me. Stranger as we leave, he says. Rushes out the door. Everyone turns to watch him.

Over in the convenience store I flip through the magazines. Lots of hunting magazines: men in green overalls with big long rifles, or crossbows, standing in the forest, grinning. They don't have any really good comic books in the convenience store. They have a few superhero comics but nothing I haven't already read. Nothing new. The only new issue is *The Mysterion*, there in the back row. I never read *The Mysterion* comics, 'cause all he does is talk and talk, long made-up words with nothing to do with anything. Sometimes there's wizards or devils, which ought to be exciting, but instead of blasting each other they just talk and talk. I don't know how many issues of *The Mysterion* comics you have to read before a devil blasts somebody, but it doesn't seem worth it to find out.

I pick up the new issue of *The Mysterion* and what do you know, there on the cover, her face full-size, her mouth open, her eyes closed shut, the Under Queen. I knew it! I knew she'd be back.

Eventually the last trucker finishes his coffee, crumples up his napkin and leaves his five-dollar bill on the table. Everybody waves as he wanders out the door, out across the long, quiet parking lot, to the dark row of trucks. One of the gas jockeys wanders through the convenience store with a broom, sweeping up the dirt and gravel that got tracked in from the winter all day. Hoyle goes around wiping all the tables down. She takes all the money out of the till and sits at the counter with an envelope and a calculator. Adding up numbers and counting bills. She makes sure that all the queen's faces on all the bills face the same way.

The Under Queen wakes up on the beach, driftwood, seaweed, all bleary-eyed and confused. She isn't even her old blue colour, more of a pale green. She lies there on the beach all confused. Takes her time, panels and panels. Yeah, this sure is a *Mysterion* comic. No fun at all. I flip ahead a bit. No blasting anywhere to be seen.

At the dock she tries to talk to the longshoremen in their watch caps. They see her in the light all bluey-green and slippery, and they panic and run away. Her speech balloons full of ...s and sort-of words, to show how confused she is.

How's your comic book? asks Hoyle.

I shrug. It's one of these super-villain-becomes-amnesia-cal-and-does-good-for-a-while stories, I say.

Those happen a lot?

It's bunk, I say. You have to wait two or three issues for someone to treat them badly enough for them to go back to their evil ways. What's worse is, not only have they made my favourite villain lose her memory, they've put her in this *Mysterion* story, and he's boring enough already.

What's a Mysterion?

He's this boring old wizard in a stupid cape that says a lot of made-up words and never blasts any devils.

Sounds pretty dull, says Hoyle. She closes up the cash register. Okay, she asks, you ready to go?

I guess so.

Hoyle drives a big brown van. A round bubble window in the back. Lots of bumper stickers: radio-station call letters and ski-resort logos. She pulls open the heavy door and I climb up, onto the running board, inside. Her van is all padded with carpet; in the back I can see wood-panelled countertops, a sink. Hoyle climbs into the driver's seat and starts the van. We sit in the dark while it warms up. There's enough of a moon out that you can see the dark sky coming down to meet the flat prairie way out in the east. There's no landscape, out in the east, no hills or mountains, no red blinking radio towers. Just the flat grey ground running out to the grey sky. Hoyle yanks the gearshift down. We drive out of Aldersyde.

When we get into Marvin, if you don't mind, I'd like to check something out, she says. It'll only take a minute.

Sure thing, I say. I try not to yawn. My eyes are heavy and stinging. I shake my head to keep them open.

I want to drive past that new music school, she says. You know where that is?

Music school?

Yeah, says Hoyle. There's a music school opening up in Marvin. You hadn't heard?

I guess not, I say. Blink my eyes out at the white fields.

A few of the farmers were talking about it, says Hoyle. She drives with one hand and digs in her purse with the other. Finds a pack of gum, unwraps a stick one-handed. They were planning to enroll their daughters. I was thinking I might enroll myself.

We drive into Marvin. Hoyle leans forward over the steering wheel, trying to see through her frosty windshield. So where am I headed anyway, kid?

Oh, you know, just anywhere.

Come on. Don't be stupid. I'll drop you off at home.

Down that way, I say. I make sure not to follow the street with my eyes when we drive by.

Everything is quiet, all over town – no other cars. We drive down the snowy streets and look at all the Christmas lights, up on every house. Red and green and blue, some of them blinking on and off. Strung in the trees and along the roofs. We drive down the hill. Marvin seems even quieter than usual, under all the white snow.

We stop at the four-way in front of the post office. Hey, she says, it's your dad.

I lean forward over the dash. Heart beating and beating and beating. Then I see Mullen's dad, sitting on the sidewalk across from the junk shop. Take a deep breath and sit back.

That's not my dad, I say.

Oh, says Hoyle. She starts to say something else, then stops herself. She claps her hands on the steering wheel and points. Look, she says, this is it!

There're two moving vans parked out front of the junk shop. The four-way blinkers light up the front windows, all orange and then dark, orange and then dark. Inside, the front room still looks pretty empty, but there's a sign now. A wooden sign, painted very carefully, hanging over the door: Music Lessons.

I'm going to learn to play the piano and get the hell out of here, says Hoyle. I'm going to move to Vancouver and play jazz music in nightclubs. She spreads her hands out over the dashboard, fingers spread apart like it was a keyboard, and starts to play, thumping her fingertips up and down on the plastic. No more prairies, no more gas stations, no more men in trucks, she says. Just a giant city where you can stay up all night and sleep all day.

Mullen's dad looks over at the vans. We both wave to him. His shoulders slump a little bit. He shakes his head and pinches his forehead. Then he nods and waves.

You want me to leave you with your friend then?

Yeah, I say. He'll look after me.

Okay, says Hoyle. Hey, I'll probably see you, though, when I come into town. When I learn to play the piano.

Okay, Hoyle. I put my hand on the door handle and then she grabs me by the shoulder. She pauses for a second, and then leans forward, all secret-like.

You need a jar, she says. Leans right over close, so that I can smell her peppermint chewing gum. You need the biggest jar you can find, with a lid that'll screw on real tight.

Now you're going to have to fill it really, really full, and make the lid as tight as you can. So that if whatever was inside there were ever to expand in any way ...

I nod. Why's it going to expand, Hoyle?

Well, when what's inside of it turns bad enough. Starts to really go off. You need that lid tight, though. And don't pick too thick a jar. It needs to break, see. At that climax.

I nod. Right, Hoyle. Got it.

But you can't do it, she says, Because it's too awful. No one's ever going to live there again, wherever you put it. Okay?

I'm not going to do it. I just need to know how. Just in case.

Okay, go see your friend.

I open the door and get out of the van.

Mullen's dad holds his finger up to his lips. Points across the street with his chin.

Hélène stands by the door, arms tight around her chest. A long white scarf, a knit white toque. Long cigarette, no hands, out of the side of her mouth. Five men in grey jumpsuits are in and out of the vans. Cardboard boxes, taped shut. Wooden chairs stacked in twos. A bookcase. They use a dolly to haul out filing cabinets, the drawers held closed with black electrical tape. One of them brings a piano bench, hugged against his chest.

Did you see the licence plates? he asks. I squint across the dark street. I can't read that. *Je me souviens*, says Mullen's dad. Digs in his pocket for a yellow pencil. Chews.

Made it all the way out to the truck stop again, eh?

I sit there and don't say anything. He chews on the pencil.

When I drop you off –

No, really, you don't have to.

When I drop you off, I'll come in. Have a few words.

Look, I say, you can't. Okay? You can drop me off but you can't come in.

I'm sick of –

You can't, okay? It's fine. I mean, it's fine.

Kid –

Promise, okay?

Mullen's dad chews on the pencil. Across the street one

of the movers pulls up his shirt and tightens the padded back-brace underneath.

My wife owns a country-and-western bar in Whitehorse, says Mullen's dad. Big jukebox, peanut shells on the floor, swinging saloon doors. Every night at last call it's 'Four Strong Winds' by Ian Tyson.

I won't divorce her because I don't want her to see Mullen. She won't divorce me because she likes being married. Keeps a Polaroid of me behind the bar, on the brandy and cognac shelf. I'm pushing an Oldsmoblie out of a ditch. All covered in mud. My husband, she tells people. She sends Mullen pictures of herself on snowshoes, on dogsleds. She has a bank account for him, for school, someday. Nothing I can sign for.

He stares across the street. Chews into the pencil. Little flecks of yellow paint on his lips.

I don't know why she even has cognac in the bar. I doubt she's ever sold an ounce.

Promise, I say.

The men in jumpsuits all go up the ramp into the second van. The whole van rattles. She paces around, watching them, shakes her head, says something angry in French. Holds her hands up. They shout back. She points and hollers.

Upright? asks Mullen's dad. Baby grand?

They start to wheel the piano down the ramp. A brown upright, on wheels, a black blanket half-draped over the top, not quite covering all the keys. They huff and heave it down the ramp. Stop to get their breath, clap their hands, find their grips. Brace their shoulders and huff, push it down to the street, then they all squat and catch their breath, and hup the piano the few inches onto the curb. Clap their hands. She smokes and smokes. Then grunt and up, they stop mid-heave, wait, one second, two, then up more and the whole thing onto the sidewalk. They pant. Hold the smalls of their backs. Then shoulders and groans and they push it up to the store.

After a long break, they bring the second piano down the ramp, black and long, like on television, in black-and-white movies. It looks even heavier. Mullen's dad whistles. She smokes and sometimes looks over at us but doesn't really pay attention. Just watches, smoking, until both the pianos are inside, then she follows them and shuts the door.

After school I like to go over to the Russians'. Pavel and Vaslav sit out on the porch in their heavy coats. Pavel shuffles cards.

Where'd you sleep last night? I ask them. Are you still sleeping at Mullen's?

Vaslav coughs. I'm getting a cold, he says. I just want to do my laundry. I want to shave in hot water and leave my razor on the sink. He coughs. Drums his black leather fingers on his coffee mug.

Don't you ever go home? Pavel asks me.

Sure, I say, every night. Just like everybody else.

Right, says Pavel. Just like everybody else.

You guys are from Russia, right? I ask. Russia the country? How come you guys never talk about Russia?

Vaslav coughs, spills some of his coffee. What is there to talk about? he asks. Pavel deals us cards. Five cards for each of us, six cards, seven cards. Slow down there, says Vaslav. Fans his cards out.

Solzhenitsyn drives up in his hatchback, the engine rattles to a slow stop. He gets out with a paper bag from McClaghan's. Walks up to us, sitting around on the porch in our mitts and blankets, doesn't say anything. He pulls cardboard boxes, new ratchet bits, out of the bag. Something small, with wires and a dial. Rubs his red eyes. He pulls a little white mask over his mouth and nose, ribbed and a bit fuzzy, the elastic strap tight around his messy hair. Fills his pockets with screwdrivers, a hammer, other tools I've never seen. He opens the door of their house and goes inside.

Got any sixes? asks Pavel.

Fish.

In Petersburg, says Vaslav, there was this guy, Ivan Mortz was his name.

Don't tell him that story, says Pavel. He's just a kid.

It'll be good for him. Shake him up a bit. You think you've got a pretty good handle on things, don't you, kid?

I shrug. Got any jacks?

Vaslav makes a face and hands me a card. Ivan Mortz was into some bad stuff. Real bad. I can't even tell you what Ivan Mortz was into, you'll get bad ideas. Stuff you've never heard of here in feedlot Alberta. You're better off thinking people go about their business, that life turns out all right.

Play cards, says Pavel.

I'm playing cards. Any fours?

Fish.

Ivan Mortz wasn't from Petersburg, he was from Edmonton, Pavel says. Remember when we lived on Jasper Avenue in Edmonton? You worked in that print shop, Gus's Print Shop.

Play cards, Vaslav says.

Vaslav leans close to me. Ivan Mortz thought he was a big-time crook, stealing cars and selling dope all over Petersburg. He'd buy dope at whatever Asian border and sell it cheap in Petersburg, in Kiev and Minsk. Drove this old Volvo, must have had 500,000 kilometres on it, he was back and forth so often across the Ukraine, Russia, Azerbaijan, Georgia.

Don't tell him this story.

I shuffle my cards. I know about gangsters, I say. I watch television. Selling dope is selling drugs. There're some kids at the junior high school that sell drugs.

I bet there are, says Vaslav. Anybody have a queen? It's not your turn, I tell him.

Gus's Print Shop did most of their work on takeout menus, see, Pavel says. Pizzerias and Szechuan, and Thai and Vietnamese. Any kind of food you could imagine. Vaslav here used to mix the ink and sort out the letters for Gus, and then

Gus would set the type and run the menus off. You could ask Vaslav here about any item from any restaraunt in town, he'd tell you.

Shut up, Vaslav says, drinking coffee.

Hey, Vaslav Andreiovich, you could say, how much is the pork vermicelli at the Double Greeting House? Number seventy-two, he'd say, $4.50. He could tell you the phone number for Ernie's Chicago Style Deep Dish, and what neighbourhoods Lee's Noodles would deliver to for free. Sure was handy, having Vaslav around.

Ivan Mortz ran out of luck, Vaslav says. They duct-taped his head to the pipe under the sink and gave him a syringe full of bleach. He makes a choking sound, rolls his eyes into the back of his head. That was the end of Ivan Mortz.

Ivan Mortz lived down the hall from us, Pavel says, in this old building on Jasper Avenue. He did his laundry wearing a pair of wool slippers and a tiny satin housecoat. He liked to sit in the hallway and read the classifieds in the *New York Times* while his dishwasher was running. Always looking at the job ads in the *New York Times*. Senior Executive, Accounts Payable, he'd say, I could do that. Remember that, Vaslav? You always said his dishwasher was too loud.

Solzhenitsyn comes out of the house. He smells like burnt hair. Sits down heavily on the step, lets the hammer fall out of his hands into the snow. He glares ahead and pulls the mask up off his mouth. A white circle where it pressed on his raw skin. Just leaves it on top of his head, his hair sticks out all around. Glares ahead. Across the street Constable Stullus sits in his car, reads the newspaper.

Did you sleep at Mullen's last night? I ask him.

I slept at Mary's, Solzhenitsyn says. I couldn't sleep, because of her cats. Like steel wool in my throat. Trying to sleep under this catty afghan on the couch while she sits at the table in the corner, flipping through the Sears catalogue.

Is that Mary works at Steadman's? She has a lot of cats?

The cats sit on the countertop, Solly says. One of them sits in the kitchen sink. Me wheezing, with an open mouth, trying to breathe. He glares at Stullus, across the street.

He probably isn't even in there, shouts Solzhenitsyn, his voice cracking. Stullus rolls up his window.

He's learning to check by multiplication, says Mullen's dad. Leaning out of the not-so-open door. I fidget on the step. He leans out the door and I stand on the step and he sighs. You want to take the toboggan out? he asks.

No, I say, that's all right. I'll just go home.

Home? says Mullen's dad.

Across the street, in Deke's house, hammering.

The voyageurs paddle their caravans from every direction to the steamship. Banquet halls and chandeliers, the heavy paddle wheel, chugging through the sand. It's not easy, working for the Petersburg Steamship Company. You could end up in the boiler room, shovelling coal, or polishing the steam stack, on a scaffold, way up in the air. Good thing I know how to make manhattans and mint juleps. They give me a little tie and a white shirt. I have to roll up the sleeves. They give me a tea towel. Every day I polish all the different glasses, make sure we have all the right bottles. I put cherries in bowls and fill a bucket with amaretto, for washing. Every night the voyageurs come in and sit at the checkerboard tables and play cards. I pour two glasses of beer at a time, one in each hand.

We sail the ship through the desert, steaming away, past Azerbaijan and Kyrgyzstan. We steam through the Ukraine, past all the aluminum smelters, smokestacks as far as the eye can see, puffing away into the dark sky. We pass signs, arrows point in different directions, China, Russia, Georgia. The Municipal District of Foothills, 6,000,004 miles. Just doesn't seem far enough.

Then it's time to go underground. We all go down and shovel coal into the Gravity Boiler. It steams and groans, its pipes and bellows blow steam. Voyageurs take their shirts off, wrap their sashes around their foreheads and heave the pumps. We shovel and pump and the huge iron Gravity Boiler gets hotter and hotter, and the hotter it gets the heavier the steamship gets. We make the Gravity Boiler so heavy that the steamship starts to sink. We sink right through the sand, down into the bedrock.

When I'm not shovelling I'm pretty busy bartending for the voyageurs. The hotter it gets, the more they have to drink. I throw my white towel over my shoulder and pour them Cuba Libres and Singapore slings. I wash all the glasses in the amaretto sink.

We sail down, down, down. We sail deeper into the rock, until it gets all red and molten, and we sail down into the lava, where it gets so hot we have to put on our welding masks and oven mitts, and shovel, shovel, shovel. Maintain radio silence! hollers the captain. Watch out for leaks! We run out of coal. We cut up the cupboards, the card tables, the pool cues and shuffleboards, and burn them in the Gravity Boiler. We throw in our leather jackets and workboots, and all the empty amaretto bottles. It's sure a lot of work, this sailing underground. Hopefully we get there before we run out of stuff to burn in the Boiler. I'd hate to get stuck, somewhere in the hot red rock strata, not even at the centre of the earth.

In the hallway Dwayne Klatz sits leaned up against the wall. An empty plant pot between his legs. His face, his hands, all smeared with dirt. Clumps of dirt all over the floor. A few scraps of plant leaves, some branches.

Dwayne?

Dwayne squeezes his eyes shut, groans.

What happened, Dwayne? Pete Leakie crouches down, puts a hand on Dwayne's forehead. Damp and pale. What's going on?

Dwayne opens his mouth. His teeth black with dirt. Tries to talk but his mouth is too sticky, his tongue too big.

Did you eat a plant, Dwayne?

He nods. He coughs, spits out some muddy spit on the floor.

Okay, Dwayne, Pete says, you have to stay right here, all right? Stay right here and don't go anywhere. He stands up and grabs me. We have to go find a telephone, he says. What's a telephone got to do with eating plants? I ask him. Just come on, says Pete. Dwayne lies on the ground, spits out some more mud.

Come on, says Pete. We creep around the hallway sneaky-like. At the pay phone outside the office Pete picks up the receiver. Dials just one number. Hello, he says after a while. Yes, I'd like to speak to the poison-control people. Yes, poison. Well, he says, that's what I need to find out.

I ate wax once, Pete tells me, his hand over the receiver. And my mom called the poison-control people. They told her not to let me drink milk, and to make me throw up. They'll probably tell us to make him throw up. But we should find out, just in case.

Hello, says Pete. Yes, well, my friend ate a plant. Well, I don't know, because he ate the whole thing. There isn't any left. Yes, all the leaves and branches. He even ate the dirt. No, I don't know what kind of dirt either. I could go back and look. What's that? Well, I guess I can wait. But he doesn't look good.

We wait in the hallway.

They don't seem to know, Dwayne, says Pete Leakie. They don't seem to know what we're supposed to do. Dwayne lies on the ground, curled up in a ball. Gags and heaves a bit, choking sounds.

My stomach hurts, says Dwayne Klatz.

I bet it does, Dwayne. I bet it does.

I just want, he says, I just wanted, you know. How come she pays attention to that guy? What's he done?

I don't know, Dwayne. I don't know.

I think we should make him throw up, says Pete.

Some teachers come around the corner, cups of coffee, piles of notebooks. Shouldn't you boys be outside for recess? asks a teacher. Pete Leakie starts to say something and Dwayne coughs up a clump of dirt, some leaves, onto the floor.

We sit on the bench outside the office. Heaving and choking, wet splashing sounds come from inside. We swing our feet above the floor. Pete stares down the hall, where a grey window shines down on the streaky floor. He looks over at me, panicked.

We're moving, he says.

Where are you moving, Pete?

My dad bought an acreage. Out in the country. It's all outside. There isn't anything around.

An acreage in the country?

What am I going to do?

I think about it for a while. I sure would like to live on an acreage, I say. Think about it, Pete. All that time to yourself. All that space. Is there a forest? Are there hills?

Pete's wide, wide eyes don't blink. He looks away, down the hall, then down at the floor.

Sorry, Pete. Sorry about that.

We listen to the gagging and splashing inside the office.

Vaslav bangs on the window of Solzhenitsyn's hatchback. Bangs with both fists; he has a brown leather glove on one hand, a yellow wool mitt on the other. Two scarves, his big leather hat, the wool lining scraggly and brown. I think he has a toque on under the hat, it sits back on his head like there's a cartoon lump, hit with a hammer. His beard is black and thick now, except for a pale sliver of a scar on his chin where no hair grows. He bangs and bangs on the window.

The car shifts, something bangs hard against the roof with a dull clunk. Thick Russian shouts inside. The door opens and Solzhenitsyn crawls out, his hand clutched around his forehead. Stands hunched over, his red eyes narrow, staring at the ground.

I can't curl.

Shut up.

I can't curl.

Shut up.

If I can't sleep then I can't curl. I haven't slept all week.

We need to stop for coffee, says Pavel.

I'm going back inside.

Curling! barks Vaslav. It's our sworn duty to humiliate every curler in this whole Municipal District of Foothills. Better rocks. More points. He shakes Anna Petrovna.

We can't drink that Okotoks coffee, says Pavel. It gets my ulcer. We have to stop at the Red Rooster.

I can't curl, says Solzhenitsyn. Holds his hands over his ears. Vaslav grabs him by the shoulders, hauls him over the icy sidewalk to where his truck idles. Opens the door, pushes him in. Solly keeps his hands tight over his ears. Vaslav spits on the ground. Reaches over and pulls Solly's seat belt over his waist, snaps it shut. Pulls the strap tight.

Can I sit in the back? I ask. Vaslav shrugs. Are you dressed warm enough? I hold up my mitts. Don't sit in the snow, he says. I got snowpants, I say. See? I can sit anywhere. Keep your head down, he says. Pavel Olegivich, don't crash the truck.

We drive out to Okotoks. I bump up and down against the straw bales. Out, up the hill, out of town. Houses go by, their driveways covered in snow, belts of poplar trees here and there in the fields. I watch Vaslav, in the cab, talking non-stop. Pavel drives with one hand, a Styrofoam Red Rooster cup in the other, lifting up and down when the truck bumps to keep the coffee inside. He should have gotten a lid. I wonder how Pavel can drive with only one eye. I wonder if his eye gets tired. I close one eye for a while, try to watch the road.

Solly stares straight ahead, sunk down low on the seat, hands still over his ears.

We go left at the highway. Up over the hills, the Sheep River Valley cutting by. You can see the radio towers from here, way up in the hills, blinking. I think they're radio towers. What else would be so tall and blink? Maybe they're signals for airplanes. Maybe they're thermometers for the centre of the earth. I wonder how tall they are. I wonder if they have a fence to keep you away.

Okotoks is the biggest town around, all right. Every time I come there's a new subdivision being built. Pink stucco houses and blue aluminum-sided houses. They've built streets and sidewalks in an empty field, the ground all dug up, bare and frozen, no houses yet. I guess they'll build houses around them when winter is over. Looks like a town blew away, like all the houses and garages scattered in a tornado, leaving just dirt holes and curbs.

In Okotoks they've got fast-food restaurants with drive-throughs, car dealerships with big flags and banners, rows of new trucks with the prices written on the windshields. They've got an elementary school and two junior high schools, they've even got a Catholic high school. We stop at a set of stop lights and I make sure to stay real low in the box of the truck. You never know what sort of things people in big towns like this will get set off by.

We pull up into the icy gravel parking lot at the Okotoks Recreation Centre. Curlers from High River and Nanton stand around their trucks, smoking, filling out their forms. The Russians' second stands by his truck, tugging on his moustache. I sit in the back of the truck while Pavel and Vaslav undo Solzhenitsyn's seat belt and pull him out onto his feet. Hands over his ears.

Now, this isn't Kreshick's ice, recall, says Vaslav. Be ready for uneven surface, vague and shifty pebble. Who knows what the temperature is like in there? The humidity? Don't take anything for granted is all I'm saying.

The Marvin Pentecostals drive up in their big brown station wagon. The Pentecostal reverend turns off the engine and gets out, opens the doors to let out his team. They wave to us and don't smile and head inside in single file.

Solzhenitsyn opens his mouth and doesn't make any sound. I can't curl, his lips say.

Call shots, says Vaslav. Skip. Lead.

Solly opens and closes his mouth. Blinks his red, red eyes.

Vaslav wraps both hands around Anna Petrovna back near the end of her shaft. Heaves her behind his head like a baseball bat, and swings, cracks Solzhenitsyn square between the shoulders as hard as he can. Solly pitches forward face first into the side of the truck and slumps down into the gravel. A few curlers whistle, take off their hats. The Russians' second crouches down beside Solly, face first in the snow. Turns him over onto his back. Solly coughs.

You've got to have some dignity, says the second. He stands up and walks across the parking lot to the recreation centre.

So Milo Foreman walks into Jarvis's office, says Solzhenitsyn.

I don't want to talk about Milo Foreman, says Vaslav.

So Milo Foreman walks into Jarvis's office. I had this dream, he tells Jarvis.

You can't sleep because someone fell in a rendering vat?

You can't fall into a rendering vat; you have to jump. I can't sleep because there's an icicle in my kitchen sink. I stayed at that junior high school art teacher's place.

The kid, says Vaslav.

She said I was overheated. She gave me some pills but I still couldn't sleep. Milo had this dream.

I don't want to talk about Milo Foreman, says Vaslav. He bends down and grabs Solzhenitsyn under the armpits, grunts and heaves him up.

The Pentecostals are going to make a mess of us, says Solly. Vaslav pats him on the shoulder and nods. We all walk slow-like into the Okotoks Recreation Centre to watch the Pentecostals make a mess of the Russians.

We wait for the truck to warm up, afterward. Pavel stands a ways off in the parking lot, staring out at Okotoks, arms at his side. Exhaust drifts past his ankles. He stands there and then bends down, picks up an old pop can. He throws it at the wall of the recreation centre. He shouts, something, Russian I guess. He picks up a rock and throws it as hard as he can at the Okotoks Recreation Centre, shouting in Russian. We wait for truck to warm up.

Hey, kid.

Constable Stullus leans out the window of his car. I stop, hitch my backpack up on my shoulder. He waves me over.

Get in, kid, he says. I pull open the icy back door.

The man in the passenger seat wears a heavy wool jacket, a white shirt and black tie. Thin black glasses. They turn in their seats and crane their heads around to look at me. I pull the door closed and pull off my mitts. Rub my cold fingers together in the warm car air.

Everything all right, Constable?

He gives the man with the tie a long look. The man with the tie starts to dig in a leather briefcase.

Where's Howitz? asks Stullus.

I shrug. I haven't seen him in quite a while.

Quite a while, says Stullus. You been in his house lately?

Deke doesn't let anybody in his house, I say. He told the Russians that he'd shoot them, even though their boiler exploded.

The man with the tie pulls some paper out of his briefcase, and a heavy, metal pen. I watch his lips move while he writes That He'd Shoot Them.

What's going on? I ask.

Well, says Stullus, we're heading over to your friend Deke's house. Just to ask some questions.

Are you a policeman? I ask the man with the tie. He chuckles to himself. No, he says, I'm an accountant. I'm much more serious than a policeman.

Stullus puts on some mitts, pulls the earflaps of his big black hat down. We all get out of the car and walk up to Deke's door. Stullus knocks with the backs of his heavy knuckles.

Howitz, he shouts, Howitz, you have to let us in. I have someone from the federal government who's interested in seeing you. He bangs again. We wait quite a while. We wait, and Stullus rattles the door handle. He twists up his face. Leans over to try the closest window; it pushes right in. He reaches inside, grunts, strains.

Say, he says, is your arm long enough?

The accountant sticks out his tongue, reaches through the door, stretches as far as he can. The door unlocks and swings open.

Deke's house is a mess: the sink full of dishes, IGA bags full of empty ravioli cans, red sauce dried, lids folded back. Dust; white sawdust on the counters, marked with fingers, coffee rings. Dirt on the floors, brown bootprints and dried puddles.

Stullus steps past the open dryer door and the half-folded ironing board and opens the door to Deke's cellar. He reaches into the dark and pulls a string. Somewhere down the steps a light bulb comes on. Exposed studs with no drywall, old bricks, cobwebs. We walk down the narrow wooden steps.

The cellar isn't so much a room as a big hole. Dirt floors that curve up into old brick walls, nothing flat. The accountant has to duck his head. A light bulb hangs on a wire.

Stullus pulls his big black flashlight off his belt. Passes the beam around. There's piles of dirt all over, scraps of wood. Sawhorses, a circular saw, the cord just lying on the ground. Two-by-fours and what's left of forklift pallets. Dirt everywhere, some of the piles as high as the cellar roof.

In the corner there's a hole. No, a tunnel. Stullus shines his flashlight on the dark gap. Narrow and rough, heading a little down. Some two-by-fours wedged between the top and bottom.

You've got to be kidding me, says Stullus.

I've never seen a tunnel. Tunnels on TV and in comic books, but I've never seen a real tunnel. Wood beams, four-by-eights, hammered together, brace the ceiling, the walls. The flashlight shows rough walls, tree roots. The tunnel narrows, none of us can see where it ends up. The accountant peers down the tunnel.

How old is this town? he asks. I mean, it can't be more than ninety years old. There haven't been any floods or landslides. Surely nothing overtly geological in the last hundred years.

Absolutely unbelievable, says Stullus.

Do you think he's down there? asks the accountant.

I am not crawling into a tunnel dug by Deke Howitz into the gullet of hell. Spelunking? He shakes his head. I never thought he was actually going through with it.

He can't be far. You've got a flashlight. How far back can he have dug?

It's not how far back he's dug, says Stullus. God knows where he is.

What do you mean? I ask.

Stullus looks at me kind of funny. Shines the beam down the tunnel. Well, he says, depending on who you believe around here, Howitz wouldn't be the first Marvin resident who's taken to digging over the years.

Deke Howitz, shouts the accountant, hands cupped around his mouth, down into the tunnel. Mr. Howitz, my name is William Rutherford, I'm from Revenue Canada. Mr. Howitz, we need to discuss irregularities in your accounting practices. I need information from you, to forward to the Alberta Securities Commission. Regarding a company called Davis Howe Oceanography.

We wait. The cellar is cold, even colder down in the tunnel. I almost think that I hear ringing, somewhere in the distance, in the dark.

Can't we just go loot his filing cabinet? asks Stullus.

The accountant shakes his head. Hardly ethical. Of course, he says peering into the dark, most tax frauds don't escape underground, either.

Get out of here, kid, says Stullus.

Thanks for all your help, says the accountant.

I blink. Oh yeah, I say. Right. Well, anything to help Revenue Canada, I say.

They stare down the tunnel, the flashlight beam not quite reaching far enough to see.

The mailman comes up the street, whistling. Stands on Mullen's porch and digs in his bag. Drops in a few letters and a rolled-up flyer. Hitches up his sack and walks up the street. I stand on the opposite sidewalk, hands in my pockets. Sometimes I shake around to get the snow off my shoulders. Sometimes I blow on my hands and rub my cheeks.

Mullen's dad comes out of the house. Stops to take off his plaid scarf and retie it around his neck. He looks in the mailbox and makes a face, lets the lid clang shut. He pulls his toque down further on his forehead and walks out to his pickup truck. I watch him roll up the extension cord. He sits in the truck for a while, exhaust puffing out the back. Once the truck is warm he drives away.

I knock on Mullen's door. Kick at the new snow. He opens the door with a spoon in his mouth, barefoot. The sleeves of his grey sweater down past his hands.

Hey, do you want to sell lemonade today?

Mullen thinks about it. Takes the spoon out of his mouth. I guess there isn't much else to do, is there?

I guess not.

Well, let me get dressed then.

We sell lemonade. I cut up lemons with the long knife and drop them in the pitcher. What I do is, I cut up a bunch of lemons into wedges; cut them in half, then halve the halves and put the wedges in the pitcher with the ice. We have this other jug, and I put in a little bit of water, and then the sugar. I stir the sugar into that little bit of water 'cause it dissolves easier, when it's cold, a bit at a time. We learned about dissolving in science class, and that's when I thought of lemonade.

Mr. Weissman said that water is the universal solvent, which means it can dissolve anything. I squeeze about a third of the wedges out into the thick syrup until it turns yellow. I pour in more water, stirring with the wooden spoon, and then I pour the whole jug into the pitcher, with the ice and other wedges.

Mullen sits in his snowpants on the step, the fuzzy white snow not too hard on the steps and on the sidewalk. Mullen blows a bubble. Kicks his boots on the porch. I sit down beside him on the step. We watch it snow. Mullen reaches a foot down onto one of the lower steps and stamps in the new snow. It puffs out, like ripples in a puddle. White flaky ripples. We watch it snow.

You walked all the way to Aldersyde?

I got a ride most of the way.

That sure would take a while, walking all the way there.

Yeah.

Much going on in school?

Not so much. I don't follow geometry very well.

Right.

Hey, says Mullen, do you think you can take some books back to the library for me? I've still got all these books about David Thompson. All the good they did me.

Yeah, I say. I'll take them with me tomorrow morning. Are they pretty overdue?

He shrugs. Probably.

Right, I say. Probably.

Sometimes it gets cold in Marvin, real cold. Low sky and windy, snow drifts over driveways, cars stuck. Country kids miss school when the buses can't make it down their road. It gets so cold you need to be inside, even when you don't want to be.

Sometimes you can sled, with a scarf, with snowpants. You get wet socks, your nose turns pink and runs and the snot freezes to your face. Sometimes the wind blows down off the mountains, out of that chinook arch, and it's like fall again: snow melts, people walk around with their jackets open. We throw snowballs. But sometimes it gets cold.

Halfway to Mullen's house I stop, pull my scarf tighter around my face. I pull my coat sleeves down over the tops of my mitts. If I'd worn long johns, my legs would be warmer, but I didn't. The cold stings my face numb, makes it hard to move my legs. I hunch my shoulders up around my neck and try to walk as fast as I can. The cold burns inside my chest when I breathe.

Most places on Main Street are already closed, although it can't be much later than five o'clock. Hardly any cars parked on the street. The credit union locked up, and the post office.

Someone in a heavy parka walks up to McClaghan's door, hammers on the wood with his fist. Maynard! he hollers. It's Morley Fleer. He hugs his parka tight, waits at the door. I step back into a closed doorway, peek around.

What's so damned important, Maynard? shouts Fleer at the door. It's subarctic out here. What's the damned rush?

McClaghan's door crashes open, he pushes out onto the sidewalk, no jacket. Wet up to his ankles, feet squishing in his shoes. He runs right into Fleer.

I'll kill him, says McClaghan. I should have killed him years ago. It'd be self-defence, Morley. I'm entitled.

What the hell are you on about?

McClaghan pushes past him, looks all up and down the sidewalk. The wind blows at his loose shirt. Howitz's trying to murder me! You've got to help me get him, Morley.

You do not make an ounce of sense.

The goddamn ... He flooded my basement, Fleer. There's water everywhere. Inches! He holds up his foot, yanks on his soggy pant leg. You see that? In this weather? Do you know how much stock I've lost? It's sadistic.

Howitz didn't flood your basement, Maynard.

McClaghan grabs Fleer by the front of his coat. There's a smashed water main with a shovel blade sticking out of it, Morley. He dug into my basement and flooded me out.

Come on, man. Howitz didn't dig into your basement. He's one man with a shovel. How far can one man with a shovel dig in a month?

McClaghan lets go of Fleer, staggers out into the road. He wanders out into the middle of the street, kicking at the snow. McClaghan kneels down in the street, digs at the brown snow around the manhole. Hammers on the iron cover with his fist. Howitz! he shouts. Howitz, I know you're down there! You'll never see the sun again, Howitz! I'll plug up every goddamn hole!

A car fishtails, pulls to a bad-angle stop in front of McClaghan. Sits, idling, waits.

And you're evicted, says McClaghan. He cups his hands around his mouth, puts his face right down on the iron. Evicted! Another car comes up the other side of the street, comes to a slow stop. Fleer puts out his arms, walks in between them. Yanks at McClaghan's arm. More cars stop. Someone honks their horn.

Solzhenitsyn's hatchback slides to a stop, just misses the back bumper of the car ahead. The door opens, Solly looks out the side, past the black garbage-bag window. Winces at the cold. Kid, you can't be walking around in this weather.

I was going for a walk, I say. Maybe out to Aldersyde.

What? Kid, you can't be out walking a block, let alone fifteen fucking kilometres to Aldersyde. You can't be out at all. Feel that wind? Your skin will freeze. You'll get pneumonia. Get in the car.

I sigh and sit down. Pull the door closed. Inside it's cold. I cough, my eyes swim. I cough and he revs the engine, pulls down off the sidewalk.

It smells like gas, Solly. I cough. The whole car is thick with fumes.

It does?

The air in the car wavers under the street lights. Gas fumes dance like hot pavement, my head reels, breathes. I feel my stomach clench and rise, like when you swallow cough syrup.

I'm having a bit of a problem, says Solzhenitsyn, with the fuel line.

I look down at the floor between my feet. The mat is soggy, but I don't think it's the slush from my boots. Gas fumes swim all through the car.

Why are we stopped? What's going on up there? Solzhenitsyn cranes his neck up, can't see over the car ahead of him. He rolls down his window.

McClaghan is evicting Deke, I say.

Howitz is out there?

McClaghan thinks he's under the manhole. Where are we going, Solly?

Hell, I don't know, he says. He puts his stick into reverse, backs up a bit. Turns the wheel hard around all the way and turns into the other lane. Drives back the way he'd come. I just wanted to go for a drive.

We drive down Main Street, faster and faster. The white street lights bleed in front of my eyes, like through a foggy window. The light spreads out all in front of me. Solzhenit-syn drives faster and faster. We drive right through a stop sign.

Damned if I know how it's getting into the car. Where it's seeping from, he says. Must have eaten through something.

Solly, I say.

He goes to roll down his window, but it's already down. The car lurches. I take deeper and deeper breaths and the lights bleed further out across my eyes, running watercolour paints, squinting. My chest gets heavy. Solly drives faster and Main Street narrows down. The Short Stack swims by, red, dark. I fight for breath in the heavy gasoline air.

Solly opens and closes his mouth.

What? I shout. Cold air blasts in the open window.

It gets easier to breathe when I drive faster, he shouts. All the fresh air.

The slow rise, up the hill, out of town. The scrubby little trees, dead, everything dead all around us. Everything white and grey and the air, the ice, the not-quite fog. Nothing sepa-rated from anything else. Up the hill, the road, grey and white and ice, black wheel tracks, sometimes you can see the painted lines on the road, under the snow. We drive not quite in a lane. The flat, long road, the fences, under snow. Patches of long grass, out of the white. We drive faster and faster. Red lights blink, sometimes farmhouses, sometimes signs. Speed limits, and deer, in triangles, and how far to Black Diamond. Noth-ing separated from anything else.

What's going on, Solzhenitsyn? I shout.

He opens his mouth. The car leans into the other lane. He slowly veers it back. I want to open my window, but on my side it's the taped-on garbage bag.

I said, he shouts, I lost my job.

You lost your job?

At the meat-packing plant. Jarvis fired me yesterday. He said – Solly takes a hand off the wheel, roots in his shirt pocket – he said I've become unreliable.

Your ice-smashing job?

Solly looks down at me. I'm a mechanical engineer, he says. I do plumbing and heating. I'm really good with coolant. He coughs.

Solzhenitsyn pulls a cigarette package out of his pocket. Looks over at me. We swerve out, then back. I started smoking again, he says. When I breathe in he gets bigger, when I exhale he shrinks, maybe blurs.

Solly, I say.

How many years ago did I quit smoking? You get so far in life, you know. You get on top. I had a house. I kept all that fucking meat frozen. And then, all these little things.

He pushes the package open. Pushes out a cigarette.

Solzhenitsyn, I say.

He leans down with his mouth open, closes his lips around the filter. Pulls it out of the package.

Solzhenitsyn, I say. I try to be loud but my chest closes up.

He pulls a plastic lighter from his pocket. I reach over and grab his hand. I grab his hand and he startles, lurches, and then the hatchback jumps over into the other lane. He drops the lighter and there's headlights ahead. He jerks back into his lane, we skid, and then the sky spins around and fenceposts and my head bangs against the car roof and all of a sudden we're stopped, backward, in the ditch. I reach out and wrap my fingers in the garbage bag, yank it off the window. Cold air pours into the hatchback and we sit and try to breathe, a funny angle, backward in the ditch.

Solzhenitsyn holds his hands out in front of his face, fingers spread apart. Stares at the backs of his hands. There's no feeling, he says, in the tips. He screws up his face like he'll sneeze, tilts his head back, a deep breath, waits. Face red. He doesn't sneeze. Tries to put his face back in order.

We went out with Milo Foreman back in October ...

I don't want to hear about Milo Foreman, I say.

Goddammit, says Solzhenitsyn, his fists up near his face. Won't somebody please just listen to me?

We sit there, in the car, in the ditch, for a long time.

Why did Milo jump in the rendering vat?

Solzhenitsyn coughs and coughs. He squeezes his cheeks with his fingers.

I don't know, he says.

We sit in the car, in the cold. The windows open, the fumes mix with the cold, cold air. Our breath blows through the fumes. I feel my feet get cold, my legs, I rub them with my mitts. Solzhenitsyn takes long, deep breaths.

You can't go out walking around when it's cold like this, he says. It's too cold. You'll get sick. You have to take care of yourself, kid. There'll be times, people won't be around to look after you.

Sure, Solly. Take care of myself.

He breathes, as deep as he can. He breathes and waits for his chest to get regular, up and down. His nose pink, his cheeks red. Twitches his fingers.

I had this dream. I'm with all these old men with white hair, trimmed moustaches, sweater vests. We walk through the forest in the autumn, and in a meadow there's this big hollow tree. What's inside? the old men want to know. So we all climb in.

It's big inside this hollow tree. They're always bigger inside. And at the back there's a tunnel, we crowd around the opening and peer inside. You ought to see what's at the bottom. Food – hot, lit-up food: roast turkeys, racks of lamb, melons and bananas, a barbecue pig with an apple in its mouth. The old men drip at the mouth and crowd around and they jump down the tunnel, and me, the last one to jump, I think, This is not good.

Now the tunnel isn't a tunnel anymore, but a chute.

We all slide down the chute and it's long and dark, and right before the tunnel ends there's this screen, this wire mesh screen. We all shoot right down and schuck, right through the screen, and it's like we come out of a garlic press, minced right up. Schlup. And all our wet, minced, pulped bodies fly out of this chute, and into this lake, this big, slurried lake.

So I wake up, in this dream, I climb out of the lake –

Wait, I say, I thought you were minced.

I was minced, says Solzhenitsyn. Minced and stewed around, and when I climb out, soggy and dripping, I'm not me anymore. I'm a bit of all sorts of people, all the other pulped people who ever jumped down that chute after that barbecue pig. I'm this whole other guy now. I remember, dimly, that I used to be someone different.

We live underground. In a dark city, underground. The city has windows and aluminum siding and auto-body shops and all the rest of it. And all of us who live in the city are sad, because we all dimly know that we used to be someone else, and now we're not, and we can't be the same.

We stare out the window. In the distance, red lights, maybe radio towers, blink in the dark.

How are you going to get Jarvis back?

He looks over at me. What do you mean?

I mean, what are you going to do to him? To stick it back to him?

Kid. Listen. Jarvis didn't do anything. I screwed up. Okay? Look at me. You don't get back at people when it's your fault.

Oh.

I'm sorry, kid, he says.

I know, Solzhenitsyn. But it's too cold. We have to go home. I want to go home.

Yeah, he says. His face soft and red, and tired. I don't think I've ever seen anybody look so tired. I'll take you home.

Maybe you shouldn't drive, though, I say.

He thinks about it.

Yeah, he says, that's probably a good idea.

We stand on the roadside, in the cold, I hop from foot to foot. Headlights zoom up. Solzhenitsyn waves his arms. Holds out his thumb. Too skinny in the dark, against the lights.

Hey, Solly.

Yeah?

What about the times when it's not your fault? Is that when you stick it to people?

He thinks about it. Well, kid, I guess where we're from, that's when you stick it to people, yeah.

Eventually someone slows down. Solzhenitsyn explains about his fuel line, in the back of the hot car. I blow on my hands. We get driven back to Marvin.

To hell with it, I decide on the last day of school before Christmas. Kids hang up their coats, put on their inside shoes. I head straight for the stairwell.

The stairwell behind the library, up to the sixth-grade floor, gets a lot of use. There's always some sixth-grader going somewhere. And the stairwell at the back door opens right out to the parking lot, where the teachers go to smoke, so that's out. But no one ever uses the stairwell under the gym. Just a caretaker now and then, down to the storage locker, or checking the furnace in the basement. Instead of the white fluorescent lights all over the rest of the school there's just a dim bulb. I head down, duck around and sit under the stairs. I take a deep breath. I find it easier to breathe down here, out of the way, where no one's likely to find me.

I read *The Mysterion* again, in the pale light, just in case. The Under Queen lies on the beach, gasps. After the long-shoremen run away, she wanders through the alleys, collar of her stolen overcoat up around her greenish face. They draw her pretty good, I guess, the *Mysterion* artists; all the inky shading makes her face real expressive. Doesn't need a lot of talking to see how she feels.

Meanwhile, the Mysterion ponders his mystic maps. Surely the theolurgical poles cannot have shifted so nefariously so soon? he says to himself. I don't even want to know what that means.

Footsteps come down the stairs. I fold up the comic, pull my knees tight around my chest. Try to be small in the dark. Wait for the caretaker, or whoever, to open the storage door.

Jenny Tierney swings around. Sits down in a heap, her heavy coat flops on the ground. She takes a deep breath and then notices me, and yelps and claps her hands over her mouth.

Jesus Christ, she says after a while.

I can, well, I can go, if –

No, she says. She frowns and sighs. Some scared little boy will be around any given corner in this stupid town. Stay there.

She rolls her shoulders forward, pulls off her jacket. I try not to stare. She stops and looks at me. I fidget with the comic book and look over at the wall. She watches me and takes off her jacket.

Do you come down here a lot?

I usually go out to the equipment shed, she says. At the end of the playground. Where they keep the lawnmower. I get left alone. But it's too cold out there now.

My stomach feels real tight. Like getting on a ride at the Calgary Stampede. Something that swings way out high in the air, and what if your little seat snaps off and you shoot out into the sky?

How old are you?

I'm ten.

Ten, she says. I was ten.

I guess you'll kill Dave Steadman today, huh?

She watches me. In a few more days. During hockey practice, I think, in front of his friends. I need his face all wrecked still on Christmas Day.

What did he say to you?

She smiles. I've never seen Jenny Tierney smile like that. If I told you, you'd know, she says.

But it must have been pretty bad.

She thinks about it. Then she isn't smiling anymore. You're probably right, she says. I'd probably better just kill him today.

I fidget with the comic book. We sit under the stairwell. Far away the bell rings, feet hurry all over.

Jenny Tierney is skinny, skinny shoulders, red elbows. Her black T-shirt worn out around the hems, a few holes around the waist. She leans against the back of the stairwell, her jacket beside her in a pile, her long arms loose beside her. A few red patches on her face, behind her long black hair hanging in her eyes. Jenny Tierney is skinnier than I thought, right here up close to her. I can smell her damp cotton socks, nicotine.

Are you scared of me?

No, I say.

She leans forward. She crawls toward me and I back up and she pushes me down. She climbs on top of me. She grabs my wrists and holds them up above my head, she covers my mouth with her other hand. Heavy on my chest, her thighs tight around the sides of my chest. My breath is hot and wet against her palm, like the inside of a scarf in winter.

Scared little boys, she says. Scared little boys everywhere. She holds me down. I stare up at her, her black hair hangs down between us.

There's more and more of them, the older you get, she says. Scared little boys, with trucks and scraggly moustaches, that suck on your tongue, that try and put their fingers in your panties. That can't undo a bra. She watches me. I try to breathe slowly. More scared little boys, she says. But I was ten once.

She shifts her weight, her hips, on my chest. Holds me down on the ground. I stare up at her. Far away there's fewer and fewer feet, and then quiet.

You'll think about me more and more, she says, the older you get. You don't know yet, but you will. Someday you'll think about me, and you'll realize what I meant. And you'll always wish you had right now back. She takes her hand off my mouth. She lets go of my hands and leans back, me stuck underneath. She's careful when she stands up not to hit her head on the bottom of the stairs. She gets her coat and disappears. I listen to her feet, far away, back up there.

I lie in the dark where she left me. Damp and sweaty where she was heavy on top of me.

The last bell rings and all the Dead Kids put their duotangs and textbooks back into their bins. All the kids push in their chairs and some of them wave to Mrs. Lampman on the way out the door. We get our coats down off our hooks, we take off our inside shoes and put on our winter boots. The hallway is dark and wet, wet from soggy jackets, from mitts and scarves all full of snow, from wet boots.

Town kids all head out the door, friends who live together walking together, and country kids all head over to the bus loop, where the big yellow school buses sit and idle, the drivers reading the newspaper or listening to the radio. You never know how long they've been sitting there, waiting to fill up with kids. Some country kids have to wait quite a while before their bus shows up.

I stand in the hallway getting ready to head outside. Christmas vacation, two weeks no school. Two weeks to see Mullen every day and do whatever I want.

Dave Steadman puts on his shiny ski jacket, all neon blue and fluorescent yellow; he pulls on his white boots and picks up his backpack and starts up the hallway. He stops at the water fountain and has a long slurp. He wipes his mouth, then thinks about it, pushes open the washroom door and goes inside.

Jenny Tierney comes from around the corner, just walks right up to the boys' washroom door, and she sees me standing there, and winks, and waves, and says, See you some other time, kid, and pushes open the washroom door. Pushes it open with her brown-paper-wrapped math textbook and goes inside. And then the noise starts.

McClaghan comes up the sidewalk, shuffling like he does. In one hand, a wooden stake, with a big, flat sign. A mallet in the other. Mullen and I see him and run up onto the porch, we crouch behind the snow-covered lawn chairs and peek around.

McClaghan stops on Deke's lawn. He grunts and hammers the sign into the snow. He slips, knocks down a corner. Swears to himself. He hammers the sign into the cold ground with his mallet and spits on the ground and walks back up the street.

FOR RENT, says the sign, dog-eared like a library book. Mullen whistles. We crouch behind the lawn chairs and watch McClaghan, not really moving his knees, shuffle away.

The door is locked. I push on the window and it opens up, just like the other day. I wait for a while, trying not to breathe too loudly. The house is dark and quiet. I wait, on the porch, in the snow, under the white moon. Then I pull my backpack off and push it through the window. Let it drop down onto the floor, to thump in the empty house. But the light doesn't come on and he doesn't come out into the kitchen. So I pull myself up, over the window sill, and drop down inside.

The kitchen is just the way we left it the other day, me and Stullus and the accountant. The same overflowing garbage bags, the same muddy footprints all over the floor. I unzip my backpack. Pull out my heavy black flashlight. I don't turn it on, though. I wait until my eyes have adjusted to the dark, hitch up my backback, head inside, careful about the sound of my boots.

The light is on, down in the cellar. I stand at the top of the stairs and crouch down to try and get a look down there. Hey, Deke, I say. Not too loudly. I lean in a bit and cup a hand around my mouth. Hey, Deke. Are you down there? Don't shoot me, okay? I crouch at the top of the stairs and wait. If he's down there, he doesn't say anything. I head down the stairs, careful not to creak too much.

I can't tell if the heaps of dirt and gravel have gotten bigger, down in the cellar, around the dark mouth of the tunnel. I walk up to the entrance. The dark swims around in front of my face. The dark swirls like a snowstorm. I reach my hand out into the opening, stretching out fingers, pushing into the black. I feel dizzy. My throat catches and I have to lean back and take a few deep breaths. The dark swimming around my face.

I think about Vaslav's mustard. Lucky mustard, I say to myself. We made lucky mustard, first-snow mustard, so everything will be fine. I flick on the flashlight. The dark hisses and pushes back, spinning and swirling, back into the cracks and rough patches in the dirt tunnel walls, the craggy sides, the wooden supports. I wave the beam down the tunnel and step in.

You can see the shovel marks in the dirt walls, the flat cuts into the earth. Sometimes rocks and hairy tree roots stick out of the hard dirt. Up ahead there's a pipe jutted out from the side, the iron flaking off in red metal scabs. The crooked ground runs up and down, covered in loose gravel and clumps of dirt – it gets really steep in places. My boots catch in little nicks and cuts. Sometimes I need to heave myself up over ridges, rocky steps that he couldn't dig through. Sometimes I need both hands and have to set the flashlight down. The tunnel twists around, leaning in different directions to go around chunks of concrete, roots, boulders – anything that couldn't be dug through or cut out.

The tunnel gets wider. The floor evens out. More wooden braces hold up the roof, different than the four-by-eights behind me. These are old and thick, soaked in green wood preservative. Rusty nails poking out here and there, rusty bolts. Wooden beams frame a black doorway that leads down another tunnel.

I stop and think really hard about how far I've walked already. I try to remember all the turns. I think about the alley up there, about walking down the alley and how many different backyards and garages there are, how many garbage cans and latched gates. I shine the flashlight around. I keep walking. Sometimes the ceiling comes down, and I have to duck my head. If I were a grown-up I'd have a hard time fitting down here. I try to imagine stabbing into the walls with a shovel, or trying to swing a pick, down here in the tight space. I walk past more side openings – they look rough, a few of them just cutting a few feet into the tunnel wall and then stopping. I have to hold my breath and run a little every time I go by one.

It's so quiet. There isn't anything at all to listen to. Up there you hear stuff all the time: classroom fluorescent lights, cars idling, furnaces, TVs, ringing telephones, and sometimes, way off in the distance, train whistles, going wherever it is they go. Down here it's just quiet. Nothing to listen to. Nothing you can even try and listen to. Like up above me the whole town just blew away in a stiff wind.

The tunnel opens up again, and the floor gets flat enough that I can walk pretty quickly. I walk quite a ways, underground, in the dark. I see an old dusty lantern hanging off one of the braces, like you see in antique shops. The dirty glass all cracked and full inside with spiderwebs.

Then I hear the sound: heavy clanking, metal hammering into something, echoing down the tunnel.

I run, stumbling on the rough floor, the flashlight beam skipping back and forth in front of me, throwing dirt corners and shadows into a jumble. I can feel that damp, wet dark breathing on the back of my neck. I run and run with the old wooden braces whipping past, all sickly green and bent.

There's a split in the tunnel and I run up the other way, through a round passage. The tunnel gets tight and heads up. I'm sure it's going up. I pant and creep forward, following the flashlight.

A mouldy, tattered old blanket stretches across the front of the tunnel. I stop. I can hear the dark, hissing and rushing behind me. I hold my breath and push on the blanket. Push it aside and step through, wincing when the dusty, oily cloth touches me.

Red coils glow down on a concrete floor. Hot red elements glowing and lighting up the shapes in the room. An old hot-water tank stands on a square of plywood. Pink insulation peels down from wall studs. Pipes hang from the ceiling, thick with tinfoil, pinched in bands with masking tape.

And there in the middle, a metal box. Pipes coiling down around it. A pale blue pilot light flickers underneath it.

Somewhere behind me I hear the clanking sound. I let go of the old blanket and creep across the room. I creep through an open doorway.

The room is full. I run my flashlight around and everywhere shapes jump out in the light: jagged, rough things, horns and springs, antlers, yellow smudges, metal fingers. I turn around and shine the flashlight around and stinging light stabs out into my eyes. I see hooks and claws and iron bars, jagged bones and spines, wires, beaks. There's no way out. I'm surrounded, boxed in by spikes and saws, tearing, chewing. I put my hand over the flashlight. The light squeezes out, just a red glow that spills out from between my fingers. The shapes all push back into the dark. I try to make my breathing slow down. Lucky mustard. I wait, wait for all those hooks and fingers and teeth to jump out of the dark. But they don't. I wait, shoulder tight, eyes squeezed shut. I don't get torn to pieces, alone in the dark.

I sit down on the concrete. I hear the clanking – I think it's getting further away. The dark pushes in and out at the corners of the room.

I have to stay somewhere. I'm not going back into the tunnel, and I'm not going back up, so this is it, I guess. I try not to look up at the walls. If I'd waited till later to come down here, the sun would be up soon. But I didn't, so it won't. I take my backpack off and set it down. I turn the flashlight off. Everything turns off. I wait in the dark.

I wake up in the corner, my neck all stiff, eyes gummy. At first I can't see anything, just blurry dark, like when you close your eyes and press on the lids with your thumbs. I sit up and tilt back my head. Above me, a ladder runs up the wall to the white-rimmed edge of the cellar hatch. Light peeks in here and there through gaps in the plywood.

It takes me a second to realize that I'm not scared. All I can remember from last night is being scared. I get up and stretch, try to stretch out the kinks in my neck. I reach down and touch my toes.

My eyes start to make things out in the dark. The basement is small and packed to the ceiling. Mattress springs and cardboard boxes, black marker scrawls, bicycle handlebars, rocking chairs stacked one on top of the other, leaning over me. A bookshelf crammed with yellow *National Geographic* spines, cabinets and chests, open a scary crack. There are old mirrors, with writing etched into the glass. Plates and teacups and deer antlers, a rusty old lumberjack saw, rakes and shovels. Coiled extension cords hung off nails. Wires run across the ceiling, stapled to the old wood beams. Metal pipes, ducts, all uncovered. The pipes creak and groan; they strain against the beams and sound like they'll jump right out of the roof, rattle and hiss, snake down the hallway dragging old stools, brown coffee sacks, window grates with them.

Above me, feet pad across the floor. I sit as still as I can. Clanks and rattles. Heavy things set down on the floor, then the feet again. A scuffling sound, then clomping steps, shoes I guess. A door squeaks, shuts. A lock rattles.

The first thing I've got to do is block off that hallway. I can see it, further than where the light reaches – the real dark.

Breathing and waiting. I unlace my boots and set them on the floor. Take a deep breath and turn on my flashlight. At first the white beam stings my eyes. Dust and dust, strings of dust hang from the roof, dust, cobwebs, balls of dust like tumble-weeds in the corners. The whitewashed doors hang there, more leaning-like I guess, and behind the hall is black and sleeping dark – or at least I hope it's sleeping.

It's pretty easy to shove a lot of the boxes over in front of the hallway. I pile up heavy boxes, must be full of books and magazines, one on top of another. Under cracking leather luggage and picture frames I find some wooden cabinets, a chest. It takes quite a lot of heaving but I get a good wall of furniture shoved in front of the door. I fill cracks with ency-clopedias, stuff an overcoat here and some striped pants there. I bank the whole wall with some wrought-iron chairs, wedged up into ledges. I get dirty and tired.

I eat some sandwiches. The bread soggy, the crust stale. When Dwayne Klatz's mom makes a sandwich, it just seems to stay good all day. I sure can't make a sandwich that good. Now my mouth is sticky, peanut-buttered. I smack my lips. I run my tongue over my teeth for clumps of bread.

I try not to think about rats, their teeth. Centipedes, their little feet. Mould, flatworms, rotten fruit, leeches in ponds.

Once you get used to the cracks and seams of light, you can make out lots. I set a chair under a pretty good sunbeam by the wall, where the wood above the foundation is thin and splintered. I flip through the brittle pages of magazines: old-time magazines with fancy cars, women in long skirts, iron-ing boards, canned ham. Some of the magazines in French. I look at *National Geographic*s: rainforests, Arctic sled trips, Hawaiian volcanoes.

I find pictures. Curling at the corners, the colours all faded to brown and yellow. None of them in albums or frames, just jumbled in a box, jumbled and dusty. There's a little town, on the side of a harbour, with sailboat masts in the background. On all the poles and stop signs a flag, three bars like a French flag, only with a yellow star at the one end. And there's a table in the middle of a long room, white light bulbs, a tablecloth. People sit all around, the women in dresses, the men in high collars, their hands down. The colours all real old, like on the CBC dramas. At the end of the table a large man in a grey jacket, a thick beard, arms out.

There's a little girl at a piano in a velvet dress, all serious-like. Straight hair tied back in a schoolteacher bun, fingers just above the keys. Looking black and white at the camera, eyes very hard.

Old men. An old man with a thick beard and cowboy hat. The other, a skinny face and a moustache like the villain in a black-and-white movie. And there she is. Only younger, a lot younger. A black leather jacket, a skinny black tie. In between the two of them. Around a table in a bar, all smoking, with whisky glasses.

I look at the little girl at the piano. At the woman with the skinny tie.

I snooze for a bit.

What I really need is some water. I smack my sticky mouth, my fuzzy tongue. I shine the flashlight around the uncovered ceiling, on the ducts and wires, stapled to the floorboards. I follow copper pipes with the beam but they disappear, down the hall, to Over There. I try to keep myself busy. I snooze, sometimes, when I run out of stuff to do.

I wake up and her face leans down over me. I holler and try to crawl out of the way and she puts her hands on my shoulders and I yell and flail my arms and she grabs my wrists and pushes my hands down and then she lets me go.

I crawl up on hands and knees and scuttle away, but the washboards and buckets, the meat grinders missing cranks, the lantern frames and Christmas ornaments and thick yellow dust are everywhere. I stop and turn around. Hélène sits where she was, sits back on her calves, her palms flat on top of her thighs. She looks around the basement. Looks at me. She looks at her hands, smeared with the white dust. White smudges, handprints on her black pants. I look at myself: I'm covered in dirt, dust, my hands black and smudged, my clothes grey, like I've rolled in dirty flour. I open my mouth and it's sticky and I just smack my lips a few times and watch her, palms flat on top of her thighs. She doesn't stand up.

After a while, she asks, Is anyone going to look for you? Her French accent making every word sound careful in the quiet basement.

I think about it. Somebody will, I say. Probably.

She nods.

Is it warm enough?

It's not too bad.

She nods. She stands up and goes to the ladder. On the floor there's a jug of water and a plate of sandwiches. Tomatoes and white cheese. I wait for her legs, calves, feet to vanish up the ladder.

Her shoes clatter from one room to another. She stops, a soft plunk, then barefoot, soft steps. Something scrapes. A chair? A bench? I try to be as quiet as I can. Nothing but the buzz from down the hall.

Sometimes she plays soft, just barely music. Sometimes she hammers on the keys, shrill chords over and over and over and so many times and so long, I can't believe anybody could do the same thing for that long. Sometimes she plays the sad, dramatic – I guess you call it classical music, what the composers wrote. She drifts in and out. Sometimes I hear her walk across the floor and stop, there's a pause, then she hurries over to the piano and plinks out a few notes, maybe a little trill or run.

I don't know much about music. At school, when Mr. Hyslop plays the piano it's one chord at a time. One chord with his left hand and then the melody you're supposed to sing with the right, his back straight, his elbows high. Slow and careful. She doesn't play the piano like that at all.

Sometimes, just the tap tap tap of her foot, keeping time to something I can't hear.

Sometimes I hear digging. Pick pick picking, ringing on the rocks. He's out there somewhere. Digging away. Deeper and deeper and further and further away.

It's tough to sleep in the basement. My backpack isn't much of a pillow. My jacket isn't much of a blanket. I listen to the digging. The clank and scrape of metal on rock. My knees are sore. My back is stiff. I stand up and reach my arms up toward the ceiling, feel my stiff back tug and roll over.

I don't know how long I've been down here. I thought someone would have come looking for me by now. Maybe I finally hid too well.

The house is quiet for a long time. Then I hear the floorboards shift. The light out of one vent, the cracks around it, smothers out. Her voice comes down the vent.

How did you know about the ringing? she asks. Her voice really close to the vent. It gets all echoey and funny-sounding, coming out of the duct. How did you know about the ringing in my ears?

Well, sometimes you grab your head, I say, like it hurts.

No, she says, you were very specific. You asked about the ringing in my ears. Because you know about my grandfather.

They were talking about him at the hardware store, I say. They said he came here to make the ringing go away.

The hardware store, she says.

Fleer has a thermostat, I say. McClaghan told him not to give it to you.

Of course he did.

So your ears ring just like your grandpa's did?

Some cigarette smoke puffs down the vent. The floor creaks while she stretches out. It can't be comfortable, lying on the floor, talking into a vent.

In Halifax we had a weekly engagement, she says. Three one-hour sets in a cocktail bar, down a long flight of stairs. Red lights and black granite and thin, languid people with long, strong drinks.

Marcel would come in an hour before the set started, while the staff was still sitting at the bar, polishing the silverware with vinegar, rolling it up in paper napkins. He'd set up his drums; he had all this little jazz hardware which the pieces of his kit were too big for: this deep, awful-sounding snare, one floor-tom – no rack – and these cracked, appalling cymbals. And he'd hit them a few times and make no effort to tune them. Then he'd start to play.

This thumping starts on the floor; she's drumming on the floor with her hands. I try to imagine Mr. Hyslop counting along to it – one*two* one*two* one*two* one*two* – the second beat always right on the heel and harder than the first. She drums along on the floor like that for a while and my head starts to bob up and down along to it.

And he'd just play that, she says. Kick snare and a rasp on the hi-hat for each quarter, never opening it up, and he never touched the floor-tom and he never touched those other cracked cymbals.

And people started to show up, coming down the stairs, unwinding their scarves, pushing themselves into their favourite booths, and Marcel would still be playing, nothing changing, one*two* one*two*, and sometimes the waiter would bring a drink by and hold it there for him to sip at with a straw. Then I would show up and play the piano. Luis would play the guitar.

I put a microphone into the top of the upright piano they kept in that bar. I ran it through a tubed PA head. Two four-by-ten guitar cabinets.

What does that mean? I ask.

That means we were loud, she says. We billed ourselves as the loudest act in the Maritimes. We played one-chord songs to Marcel's beat, as long as we could manage. Over and over. Luis would hold his guitar upside down with the headstock planted against the head of his amplifier making white noise and I just played that one chord, over and over, to that one beat. We never found out if Marcel knew another beat. People would sit there drinking their drinks as long as they could stand it. They'd get up and their knees would buckle, because it was so loud that it changed the pressure in your ears. Luis would stand there with his guitar feeding back and the pitches changing as people moved through the bar. As they changed the angles of reflection. People would walk around the bar with their hands over their ears, changing the pitch of the guitar feedback with their bodies, and I'd change the piano chords to accompany the new tones. That's how loud we were.

We played on Sunday nights and my ears would ring all day Monday. And after a while they would start to ring later in the week. Later, after we got fired, and I was living in Montreal, I was sitting at a bus bench. And my ears started ringing. Much, much louder than they ever had before. I sat there holding the sides of my head and the bus drove up, and the door opened, people got out, the door closed, it drove away, and I couldn't move. I remember sitting there holding the sides of my head, unable to move. And my whole life I'd known that it was coming, but at least now it might have been my own fault.

You wanted the ringing in your ears to be your own fault?

I couldn't let him have all the bad things, she says. He had too many already, my grandfather. Too many bad things.

Worse things than your ears ringing? I ask.

Much, much worse.

I think about it for a while.

You sure have lived in a lot of places, I say.

She's quiet for quite a while. When you leave early, she says, you have more time.

Why would anybody move to Marvin? I ask. Sitting on the dirt floor with my arms around my knees. Her feet stop moving. I start to breathe fast and heavy. Why would anybody move to Marvin? I shout, as loud as I can.

I wait a while. The floor doesn't creak right away. Her voice comes out of the vent.

You can't stay in my basement, she says. You have to go home.

Go home, I say. I don't think loudly enough for her to hear. I sit there with my arms wrapped around my knees, staring into the dark. The dark in the corners of the basement pulses and breathes. I'm lucky 'cause it's asleep. Eventually the dark is going to wake up and find me, though.

You have to go home.

And what good will that do? My face is all hot. Huh? I say. What then? If I just go home again. Without – without making them do anything about it. Again.

Again? she asks.

Yeah, I say, and it's hard to be loud this time because my voice isn't really sounding the way I want. I want it to sound all tough but it sure doesn't sound that way. 'Cause if it just happens that way again, I say, I don't know how I'm ever going to make them do anything about it.

Again.

Right.

She doesn't say anything. The floor gives a big creak, I guess she's standing up, and I hear her walk away out of the room. Somewhere water starts to move through the pipes; a few of them start to shake in their brackets, up there in the beams. A rushing sound and a high-pitched whistling sound.

I hear some splashing and clanking, sounds like dishes getting stacked. In the corners the dark just breathes and doesn't do anything. What if it's already awake, and just waiting? What if it's just waiting, watching me, taking its time deciding what to do? I sit there and hug my knees and want to get the flashlight out of my backpack and run around shining it in all the corners. But I don't. I sit there hugging my knees and wait.

I start to smell cigarette smoke, down from the ceiling. The boards creak when she shifts on the floor. She must be lying out straight, smoking.

Is it cold out? I ask.

There's, how do you call it, the strong wind, and the clouds make an arch above the mountains.

A chinook, I say.

Windy but not terribly cold, she says. It gives me a headache.

I stand in the boiler room, watching the red pulse of the space-heater coils. They make a really quiet sound, too quiet to be a buzz. Almost a sizzle. I hitch up my backpack, stuffed full again with all the used sandwich wrappers.

I guess I had always thought that a boiler would be huge: pipes and hoses, bellows and valves. Hélène's boiler just sits there, sits there in the middle of that knot of pipes, thin copper pipes and thick black plastic pipes with heavy joints. Sits there, quiet, all red-rimmed from the space heaters. Up ahead the old blanket stretches across the tunnel. Behind it that heavy tunnel darkness waits. I guess I've gotten away from it long enough. There's thin window-grey dark and space-heater red dark, and then there's tunnel dark, and tunnel dark sure is dark. It's cold. My heart beats real fast and I want to pee. I really want to pee. I should turn around, back into the basement, run up the stairs, pound on Hélène's door. She'll open the door and pick me up, carry me up the stairs to where she lives. Carry me up there and fix everything.

The damp, soggy dark blows out of the tunnel, soaks my clothes, makes me heavy, sticks me to the floor.

I take a step and trip on the space-heater cord. I pitch forward and drag the heater with me and the cord pulls out of the socket, and I hit the ground in the dark.

That's when I just disappear altogether. I knew it would happen someday. I take a deep breath and let it out, and it just goes, that breath, and I feel my lungs and insides just puff away, like ice on a stovetop. Everything inside me just steams and blows away down in the dark boiler room, and there's this cold feeling as the rest of me follows along in that long, cold breath, until everything blows away and I'm gone. And I guess what I mean is, I'm cold and I'm lonely and I'm scared.

Some light comes into the room. I lie there and watch the light move around, parts of the boiler room appearing, cords and nails and drywall, rough hard-packed dirt. Making the room out of nothing as it pans across.

The light gets close and shines right in my eyes, just blinds them right out, like truck headlights in the night. I squeeze my eyes shut. I open them slowly when the hot light moves away.

Mullen sits beside me, cross-legged. His hard hat turned to the side, so that the miner's light in front doesn't shine right into my face. He sits beside me and I lie there on the ground and try to breathe more slowly, try not to gasp and pant so much.

You're crying, says Mullen.

Yeah, I'm crying.

Why are you crying?

I think about it for a while.

I really like the sandwiches Dwayne Klatz's mom makes, I say. It was tough, at the end of school there, when he had to stay home sick, from eating all that dirt. I couldn't trade sandwiches with him. That was a pretty lousy week.

Most kids would love to have a pizza sub from the store every day. Those things sure taste great.

Most kids don't know much, I say.

Yeah, says Mullen. Yeah, most kids don't know much.

I sit up. I crawl across the floor, feeling in the dark with my hands. Mullen looks over with his light, across the cold floor, to the cord, lying a few feet from the socket. I plug the heater back into the wall. We watch the dark coil slowly turn red. Mullen's light twitches around the room, never stays on anything long enough to get a good look. I guess that's how things look to Mullen all the time: jumping around like the boiler room, twitchy and brief.

We hear it, off somewhere underground: the clanking. We both sit and listen: clank clank clank, all muffled and ringing, coming through the ground, through the walls, through the dark hole behind the old curtain. It rings for a while and then fades away, and after a while we can't tell if it's even there anymore.

What's behind that curtain? asks Mullen.

It's a tunnel.

Mullen's eyes get real big. No kidding, he says. Really a tunnel? All dug down into the ground? No way.

Have a look, I say. It's pretty dark.

Mullen pushes the old curtain away. He whistles, the hard-hat light passing around on rough dirt, old beams. They hold the ceiling right up, he says. Look how old the wood is. This must have been down here forever.

Why did you come and find me? I ask.

They must have dug this years and years ago. Braced, that's what they call it, all this wood. It's like a mine shaft. My dad has all sorts of books with pictures of mines, they've got these wood beams. He leans into the tunnel. I can't even see ... He stops. More ringing. Maybe even someone talking, or shouting – it's tough to tell, like hearing a quiet radio in another room. You can tell there's sound, but not what it is.

Mullen runs his hand up the beam. Grey old splinters bend out into the fabric of his mitt. I bet he could use a hand, he says. We could help him carry dirt; he's got to carry the dirt back up somewhere. How much do you think he's dug? How close do you think he is?

He doesn't want anybody to find him, Mullen.

What do you mean, he doesn't want any–

I know about wanting to be found. He doesn't.

Mullen keeps looking at me. I have to squint in the white light. It leaves blue circles scratched everywhere I look. He looks down the tunnel, down the rough dirt walls, the green-stained wood beams, everything dusty and old and dark.

My dad told me you were down here, says Mullen. Go find your friend, he said. He's in the junk-shop basement. I asked him how he knew and he wouldn't say. It's time he came out of there, he said, time he came back up. Wouldn't say how he knew. The light wavers out of Mullen's hard hat. He reaches up and fiddles with the bulb, it flickers and goes out for a second, leaves us a flash of dark, then the beam comes back, a little dimmer maybe. We stare down the tunnel, listen to the clanging, far away.

Your dad told you.

Yeah.

Well, why wouldn't he? I say. Why wouldn't your dad decide when it's time for me to come back up?

I can't see Mullen's face behind the white light.

I know how to make the Milk Chicken Bomb, I say.

The what?

The Milk Chicken Bomb. You remember when Paul Grand told us about the Milk Chicken Bomb?

How did you get him to –

I figured it out. I know how to do it.

You figured it out, he says. He has another long look down the tunnel. We ought to go back up there, he says.

Yeah, I say, I guess we should.

At McClaghan's I go straight to the counter. Mullen wanders around the aisles, poking at rakes and garbage bags. I stand up on my tiptoes and rest my arms on the counter. McClaghan sits behind the counter on his stool, arms crossed, chewing, watching his television. The quiet newsman behind his desk, saying something none of us can hear. A map of some country behind him.

McClaghan chews and looks around for his jar on the counter and leans over to spit black juice into it. Spittle trails down into the jar, he waits for it to stretch and thin out, longer and thinner, finally snap off. He pushes the jar back down the counter. Looks over at me.

What?

Do you sell thermostats?

He narrows his eyes at me. What did you ask?

Thermostats. My friends are having problems with their boiler, I thought that –

Get out of here, says McClaghan. He crosses his arms and looks back up at the television.

I pull myself up on the counter to get a look over the other side. They've got a gravity boiler, I say, with an airlock. I figured maybe you'd have –

McClaghan lurches off the stool and swings a heavy hand at me. Get out of here! he barks. I duck my head and slide off the counter. I jump up and grab his telephone. Do you know Morley Fleer's phone number? I ask. I start to press buttons on the phone. Fleer would probably have something like that, right? Some kind of thermostat? McClaghan grunts and comes around the corner. I run down an aisle, pressing buttons on the phone. What did you say Fleer's number was?

I holler. McClaghan jogs around the aisle after me. What in god's name are you doing, you miserable shit? Put down the goddamn telephone!

I run around the aisle, then stop and run back, straight at McClaghan. He opens up his arms to catch me and I tip over a stack of rubber garbage bins. Rubber bounces and rattles and a bin knocks down some mops. McClaghan trips and tumbles over top of me, arms flailing, crashes over into one of the rubber bins. I run around the aisle and put the phone back on his counter. If you find one of those thermostats, let me know, I yell at him. He picks himself up and kicks a few mops out his way. Red-faced and puffing. I run out the door.

Down the alley, Mullen sits with his back against the post-office wall. I sit down next to him, panting. We sit and I pant for a while. Mullen unzips his jacket. The jar in his lap, its sides thick and waxy, all tobacco brown and flu yellow.

We probably shouldn't go in there for a while, says Mullen.

No, I guess not, I say.

The chinook lasts a few days, the wind warm and always blowing, all day long, down from the mountains. The sky a blue band above the mountains, in an arch, under the high clouds.

We sell lemonade all morning, on Christmas vacation. We don't pack everything back into the garage before nine. Heck, we don't even start selling lemonade until after nine. We sit behind the table, our scarves up over our noses. Mullen pushes dimes on the table with his mitts, can't quite pick them up, to stack. We keep the lemonade jug in one of Mullen's dad's beer coolers, to keep it from freezing. When we open the lid, the lemonade steams in the cold, frost around the rim of the plastic.

Solzhenitsyn walks up the street, his thick toque crooked on his head, his collar up around his raw face. He sees us and stops. He walks up the walkway. Stands in front of our lemonade table and watches us, then sits down in the snow. Pulls his knees up against his chest.

You kids sell much lemonade?

We haven't sold any lemonade in a week, says Mullen.

Solzhenitsyn pulls off a black wool glove. Leans over and digs into his pocket. He finds a key or two, a pencil stub, a lottery ticket. A few nickels.

You know, Solzhenitsyn, it's been a bad few weeks. We can cover you, says Mullen. He opens up the cooler. Pulls a cup off the stack. Solzhenitsyn sits in the snow, arms around his legs. We pour him some lemonade – no ice, though. Sure it's a chinook, but it's still cold. He takes the cup of lemonade, has a long sip. Swishes it in his mouth, swallows. Smacks his lips, has another sip.

That is a damn good glass of lemonade. Tart. Awfully refreshing, tart like that. He has another sip.

It's pretty cold for lemonade, though, he says.

Yeah, yeah it is.

You just get the water out of the tap?

Of course we do.

Solzhenitsyn nods. Pretty good water in this town. I noticed that first thing when we showed up. I've lived a lot of places where the water wasn't so good. We had to boil it, in Petersburg, a lot of the time. You never knew what someone might have poured down the storm sewer.

Do you miss living in Russia? asks Mullen.

Solzhenitsyn shrugs. I like curling a lot. You don't get curling clubs in Russia. And your dad can carry on a good conversation, even if it is in this foreign language.

What foreign language?

English, says Solzhenitsyn. I don't know how you people do with so few vowels. He drinks some lemonade.

For a while, in Edmonton, I did instrumentation at a refinery, out past Leduc. A ways out into the field. You'd show up at the mobile shed, you'd be all sweaty and filthy, days' worth of dust worked into your clothes. You showed up to the shed for a drink of water, and they keep the water cooler beside the propane heater. Do you know that smell? That sour, pinched smell of a propane heater? Which is all you can taste, of course, when you drink the water.

Solzhenitsyn drinks some lemonade.

Milo Foreman's brother coached bantam hockey in Okotoks. Coaches, I mean. I mean, he still does. We liked to go and watch the games. They played good hockey, those bantams. None of this banging on the glass, none of this drilling kids on dump and chase, hit and wait. Milo's brother had them skating. I like that good skating hockey, carrying it in off the wing, like back home. Fast and loose.

I liked this one restaraunt in Okotoks, I think it closed. Up a flight of stairs, in an alley, low ceilings and thick steaks. Milo and I would head there after the games, while his brother got all those kids home, talked down the parents, made everybody happy. I can't recall the last time we went out there, Milo and I. I guess his brother must still coach hockey.

You should really show those Pentecostals next time, says Mullen. Really let them have it.

Yeah, laughs Solzhenitsyn. Drinks some lemonade. Really let them have it. Really show them.

Any time I smell a propane heater, I get depressed. I hated that job, twisting pipes out past Leduc. I smell propane and it's first thing in the morning, cold, waiting to start work, and you can't warm up for hours, and when the sun gets high then there's no cooling down, and even when you want a glass of water, it smells like propane.

He finishes the last of the lemonade. Holds up the cup, lets the last drop drip onto his tongue.

Hey, do you kids want to see something?

What have you got? asks Mullen.

Solzhenitsyn takes an envelope out from his jacket. A thick brown kind, like you get at the post office, probably all padded inside. The flap torn open. He hands it to us. From Toronto, it says, addressed to Vaslav Andreiovich Kurskinov.

What is it?

Look inside.

Did you open it already? Did Vaslav?

Just look inside.

We pull out the red paperback book from the plastic bubble padding. Mullen holds it up, reads the title out loud.

THE TENDEREST TEMPEST
ANDRE KIRK
Uncorrected Proof

He's always on about his pseudonym, says Solzhenitsyn. Who's going to read Vaslav Andreiovich Kurskinov's book? he always says. I think he spent more time coming up with that name than any other part of the stupid thing.

The paper cover is shiny and thick, the letters of the title pressed out, gold. Mullen opens the first few pages, looks for the start.

Troy Deville had the world, Mullen reads, slow and careful. The biggest estate in Louisiana, a house with forty rooms. He had marble columns and high glass windows with black wrought-iron ledges. Across his hundred acres would stroll the livery men to the stables, the gardeners about their business, and even an iridescent peacock. Often Troy Deville would sit in the highest window and gaze down the hill, to the port where his ships waited, their precious cargo to be unloaded. Troy Deville had all of this. But he didn't have Lucia, so he didn't have anything.

I look at Solzhenitsyn. That's her name? Lucia?

I guess that's her name, says Solzhenitsyn.

We open up the Profit Envelope at Mullen's house. We sit inside his kitchen and Mullen pours all the lemonade money out onto the white table. He piles quarters up into stacks. He stacks up quarters in piles of ten, and then, real careful-like, takes a stack of quarters and puts it on top of another. He gets quite a stack of quarters and then starts to put dimes on top, one at a time. Gets maybe two dollars in dimes on top before it all spills over and we have to recount everything. We put aside enough change for lemons and sugar and put all the profits into our pockets.

We go to the IGA. We buy two litres of milk. We get the homogenized kind. We buy chicken breasts: deboned, soft, tight on a Styrofoam tray.

At the credit union, fire trucks idle, their yellow lights light up the street. The only other time I ever saw so many fire trucks in town was last year in the Sports Day Parade, when the firemen walked beside their slow-driving trucks, wearing their big black boots and yellow hats, throwing candy to the people lining the streets. Now firemen stand around the sidewalk, hands on their hips – there's a crowd to watch them, men in workshirts and a few in suits. Cars slow down on Main Street, people lean out their windows. Up at Steadman's they come outside in their white pharmacist jackets. Some old men come out of the Elks' Hall.

Constable Stullus leans against his car. Firemen open up the back of a red van. They unpack heavy boxes, root around on their cluttered shelves inside. They pull on hip waders. Like fishermen, underneath the train bridge, in the summer. A fireman pulls a pair of swimming goggles down over his eyes. His snorkle flaps on the side of his head. They go into the credit union.

At Mullen's house we flick pennies across the table at each other, our damp socks hanging off our feet, dangling down from our too-tall chairs. We flick pennies like hockey pucks, try to stop them from flying off the table.

When we get tired of that, we get McClaghan's jar and make the Milk Chicken Bomb.

It takes a while to find a lid that fits. Mullen's dad keeps all his jar lids in a drawer, with the Tupperware and old margarine containers. We find one that fits, though. Mullen holds the jar steady while I screw it on as tight as I can. It's tough, because the jar is so full, right up to the top, but we get it screwed on real tight.

So, you know where you're going to put it?

It has to be someplace warm, I say. Warm enough that it'll all spoil real bad. Bad enough that Bang! I hold up my hands, palms out. Mullen makes a face.

Ugh.

The worst thing, I say.

So you've got a place?

We'll put it behind the furnace. They'll never find it. You going to come?

Sure, says Mullen, I always wanted to see your house.

You want to sell lemonade tomorrow?

It's almost January. Nobody's going to buy any lemonade. Besides, we're on holiday. Who wants to work every day?

Yeah, I guess you're right.

We get the Milk Chicken Bomb and head outside.

An excerpt of this novel originally appeared in the March/ April 2004 issue of *Alberta Views* magazine.

Many thanks to Aritha van Herk and the students from her manuscript class of 2001. The entire writing community here in Calgary has looked after me for years, so thanks, everybody – *filling Station* and *dANDelion* magazines, Jackie Flanagan and *Alberta Views*, and everyone who read and was interested right from the start: Nicole Kajander, Tasya Moritz, Derek McEwen, Grant and Lee, Julia Williams, Craig Boyko, Romana Prokopiw. Most importantly, I couldn't have accomplished anything without the support of Jennifer Tamura and my family.

Thank you to Chad Saunders for eating so many stupid things as a child, and to Silas Kauffman for the recipe.

Finally, thank you to Alana Wilcox for understanding everything so clearly and completely right from the start, and to everyone else at Coach House for the tremendous support.

Andrew Wedderburn lives and works in Calgary, Alberta, and grew up in the nearby towns of Okotoks and Canmore. He performs rock-and-roll music in the group Hot Little Rocket. *The Milk Chicken Bomb* is his first novel.

Set in Legacy and Slate
Printed and bound at the Coach House on bpNichol Lane, April 2007

Edited and designed by Alana Wilcox
Author photo by Tyler Stalman
Milk photo by Diane Diederich
Chicken photo by Ralf Hettler
Bomb photo by Felix Möckel

Coach House Books
401 Huron St. on bpNichol Lane
Toronto ON M5S 2G5

800 367 6360
416 979 2217

mail@chbooks.com
www.chbooks.com